Born Under the Lone Star

Darlene Graham

MILLS & BOON
Super ROMANCE

He picked up on the first ring.

"Hello?" Even in that one word, a west Texas drawl, the quality of Justin's voice echoed. It was the same resonant public-speaking voice that had made Brandon's grandfather stand out in the halls of Congress.

She swallowed, then started again. "May I speak to Brandon Smith, please?"

"This is Brandon."

Markie closed her eyes. She was talking to her very own son again. Just like the first time, it was scary, but also strangely intoxicating. It took all her will to suppress tears as her mind flashed back to the pages of her journal where she had made those promises to him so long ago. Would she keep them now? Or would she injure her child? Would she hold him back?

Or let him go?

Born Under the
Lone Star

DARLENE GRAHAM

MILLS & BOON®
SuperROMANCE

*First published in Great Britain 2007
Harlequin Mills & Boon Limited,
Eton House, 18-24 Paradise Road, Richmond, Surrey TW9 1SR*

© Darlene Gardenhire 2005

ISBN: 978 0 263 85792 4

38-0707

*Printed and bound in Spain
by Litografía Rosés S.A., Barcelona*

Dear Reader,

People often ask me where I get my story ideas. THE BABY DIARIES were first "conceived" when I was reminiscing with a friend about the birth of my middle daughter, who was born when my husband was a candidate in a statewide political race. It occurred to me then that babies seldom arrive when it is convenient.

THE BABY DIARIES are three stories of three sisters, each having a baby under most inconvenient circumstances, each falling in love under equally inconvenient circumstances.

For these stories I returned to my beloved Texas Hill Country. My brother and sister-in-law, her mother, Jean, and Jean's longtime friend Helen were perfect travelling companions as we hit the trail in the minivan and explored the colourful towns and rural areas that eventually melded into the setting I have named Five Points.

One final note: authors are also often asked if their work is autobiographical. Yes and no. While my own impressions and experiences are always unconsciously woven into any story, this town and these characters are pure fiction. For example, unlike the conniving Marynell McBride, my own mother was honest to a fault and would never, ever have touched someone else's diary!

As always, my best to you,

Darlene Graham

PS I love to hear from you! Drop me a line at PO Box 720224, Norman, OK 73070, USA or visit www.darlenegraham.com. While you're there, take a peek at the next book in THE BABY DIARIES series, *Lone Star Rising*.

This first book in my new Texas series is dedicated to Rick and Jody, my precious brother and dear sister-in-law. Despite six-shooters, snakes and donkeys that bite, I will go back to the Hill Country with you two anytime!

CHAPTER ONE

If you are reading this diary without my permission, stop right now. I mean it. I want you to put this diary down. Immediately. For your information, this means *you*, Mother.

I'm warning you, if you keep going you'll find out things you don't want to know.

Okay, I know you're still reading, you snoopy old thing, so you asked for it. Don't blame me if you have a horse heart attack.

I am pregnant.

There.

And Justin Kilgore is the father. How do you like that? Me and Justin. We're in love. And don't you dare try to interfere with that. Don't you dare go and ruin the one beautiful thing—

"WHAT ARE YOU reading there, Sissy?"

Markie McBride jumped at the sound of

her middle sister's words, even though Robbie always spoke with the soothing lilt of a low violin. Not even the antics of her three little boys could make Robbie McBride Tellchick raise her voice.

"Nothing." Markie closed the cover and tried to stuff the book back down in the dusty old cardboard box where she'd found it moments ago. It had been a physical shock to look down and see, wedged in between her yellowed first communion dress and her high school letter jacket, next to a flank of musty yearbooks, the faded mauve cover that was her Baby Diary, as she had come to call it many years ago. Eighteen years ago, to be exact. Her son would be eighteen by now. Correction. Her son *was* eighteen now—a bright, exceptional, eighteen-year-old young man. Only a few days ago, she had talked to him herself, in a phone conversation that had haunted her ever since.

As her hand struggled in the tangle of drycleaner bags encasing the cloth items in the box, she realized, not for the first time, that her mother was a totally conflicted human being.

Hot and cold. Love and hate. That was

Marynell McBride. Mostly cold and mostly hate, Markie decided sadly, as her mind absorbed this latest in a long line of betrayals. *Where was the photograph?* Markie couldn't risk looking for it now.

The box had been tightly packed and the diary refused to fit back into its appointed slot. Markie pushed harder. So weird. So, so weird that she'd stumbled on the thing *now,* when she'd been compelled to return to Five Points to attend her brother-in-law's funeral. *Now,* at the very time that her son, *Justin's son,* was actually preparing to come here, as well. It was almost like some kind of…eerie convergence. Like fate or something.

"It looked," Robbie said as she leaned back with a grin and planted a palm on the saggy mattress of the twin bed where she'd been sorting old photographs, "like one of our old diaries." She craned her neck in Markie's direction. "Whose is it? Yours? Frankie's?"

With their father's encouragement, the three sisters had each faithfully kept journals in their teens.

"It's in your blood," P. J. McBride had explained quietly one Christmas as he passed each girl a ribbon-bound stack of blank journals, "like your pioneer grandmother and her mother before her." Daddy had kept those old leather-bound journals, hardly legible now, but precious as ancient Egyptian scrolls to P.J.

The girls had decorated their plain cloth-bound versions so each could immediately recognize her own elaborate designs. Ever-sensible Robbie had likely disposed of her own foolish ramblings long ago.

Markie had gotten rid of her journals, too. All but this one. She could never bring herself to part with the record of her seventeenth year. *The Baby Diary.*

The last time she'd moved, the diary hadn't shown up at her new town house with the rest of her stuff. Its disappearance had distressed her terribly. And, even more distressing was the loss of the photo. Her one picture. That broke her heart more than anything. She'd grieved, alone and in secret, over that loss especially. She should have had copies made instead of sticking it inside the diary cover. *Where,* she had fretted during many lonely evenings of unpacking, *could her precious diary have disappeared to?*

Now she knew.

She stared at the back of Marynell McBride's graying head as her mother's skinny arm furiously scrubbed at the panes of one of the high dormer windows as if it were the Queen Mother who was coming to stay instead of Marynell's own three rambunctious grandsons.

She took my diary, Markie thought with a familiar sickness of heart. *For heaven's sake, Mother, what were you going to do? Blackmail me?*

"Fess up." Again, Robbie's voice made Markie jump. "Whose is it?" Robbie was smiling pleasantly.

"Nobody's. I mean, it's nothing. Really." Markie knew she sounded guilty, probably looked it, too.

Markie could see Marynell's thin back stiffen high up on the ladder. The woman slowly turned her head and squinted down at her youngest daughter with an expression that was equal parts hostility and suspicion.

"Margaret," she demanded, "where did you get that box?"

Funny. Marynell never called Frankie "Frances," or Robbie "Roberta." And although Marynell had coined her daughter's tomboy nicknames, she reserved the use of Markie's full name for the times she was working herself into a slow-burning rage at her daughter.

"From under the bed." Markie fixed challenging eyes on her mother's face, willing her, daring her, to press the issue, especially here in front of Robbie, especially now.

Robbie, sensing the sudden shift in the atmosphere, frowned. As she stood and crossed the room, the taut silence seemed amplified by the scuffing of her house slippers and the measured ticking of their father's antique mantel clock.

Markie turned her eyes from her mother's scowl to her sister's pallid face. Robbie didn't look like herself these days. Instead of the family's slender Irish rose, she looked like a puffy, used-up, freckled hag. Her long ginger-colored hair, usually bound in a neat French braid, was shoved behind her ears, limp and unbrushed. At ten o'clock in the morning, she wasn't dressed, unthinkable for a farm wife. Her frayed pink terry-cloth robe accentuated her pale complexion and the girth of her expanding middle. As she waddled across the bare floorboards of the long attic room, Markie thought how Robbie even moved like an old woman now. So unlike the energetic sprite that had kept pace with a robust husband and three growing boys on their huge farm. But Robbie was doing a lot of uncharacteristic things lately—understandable under the circumstances—like now, for example, poking her nose in where it didn't belong.

"It *is* one of the diaries." Robbie's teasing smile returned as she advanced, having no idea what she was about to do. "Nothing else could make you blush like that." Her hand snaked out to grab at Markie's, still submerged in the box, now sweating on the cloth covering that encased the most damaging secret of her life.

When Robbie's hand tugged on her wrist, Markie pushed her sister away. "Stop it!" she snapped. "I said it's nothing!"

"Ah, now," Robbie wheedled, "we could use a little entertainment. Couldn't we, Mother?"

"That box wasn't supposed to go in this room." Marynell acted as if Robbie hadn't even spoken. Her brow was creased and her voice grew vehement as she started to descend the ladder. "I told P.J. to put it across the hall with my things. I swear, that man never does anything right."

The McBride farmhouse had a high converted attic, cleaved in two by a dark hallway illuminated by a single bare bulb at one end and a tiny window at the other. Right now, at midmorning, a thin shaft of light poured down the steep-pitched stairs that led to the kitchen. On either side of the hall, two enormous rooms stretched the length of the Victorian-era frame structure, with dormers poking out along the front and back planes of the roof.

Those two rooms had been rigidly appointed when the sisters were growing up. Their bedroom was at the front of the house, arranged like a dormitory with three twin beds evenly spaced between the two dormers and three scratched and dented dressers standing at attention on the opposite wall. The mantel clock on top of the center dresser had been the only decoration allowed during their childhoods. The long room on the other side of the hall was the playroom, later the study. Three identical desks, three plain bookshelves, three metal footlockers. No rugs. No curtains. No pictures. Marynell was nothing if not tidy. She despised clutter, her husband P.J.'s most especially.

Both attic rooms had grown fallow and musty since the girls had grown and gone. The one they were cleaning now had devolved into a repository for P.J.'s projects and memorabilia. Tucked in among the three beds were boxes of old photos and papers, childhood keepsakes from his daughters, magazines, sheet music, hunting and fishing equipment, anything that "offended" Marynell's aseptic sense of order.

The other room, dedicated to Marynell's sewing and paperwork, remained as bleak and sterile as an operating room. Marynell liked it that way—their belongings strictly divided.

Today the three women had been mucking

out this room so Robbie's three boys could stay here until she could get her life sorted out. The move back to the McBride farm had been Marynell's idea. She adored her grand-sons—the sons she never had.

Marynell was scrambling down the ladder faster than a spider backing down its web. "I'll take that box across the hall myself."

"I'd like to look through it first," Markie said evenly while she kept one hand on the card-board edge and the other inside…on the diary.

"Those are my things," Marynell protested.

"Not exactly, Mother. This is my letter jacket, these are my yearbooks, and this is *my* diary." Markie flipped her hand.

"Ha! So it *is* one of yours." Robbie suc-ceeded in snatching it from Markie's grip. "Full of dreadful teenage secrets, I bet." In fact, ex-cept for the one hidden in these pages, Markie couldn't think of a single secret between the sisters. Her heart hammered and her stomach sank as her sister started flipping pages.

"Anything about me and Danny in here?" Robbie flopped on the nearest bed as she skimmed page after page of Markie's teenage scrawl. In recent days Robbie's whole world had come down to this obsessive quest—the desire for one more word, one more photograph, one more memory of Danny.

Robbie's face lit with an expectant smile as she scanned the early pages, the first genuine smile Markie had seen in days. For the moment, her beleaguered sister looked vaguely like a teenager in love, instead of a devastated widow. "Here we go." She read aloud with obvious delight, *"Ohmigosh!!!! Robbie and Danny are getting married.* With four exclamation points—isn't that cute?"

Markie's heart contracted. This diary contained precious few entries about Robbie's youthful romance with Danny. In only a few pages Robbie would see the secret Markie was in no mood to reveal, certainly not now.

"There's nothing else. Now, give it back to me." Markie grabbed at her sister's arm, but Robbie swung away saucily as Marynell inserted her tall frame between the girls.

Markie's mother's thin face had turned as gray as the cleaning rag compressed in her bony fingers. "This is *my* house," she said to Markie quietly, ominously, "and you have no right to go through *my* things."

"*Your* things?" Markie spun to face her mother squarely.

In these last few days since she'd returned to the farm, she had finally given up hope of even the pretense of a decent relationship with Marynell, even for Robbie's sake. Truth be told, Markie had given up that hope a long time ago. Truth be told, she was never going to please her mother no matter what she did. And truth be told, if it weren't for her father and Robbie, she would never have set foot in this house again, not after… It was certainly too late now. Recently, fate—kindly or not, Markie couldn't decide—had engineered it so that she now knew exactly how much her long-ago decision had cost. It had cost her the beautiful young man who was her son, or rather, the son of a very fortunate family in Dallas.

"I will not be disrespected this way." Marynell's crepe-paper cheeks grew mottled, but for once her mother's distress inspired no mercy in her youngest daughter. "This is *my* home and I… I…" Marynell stammered before her lips clamped shut and her chin went up, her old defiant gesture.

"Oh, there has never been any question about that." Markie couldn't help her sarcasm. "That's why it's okay for us to go through Daddy's stuff like a wrecking crew, but *your* precious things must not be touched. But that happens to be *my* diary." She pointed at the volume still in Robbie's hands. "And you *took* it, didn't you, Mother?" The accusation made tears spring to her eyes. "Back when you and Daddy were helping me move from Dallas to Austin." Markie had moved a few times early in her career, but since the move to Austin a few years ago she felt settled at last. High time. She was thirty-five.

"I did it for your own good." Marynell's compressed lips were turning white.

Robbie's head came up. The sappy smile was gone, replaced by a worried frown. "Hey, you two," she chided in her musical voice. "What's this all about?"

"Your sister's husband," Marynell hissed, "has just been killed in a tragic accident." She emphasized each word as if Markie had somehow forgotten why they were all assembled here. "And she does not need any of your foolish drama."

"This isn't about *me,* mother. It's about *you,* stealing my diary. And not just any diary. *This* diary." Markie jabbed a finger at it.

"What in the world is going on here?" Robbie looked puzzled…and deeply disturbed.

"I was trying to protect you." Marynell ignored Robbie's question. "You were a very foolish teenage girl who had no idea what you were writing in those pages. You still have no idea."

"Well, *you* certainly shouldn't have had any idea what I was writing in those pages!" Markie was practically shouting now.

"Hey, now, Miss Marker." Robbie's use of Markie's old childhood nickname did not mollify her. After years of heartache she was determined to have it out with the old biddy, right here. Right now.

"Nothing is sacred with you, is it, Mother?"

"Sis." Robbie touched Markie's sleeve. "Stop it. It's just an old diary. Here." She held out the volume.

Robbie, the peacemaker, Markie thought. Robbie, Marynell's whipped little pet.

Marynell's eyes flitted to the diary, then to the pained expression on her bereaved middle daughter's face. Glaring back into Markie's eyes, she said, "You can take the thing and publish it in the *Dallas Morning News* for all I care. Whatever happens now, it's not on my head." She turned on her heel and stomped from the room.

"What on earth was *that* all about?" Robbie said after they heard the stairway door slam.

"That diary." Markie was unable to keep the creeping sorrow and resignation out of her voice, out of her heart. She sighed. "Or rather, what's in it. Read. You'll see."

"I'm not sure I want to now. Here." Robbie flapped the volume at Markie. "Take it."

Markie pushed the diary back. "No. I'm sick of secrets. Go on. Read it. I want you to. Honest." Even though she meant what she said, she couldn't help crossing her arms protectively around her middle.

To hide her pain, she turned to look out the dormer window. Out of the corner of her eye she could see her sister hesitating, then unsteadily lowering herself to perch on the edge of the bed.

Just beyond the bare yard Markie could see the windmill, like a huge leaden sunflower, fanning above the leafy tops of twin live oaks. The holding tank to the side was the same dull silver color, the color of all things utilitarian on the farm. In the foreground a rickety post-and-barbed-wire fence demarcated her father's garden, already bursting with spring foliage. An overalls-and-Stetson bedecked scarecrow, twice the size of a real man, stood over the rows with a toy gun lashed to one stuffed glove and a lurid smile painted on his pale muslin face. Markie smiled. One year her father had actually won first prize in the scarecrow festival over at Cedarville.

Beyond lay the acres and acres of gently rolling land that marked the southern reaches of the Texas Hill Country. *Will I ever get away from this beautiful, godforsaken place?* Markie was beginning to doubt whether she should stay on here to help her widowed sister. She caught a glimpse of her reflection in the glass, as if her very countenance, her very identity, arose from this land, would always be imprinted here.

Markie's love-hate relationship with the Hill Country had plagued her even after she'd made a disciplined effort to focus on a new life, a good life. Even her years as a mover and shaker among the power suits in the glass-walled urban canyons of Dallas had not eradicated the strange spell of the Texas Hill Country. Rocky gorges. Remote waterfalls. Wild rivers. Dusty rodeos. Savory barbecues. Old-time German Christmases. The memories, good and bad, always vivid, came back to her too easily as she looked out over the landscape where she had grown up. The Texas Hill Country was not the kind of place one could just *leave*.

Sometimes it felt as if she was two people. The hearty little girl who grew up running around this rustic landscape regulated by the seasonal rhythms of farming, and the sleek, sophisticated young woman who thrived in a bustling cosmopolitan culture, rushing headlong into the future. Two distinct parts, cleaved by the one event certain to change girl to woman—the birth of a child.

For some moments Robbie had been flipping pages, reading with the diary held close to her face as had been her girlhood habit. Markie noted the exact moment when she stopped. The clock ticked three times before Robbie lowered the open book to her lap, her finger touching one spot on the page, like a devotee lining a particular passage of the Bible in church.

Markie bit her lip as, with head bent, still as a penitent, her sister stared at the open page.

Robbie lifted sad eyes up to look at her sister and asked, "Am I reading this right?"

Markie didn't answer. She turned back to the view. So peaceful. So beautiful. As if nothing had ever gone wrong in this place. But everything had.

"Markie?" Robbie's troubled voice insisted from behind. "You…you had a *baby?*"

Markie stood stock still, closing her eyes, imagining again the scene of Danny's death. What a horrible way to see one's husband die. And what a horrible time to find out that your little sister is not even remotely who you thought she was. "Yes," she said without looking back at Robbie. "When I was seventeen."

"I… I don't believe it." Robbie flared a palm over her swollen bosom, where a perennial gold cross winked on a short chain. A gift from Danny, no doubt. Her sister, always the good girl to the core, would never understand what Markie had gone through, no matter how many diaries explained the pain.

Markie turned upon her sister with that uncompromising steady gaze that had vaulted her to her success in the political arena. "Well, you've got to believe it. Because it's true."

CHAPTER TWO

The maternity home is not such a bad place. It's kind of pretty from the street, actually. Quaint. A brick three-story with a big porch and tall white columns. Somebody said it's an old converted sorority house. Isn't that weird? It's a sisterhood of losers now. Girls like me who listened to some guy's sweet talk until he broke her heart.

The *home*—and I use that word in the worst sense, sort of like the warehouses where they stick old people—is tucked away at the end of a long, shady street a few blocks from the University of Texas campus. There's nothing that indicates what's really going on inside—just a little brass plaque beside the door that reads Edith Phillips Center. For Wayward Girls, I added in my head as I walked through the door.

Frankie insisted on lugging my bags upstairs, acting like she wasn't in a hurry, but I could tell she was. I could tell she wanted to beat the rush-hour traffic around the capitol. And, of course, the almighty Dr. Kyle mustn't miss his dinner.

A girl who actually looked more pregnant than me showed us to a tiny office where I met my caseworker, May, who is kind of cool. May looks as if she's stuck back in the sixties, wearing a loud afghan and a shiny Afro. Really. She even made Frankie laugh. Then we met some of the other girls, who were in the kitchen cooking dinner together like one big happy family.

My room's on the second floor. Frankie spread the twin comforter set she bought for me across the bed and set up some pictures in pretty frames on the dresser as if she was moving me into a real sorority house or something.

"Call me when it happens and I'll come right away," she told me as she gave me one last hug. "And remember, we love you."

We who? Her and Kyle? I am well aware that Kyle thinks I'm a juvenile delinquent, a stupid little slut, and I'm sure he's glad I opted to enter this free adoption program. I had to come here now so mom and dad would think I was off at the camp. Kyle doesn't mind pretending that he and Frankie are helping me foot the bill for that.

It's not bad here. Really. The backyard is pretty and secluded, with places for me to sit in the shade and write in my diary. Somebody put a little bowl of fruit on my dresser before I arrived. I'm supposed to keep up my studies here, but I don't know if I'll have the heart. I don't want to do anything. I don't want to be here at all.

But here I am. Waiting to give my baby to strangers.

ROBBIE, THE ONLY REDHEAD in the family and the most emotional of the McBride sisters by half, even when she was not pregnant, pressed a palm over the open pages of the diary as her face flushed and the tip of her nose gorged red from suppressing tears.

"Oh, Sissy, I'm so sorry," she whispered. She shook her head and gripped the diary. "I had no idea. I thought this was just going to be a bunch of kid's stuff."

"Of course you did." Markie was determined to let her sister off the hook gently for this trespass. "That's what a teenager's diary should be, shouldn't it? Innocent kid's stuff. Like yours, I suppose."

Robbie stared past Markie's shoulder, at the sky beyond the window. "My diaries were mostly about Danny. From the eighth grade on I expect my whole life was about Danny. But you're right." Her eyes snapped back to Markie's. "It was all innocent. School and proms and stuff. I just assumed yours would be the same."

"How far did you read?" Markie took two strides and lifted the diary from Robbie's hands. She angled her wrist so she could scan the page where her sister had been reading. The words *Edith Phillips Center* jumped off the page. "Oh, you got to the part where I moved to the Home."

Robbie nodded. "So I assume you…you gave up the baby for adoption?"

"Yes." Markie frowned at the loopy teenage handwriting that described the most painful months of her life. "I'm really sorry you had to find out this way."

Robbie swallowed. "Don't apologize. Do you know what…what happened to it? To him—her?"

"Him." To keep from going into total meltdown, Markie frowned at her reflection in the window. "He was a little boy. He's with a good family in Dallas." Again, to keep herself composed, Markie stated the facts simply, though living through it had been far from simple. It would never, ever be simple. The fact that she hadn't shared that experience with the sister she claimed to love so much seemed to only compound her loss.

"How in the world could I have missed this?" Robbie had the same look on her face that Markie recognized on her own. Self-condemnation.

The pattern of the McBride sisters from childhood on had been to shoulder the blame in any situation. A by-product of growing up under their mother's unrelenting domination, Markie knew. All of them had chosen different ways of coping with Marynell. Frankie fled. Markie rebelled. But poor Robbie had stayed on in Five Points, trying to appease a woman who could never be pleased. She had ended up feeling responsible for everybody else's happiness. And now even the buffer of happy-go-lucky Danny was lost to her. The last thing Robbie needed was more guilt.

"It's not your fault. I intentionally kept it from you." Markie took two more steps and sat down on the twin bed next to her sister, grasping her hands. "And it wasn't the end of the world. I survived. I know I did the right thing. I know he's happy and well." *And brilliant and handsome and brimming with charisma and a natural-born leader like his father.* But Markie couldn't add those things. Because how would she explain how she had come to know all of that? There was too much risk…for Brandon.

"Don't try to make me feel better. You were only *seventeen.* I could have helped you *and* your baby." Robbie withdrew one hand, draping it protectively over her abdomen as if shielding the child growing there from the sad knowledge that he or she had an unknown cousin somewhere, far away from them all, far away from Five Points.

"You had just married Danny that Christmas. And then you guys got the opportunity to buy the farm and you and Mother and Daddy ended up working so hard to get it in shape by the following spring."

"So, you were pregnant when I got married in December and then you had the baby that spring?"

"That summer."

"But how—"

"Remember when I had that bad case of mono and dropped out of school and Frankie told mother she would tutor me and take care of me in Austin?"

Robbie nodded.

"Then that summer when I was supposed to be at that Christian leadership camp for a month? Well, I *didn't* ever have mono and it *wasn't* a leadership camp."

Troubled emotions flitted across Robbie's face as she struggled to add it all up. "I remember when Frankie moved you down to her apartment. That was right before she married Kyle."

"Yes. She finished nursing school that May," Markie supplied.

"Right." Robbie nodded.

"She and Kyle got married—"

"At the courthouse. You know, I think she always resented the fact that Mother and Daddy threw a huge hometown wedding for me and Danny."

"It was Kyle's idea to skip the wedding. They were in a big hurry to settle in and set up their first apartment in time for him to start his residency. Then I popped into the picture. It was no picnic, living with young marrieds as a pregnant teenager. Kyle wasn't all that great about it. Poor Frankie. She was trying to help her baby sister and at the same time trying to please a very demanding young husband."

"And now he's a demanding *old* husband," Robbie pronounced. Kyle, barely past forty, wasn't exactly old. But Markie knew that Robbie and Danny had never cared for their uppity, sneering brother-in-law.

"Yeah. I was glad he was off on his residency rotations most of the time."

"I can't believe she married the guy, even if he is handsome as all get out. Was that it, Markie?" Robbie turned on her younger sister, eyes radiating sympathy. "Your big sisters were falling in love and getting married so you got in a big hurry to do the same? You always were trying to keep up with us like that."

"No, that *wasn't* it!" Markie couldn't keep the annoyance out of her voice. "Look," she continued more gently, "I was genuinely in love with the father of the baby. In fact, I don't think I've ever stopped loving him."

"Who was it?" Robbie asked softly. "If you don't mind my asking. I mean, I don't remem—" Robbie stopped as if a truck had slammed into her. "Oh, my gosh. It was that congressman's son! What was his name?"

"Justin Kilgore. It's all in there." Which was foolish, she supposed, having the whole thing written down like that. But even with all the pain recorded in its pages, some compulsion had kept Markie from being able to part with the diary.

"Justin Kilgore." Robbie's soft voice was full of awe. "I don't believe it. Justin and his father used to come into the Hungry Aggie back when I was waiting tables. I always kind of liked him. I remember how he'd always ask about you, how he always found a way to work your name into even the briefest conversation. And then when you guys started seeing each other…oh, my." Robbie's shoulders sank and her soft voice grew hushed. "It was partly my fault, wasn't it? I mean, I helped you go sneaking around with an older guy."

"Robbie. It wasn't your fault. I was a big girl. I made my own choices."

"I guess. But I should have told Mother what was going on. But you seemed so…so happy with him. I thought he was kind of right for you. He was so handsome, Markie. And so smart. So very nice. What a terrible ordeal." Robbie lowered her head.

Markie lowered her head, too. As she did, she brought the diary to her lips, fighting tears. "Yes," she whispered with her lips pressed against the dry, musty fabric, "it was."

"Oh, my poor baby!" Robbie wrapped her arms around her sister's shoulders. "I can't imagine how painful it was for you."

Markie struggled not to let herself feel it— all the emotion she had kept bottled up for eighteen long, lonely years. "It's nothing compared to what you're going through now."

Robbie turned her head into Markie's shoulder.

Markie clasped her sister's forearm, holding on tight, afraid that what she had kept so carefully sealed away would crush them both if she let it out now.

But when Robbie started to cry, Markie knew there was no hope of holding her own tears in.

For a moment the two wept and clung in a sisterly hug.

Finally Robbie held her sister away at arm's length. "You had a baby with Justin Kilgore." She looked into Markie's brimming eyes and pronounced each word slowly, as if trying to cement the fact in both their minds.

Markie swiped at her eyes and looked down at the worn floorboards. How she had hated this barren room as a young girl, especially after the warmth of her sisters was gone from it. "Yes. I just hate it that you found out this way, now of all times."

But Robbie, who could be incredibly strong as well as kind, shook her head. She wiped at her eyes with the sash of her robe and suddenly she looked more like her old self than she had in days. "I hate it that you suffered with it alone all this time. I can't imagine. Being so young and having a baby off in Austin, with a congressman's son, no less."

Another silence stretched before Markie said, "I wouldn't say it was *with* him." She glanced at Robbie to see if she comprehended.

But Robbie frowned. "What do you mean?"

"He never knew."

"You mean he never knew that…" Robbie hesitated, and Markie imagined her sister was still struggling with the fact that she had a living, breathing nephew somewhere in Dallas. "That you gave the baby away?"

"No. He never even knew I was pregnant."

"Mar-kie." Robbie stared at her. "He never even knew—I don't understand." Robbie tilted her head, looking disturbed now, as well as perplexed. "I mean, I can see how you kept this from me, maybe, but how could you keep such a thing from the baby's *father*?"

"He… I didn't think he wanted to know. I was young. I was convinced. People—the congressman and Mother—convinced me that it would ruin Justin's future if he knew, that there was no point in telling him if I wasn't going to keep the baby, anyway." Markie's voice trailed off as she realized how weak and sorry her excuses sounded now, coming from a competent woman of thirty-five. But back then, she had been one very scared teenager. And back then, she had felt so angry, so betrayed.

"Besides…" Markie had trouble admitting this next part even to herself, much less to her sister. "He was already engaged."

"Engaged?" This time when Robbie stared, her jaw dropped, as well. "The guy was engaged and he…he…when you were just a *teenager?*"

"He was only twenty-one himself."

"Stop defending him! Apparently all that Mr. Nice Guy stuff was nothing but an act. He was busy getting you pregnant while he was engaged to another girl, Markie."

"It wasn't like that. It wasn't about the sex."

"Oh, please. Let's call a spade a spade, okay? The guy was a creep. I mean, when did he decide to tell you about his fiancé? Right before he dumped you and went back east?"

Markie bit her lip to gain control. Robbie

could be so small town, so black and white in her thinking. She of all people would never understand what had happened between the young couple. "He never did tell me, exactly. Mother found out about the engagement from his father and she was the one who told me."

Robbie shook her head sadly. "Mother."

Markie nodded. "Yeah." Nothing more needed to be said on that score. "She took over my life after she found out about me and Justin and the fact that I was pregnant. She read all about it. In here." Markie stroked the dairy in a gesture that was resigned, gentle.

Robbie's jaw dropped in genuine shock. "*That's* how she found out? By snooping around in your diary?"

Markie shrugged. "It doesn't matter. The whole thing happened so fast. She would have discovered the truth sooner or later, anyway."

"Oh, man. I imagine she had a cow. And there you were, all alone in this house with her."

"I had Daddy."

"I meant alone without *us,* without your sisters. Was she just awful about it?"

"You really want to know?"

Robbie swallowed, nodded. They'd tried, over the years, to share the pain their mother had inflicted, to dilute it by spreading it out before them in the light of day. But they all knew it was Markie who had suffered the most at their mother's hand, though it was Robbie who could never seem to break free from her.

"One time I dashed outside because I had to puke. It was weird how my morning sickness never hit in the *morning* like it was supposed to. It hit like clockwork every day after school. I never wanted to eat dinner, but she insisted that I sit down at the table. I could feel her watching every bite. I'll never forget it. I jumped off the porch and ran around the side of the house. The sun was going down. She came up behind me while I was retching and yanked me back by the hair."

"Oh, Sissy." Robbie sweet brow furrowed with sympathy. Looking at the dark circles that had appeared under her sister's eyes since the funeral made Markie want to soften the story.

"She just fumed a lot at first. But after she

talked to the congressman, she suddenly wanted me to have an abortion."

Robbie gasped and covered her mouth.

"I'm sorry. I know that word must be hard for you to hear, especially in your condition, especially with everything else you're going through."

"Markie, will you stop apologizing!" Robbie turned to wrap thin fingers around her sister's forearm. "I care about you." She gave the arm a hearty shake. "You should have told me about this. About all of it. I don't care if I *was* planning a wedding. I don't care if we *were* buying that damned farm. I'm your sister and I would have helped you. What did Daddy say? Surely he didn't want you to have an ab...to..." Robbie stumbled over the words. "To get rid of your baby."

"He didn't know."

"*What?* I can't believe it! I can't believe you had a baby and kept it a secret from Daddy, from all of us, for all these years."

"You might as well hear the whole story. Maybe you'll understand it better then."

They arranged themselves more comfortably in the swale of the old mattress. Around them, the boxes they had been emptying were completely forgotten.

"At first I agreed to do whatever mother wanted. She was under a lot of pressure from Congressman Kilgore. He was facing a very close election and some other troubles that I've now had an opportunity to research."

Robbie frowned. "What kind of troubles?"

"A grand jury was about to indict him in a campaign-financing probe."

Robbie nodded. "Oh, I see."

Markie figured Robbie probably *didn't* see. At the mention of anything concerning politics, her sister's eyes had always glazed over, so she simply went on.

"Anyway, he was in no mood for this mess." She tapped the diary. "And he didn't want his brilliant son's life interrupted, either. Frankie was supposed to find the doctor to perform the…you know, the procedure, in Austin. She found a good doctor, a place where I would be safe. The plan was to get it done right after your wedding. But when the time came I just… I couldn't. I knew…"

Markie bit her lip to hold back the emotion, then forced herself to go on. "I just knew any baby of Justin's was bound to be beautiful, exceptional, and he became…the baby became so…so real to me." She clutched the diary, remembering the things she'd written in those pages in the early stages of her pregnancy. "So Frankie and I made up the mononucleosis dodge and then she and Kyle found the Edith Phillips adoption center in Austin."

"But how did you keep Mother from finding out that you changed your mind? How did you hide something like that?" Again, Robbie's hand slid to her bulging tummy. She was only five months along and her pregnancy—her fourth—was already obvious.

Markie's older sisters had always been utterly feminine, curvy and pretty, but for Markie it had been different. She had never considered herself all that beautiful, at least not until Justin had made her feel that way. Naturally tall and athletic, with angular shoulders and long legs, she had managed to conceal her pregnancy behind the camouflage of sloppy sweatpants and oversize letter jackets. Her plain brown ponytail, thick glasses and pale, unadorned complexion made it easy enough not to attract male attention in a high school filled with perky little blondes in skimpy pom-pom outfits.

"I think Mother made some kind of deal with the congressman. Supposedly she got money for my college education. I never saw much of it, I'll tell you that." Markie tried not to be bitter.

Her current life, the life of a successful political consultant with tons of friends, was enormously satisfying. But when she came back to Five Points the memories always surfaced afresh, and it was hard to look at her life objectively.

"How could Mother keep something like that from Daddy?"

"You have to ask? How does Mother do anything she's determined to do? Listen—" suddenly Markie's tone was urgent "—don't stay here with her."

"What?"

"Don't move in with mother. She'll only make your life miserable, bossing you around, manipulating your feelings. And you don't need that now, not when you're so vulnerable."

"But… I can't stay way out there on that

big farm by myself. I'll need someone to help me when the baby comes."

"I'll move out to the farm with you. I do most of my work on the phone and on the Internet this time of the year, anyway. And Five Points will be the locus of Doug Curry's campaign. It's in the center of his district."

"Oh, man, I just realized something. Curry's running against Congressman Kilgore. Are you sure you're not working for this guy out of some kind of old spite? I mean, to get even or something? And isn't it going to be hard for you to face the congressman, after all that's happened?"

"Now, hold on just a minute." Markie aimed a finger at her sister's nose, then quickly squelched the gesture. She wanted to be gentle with Robbie, she really did, considering what Robbie had only recently endured, considering what lay ahead. It wasn't Robbie's fault Markie had made a mess of her life so long ago.

"For one thing, Congressman Kilgore doesn't know what I really did about the baby. Nobody does, except for Frankie and Kyle, and I doubt *Mr. Big Shot Surgeon* has ever given it a second thought." She ducked her head to meet her sister's eyes. "And now that you know the truth, I can trust you to keep it to yourself, right?"

"Of course," Robbie murmured. "Who on earth would I tell?"

What was left unsaid was that the one person in all the world Robbie might tell was recently dead. Markie could see that's what her sister was thinking. She looked haunted, pained, the way she had looked almost constantly for these past few days.

And watching that expression overtake Robbie's face again gave Markie a sick wave of guilt. She looked away. Here was her sister, coping with the loss of a husband, with the possible loss of her farm, and she's berating the girl about keeping her own deep dark secret. Robbie, of course, couldn't possibly understand the stakes, couldn't possible know what Markie had discovered only a few days ago.

Brandon Smith. For one instant Markie relived the shock of seeing his picture among the applications, the shock of hearing his voice—so like his father's—on the phone.

Every campaign season she chose a protégé, a young go-getter to work alongside her in a congressional or senate race and learn the ropes. Every season, the competition for the internship got stronger. Applications poured in to McBride Consulting from all over Texas.

Markie patted Robbie's hand. "Of course you won't tell anyone. But please don't go thinking I've got some kind of ax to grind with the congressman. I didn't seek out his opponent or anything like that. Curry's campaign contacted me. Because I'm the best, remember?" She nudged her sister and got a faint smile.

"And I firmly agree with Doug Curry's positions on the issues. He's going to do a great job in Washington. Old man Kilgore thinks he's got this race all sewn up. He'll make a few scattered appearances around the Hill Country and maybe he'll even show his face once or twice in Five Points. In the meantime, we'll be slowly and surely kicking his ass."

At least Markie hoped that's the way this summer would go. Not only for Doug Curry's sake, but for her own. And for Brandon's? She bit her lip as she pressed the diary to her middle, wishing she could see her son. Would that be worth the price? No. She already knew she would do what she had to do. The safe thing. Always protecting herself. She'd done it so long she didn't know how to stop.

"So what do you say?" She affected an up-beat attitude, nudging Robbie again. "I can make Five Points Curry's campaign base if I want to. Like I said, it's smack in the middle of the district. I can stay with you out on the farm. Help with the bills and groceries and stuff. That way you can stay in your own home and keep the boys away from…" She rolled her eyes in the direction of the stairs at the end of the hallway. "You Know Who. And by the time this little darling ar-rives—" she gave her sister's pregnant abdomen a soft pat, as if everything would be hunky-dory when that blessed event happened "—the election will be over and I can concentrate on taking care of you and the baby."

"I don't know," Robbie frowned. "That's a lot to ask of you. Maybe I should just stick to the plan and move in here."

"What else has your spinster sister got to do?" Markie tried to kid her, then grew serious again. "Mother would suck the heart and soul out of you within a week and you know it."

The sisters fell silent. Both of them knew the situation to be just so. Their mother was the most controlling woman in all of Five Points, in all of Keaton County, possibly in all of the state of Texas.

And somewhere below them inside the quiet walls of·this picturesque Victorian-era farmhouse, the most controlling woman in all of Texas was seething, waiting. Waiting to pounce on her daughter Markie for daring to rebel yet again. Waiting to reexert control over the one thing she had always controlled more easily than any other—her daughter Robbie.

CHAPTER THREE

I promise you one thing, my little one, I will do everything in my power to see that your life is safe and happy. Even if that means giving you up—no. I don't want to think about that right now. Not yet. I want to think happy thoughts because if I don't, I'll cry.

And if Mother catches me crying again, she'll get suspicious for sure. Not that she isn't already. When she reads what I just wrote on these pages, all hell will break loose.

(And you are reading this, aren't you, Mother???)

P.S. I don't care what you do. There's nothing you can do to me anymore. I have my baby to think about now.

Back to you, sweet baby. You know how much I love you, my sweet, sweet baby. Hey!

Was that you? Did you just give me a little tiny kick? Awesome! Truly, truly awesome!!!

Man. I can't wait to see you!

You will be a beautiful baby, I bet. How could Justin be the father of any other kind? You will have his perfect, wavy dark hair. His dark brown eyes. Maybe even tiny baby muscles that are shaped like his gorgeous big ones.

I guess I can't think about your daddy, either, sweet baby. Because that makes me want to cry, too.

Oh, Diary! Why did he leave me? Wasn't I good enough for him? Didn't he understand how much I love him? I gotta go now. Because now I *am* starting to cry again.

JUSTIN KILGORE ROLLED INTO Five Points on one of the five highways that radiated out in a star pattern from the town, the one that angled up from the southwest. As he looked around at the familiar buildings, he thought, *For ill or good, I'm committed now.* For ill or good, he had come back here, back to the ranch land of his Kilgore forebears, back to the home of his first love, his only love, Markie McBride.

Memories of her started to flow through him as soon as he'd caught sight of a windmill on the highway. Some sweet, some disturbing.

Like the sound of her mother's voice when she answered the phone the first time he called their farmhouse.

"It's some boy," he'd overheard the woman say in a hateful tone. It was the first indicator he had that Markie's childhood had been far from gentle.

He'd heard Markie say it was probably something to do with the campaign. When she'd picked up the phone, she'd offered a careful "Yes?" and Justin got the impression the mother was listening. He could hear dishes clanking in the background.

Man! Markie's voice on the phone! Clear and sweet and sending tightening sensations through his core. Right then, he'd suspected he was falling in love with her.

He'd asked her if he could come out to the farm and pick her up and take her into town for a Coke. Later she'd told him her parents would chain her to the bed before they'd let her date a college guy. And they'd make her stop volunteering in campaigns if they knew she was meeting older guys doing it. She told him that wasn't the reason she volunteered—to meet cute guys—but it sure didn't hurt! Then she'd gone on to say the boys that do stuff like that are head and shoulders above the stupid jocks at Five Points High, but she never dreamed one would actually call her. How unsophisticated she'd been back then. How innocent.

He'd watched her that first night when they were stuffing envelopes, being so nice to the old ladies in tennis shoes. He got up and moved his stack of fliers and envelopes to her card table. The old ladies smiled to themselves, but he hadn't cared.

Some lady named Fran did all the talking, so they didn't get a chance to say much. But her eyes. Oh, my, her eyes! Every time he looked up, he felt like he was looking into them for the very first time. In all these years he hadn't forgotten how they'd thrilled him. Blue as the Hill Country sky. Sparkling with intelligence. He'd give anything to look into those eyes again.

"I'm not allowed to go out on school nights,"

she'd said. "And besides, I have choir practice tonight." It was a code to avert the shrill mother, one that he caught onto immediately.

"Where?" he'd said.

"Old St. Michael's."

"That tall old brick church that's set back off Dumas Street?"

"Uh, yeah."

"Can I come and listen in?" He'd sit in the back of a church on a handful of thumbtacks if he had to.

"Uh, yeah." She hadn't sounded too sure.

"What time?"

"Uh, seven."

"I'll stay in the back. I don't want to disrupt your choir practice. I just want to look at you," he'd said, bold as you please.

He'd looked at her, all right. And he remembered, to this very day, how beautiful she was. So many memories. All of them revolving around Markie McBride.

The divided highway narrowed as it became Main Street. The town looked about the same to Justin, spruced up a bit, maybe, because of a recent holiday or parade or whatever. The old diner, the Hungry Aggie, was still tucked in between the bank and the optician's office on Main Street.

He could see the steeple of the church where Markie had sung in the choir off in the distance. He turned the car down a side street, headed there. The priest had called him on his cell phone while Justin was out riding the fence line. Lorn Hix, the foreman out on the Kilgore, had given the priest the number. A girl, the priest said. All alone. Being held in the municipal jail. At least she had known to make her one phone call to the local Catholic church. Could Justin help? the padre asked. The truth was, Justin was buzzing with excitement at having his first case, his first real rescue.

Justin parked and went inside the small limestone jailhouse that crouched beside the small limestone fire station.

"She's another one of those illegals, probably dumped by coyotes," the guard tossed the words over his shoulder with no small amount of contempt as he led Justin to a back room. "I'm glad the priest called you. I don't have the space or the time for these people."

"We call them undocumented immigrants."

Justin laid some emphasis on the word *un-documented*, but he doubted this man would appreciate the distinction. "And she won't be that way for long." That was the reason he had started the Light at Five Points, known among Mexican crossers simply as La Luz, the Light. As he and his very bare-bones staff often told the desperate crossers, *You're an undocumented alien now, but not for long.* We will help you get your citizenship. We will help you learn English. We will help you find a job. *We will help.* It had become Justin's mantra.

"Stinkin' coyotes," the guard said. "Getting a girl this far into Texas and dumping her. Bet they took all her money and, you know, probably did some other things to her. But I have no choice but to pick up these illegals when the store managers call. I did get her name out of her. Aurelia Garcia. Stinkin' coyotes."

Justin would never say it to a guy in local law enforcement like this one, but in Justin's mind the young men who devolved into coyotes were victims of sorts, as well. They were bad hombres, to be sure. Living a subterranean life that fed off of the human bondage and desperation of their own people. But in the beginning most of them had been lured away from all that was wholesome or sacred in their culture by something that only those crushed under the weight of poverty could fully understand.

Money. Lots of money, and all that it represented. A coyote could get as much as two thousand dollars a head for moving crossers north under cover of darkness. A smart one could make nine or ten thousand dollars a day, easily. Justin knew how it happened. He just didn't know how to stop it. He didn't know how to save girls like this one or boys like the Morales brothers who had shown up out on the Kilgore last week, looking for ranch jobs, looking for food. But he was determined to try.

The deputy brought a tiny girl up out of the holding cell. She had straight black hair, nearly to her waist, huge eyes, nearly as black, frozen wide in terror. Despite a filthy face and clothes, her beauty still shone. In the few pictures Justin had seen of his mother, she looked like this. Fragile and beautiful.

When she hesitated at the sight of Justin, the guard pulled her forward by the wrist as if she were a child. And she could have easily passed for one, in the States. She couldn't have been more than five feet, not an ounce over a hundred pounds. She eyed the men with the kind of wary silence that spoke of mistrust from past abuses.

In English, Justin convinced the guard to let him speak to her in private. In Spanish, he told her not to worry and guided her over to a bench. After they sat down, he took off his Stetson. "Aurelia, I'm Justin Kilgore," he said in Spanish, "and I'm from a place called the Light at Five Points—"

"Ay, La Luz!" the girl cried, clasping her tiny hands together. "I find you! Take me with you! Padre Gusto, he told me about you! It's a miracle how I find you!" She made the sign of the cross on herself. "A miracle!"

Justin gave her the quiet sign. He didn't want the local cops to think he was running some kind of underground network. "Father Augustus?" he said quietly. This was the name of his aging friend in Jalisco. A renegade Roman Catholic priest who encouraged the natives in Jalisco and the surrounding areas to blend their native culture with Christian spirituality. Father Gus's favorite hobby was roaring around on his motorcycle and dispensing condoms to those who needed better sense.

"*Sí.* He said if I can make it to the Light at Five Points, I would be safe. Please." Her eyes pleaded. "I think Julio is already there."

"Julio?" That was the name of the youngest of the Morales brothers. A strong, quiet young man, about eighteen or nineteen, Justin would guess.

"*Sí.* My man. We are getting married."

Which might further explain why the Morales brothers had urged him to hurry into town for her. Well, he'd do his best. "We have to be careful here. You were caught shoplifting at the 7-Eleven."

"*Sí.* Please." Aurelia continued to beg. "I'll cook for you. I am a fine, fine cook. My whole village says so."

"Wait here. Do *not*—" he pointed a warning finger at the girl "—run."

Justin went back to the guard.

"She was hungry. It was only a candy bar.

Do you honestly think sending these poor people to jail helps?"

"Nah," the guard scoffed. "But you and I know about ninety percent of them are out to beat the system. They keep going around in the same old ruts, generation after generation. We can't let them overrun us, either."

Justin knew about the ruts, the patterns, the traps. Border crossers knew one another, ran in groups. Whole families, extended families, came to the States in stages. A father or a grandfather would go north and make his way, then call for the others. This process took years, sometimes spanning several generations.

"Then will this help pay this girl's expenses or her fines or whatever so I can get her out of here?" Justin had carefully folded the hundred-dollar bill so that the numerals showed.

Bribes. Common as the Texas limestone beneath their feet.

The guard peered off into the cells beyond, past Justin's shoulder, obviously looking at Aurelia, who sat hunched on the bench. He took the money.

"You're wasting your money, Mr. Kilgore," he said as he stuffed it in his pocket. "You know this kind of shit always ends badly. These people would be better off never leaving their villages. We should just press charges and send her back."

Justin thought Father Augustus might surely agree. The priest felt the contaminating influence of El Norte was ruining the simple life of the villages. But how did you convince the young people of that? Once they had seen the big TVs and the big cars and the fancy clothes? How could you send a girl back south who had journeyed more than a hundred miles inside the border through God-knows-what to meet up with the love of her life?

Back out on the highway, Justin didn't stop in town. There was no need. He had plenty of gas and the girl was skittish, being in the cab alone with him. She hugged the passenger door like a frightened kitten. Justin was relaxed in the seat but tried to keep his six-foot frame squarely on his side. No need to spook her. In Spanish he said, "You'll be all right now."

"Sí," she said, but he could tell she didn't

quite believe him. Though it was another fifteen miles out to the ranch, he was anxious to get her to Julio. So when the highway opened up outside of town, he set his old pickup's engine to thrumming. They might not encounter another car for miles now. One could put the pedal to the metal on these Texas highways with some impunity.

As the truck gained speed, the girl looked more and more frightened, yet more and more excited, as well. No doubt she was anticipating seeing her true love. Justin tried to remember how that felt. Somewhere deep inside him there was a spark of the love he'd once cherished for Markie McBride. But out of sheer emotional survival he had quelled those feelings long ago.

He glanced at Aurelia. How had she made it? he wanted to ask her. She had mentioned the sign of the Five Points.

"Did Julio send you a star?" Justin asked her in Spanish. He wanted to know if word of his organization had begun to spread yet among the crossers. He hoped so.

"*Sí.*" The girl slashed a quick star in the air with an index finger.

The Five Points of the Lone Star. The signal that a crosser had made it as far as the Texas town where five highways converged in a radiating pattern. Crossers sometimes sent a Lone Star home to their relatives in Mexico in one form or another—a trinket, a postcard, a pattern stitched on cloth.

Justin had chosen Five Points as his location partly for that reason. Once they got that far, crossers felt safe enough to rest before fleeing in five directions to hide in the caves and canyons and remote ranches of the Hill Country. If he could get to them at that stopping place, he felt he had a chance to make a difference, a chance to interrupt the cycle.

Five Points.

Outside the truck window, the country Justin had loved since he was a boy rolled by. Evening was coming on and the dark hills undulated endlessly against the purple sky.

When they pulled into the ranch drive, Aurelia spotted Julio. He was high up on a two-story scaffolding, repairing some crumbling limestone on a corner of the immense Kilgore ranch house. Justin had been pleased to learn that the Morales brothers were local Maya stonemasons in their home village, as skilled as their ancient counterparts. The renovations they had accomplished on the aging ranch house were nothing short of art. Even in its current state of decay, the house was an architectural monument of symmetry and well-crafted stonework. Constructed more than a hundred years ago by one of Justin's Kilgore forebears, the place had a Romanesque simplicity that Justin loved. Rows of limestone pillars defined the first-story veranda. It would take plenty of fresh limestone to restore it, and Justin knew just where he could get it on—the Tellchick farm.

Justin's father no longer made a pretense of keeping a residence in Texas, and the place had been virtually abandoned until Justin returned to it a couple of months ago. The inside was caked with dust, its timeless beauty only enjoyed by the occasional stray cow or shelter-seeking snake. But Justin had come to the house often as a youth, dreaming of restoring life to it.

And of course, he'd brought Markie McBride here often to share that dream.

Aurelia had rolled down the truck window

and was hanging out of it, waving her arms and screaming, "Julio! Julio!"

Julio scrambled down off the scaffolding like an ant off a mound. He ran, his boots kicking up dust, until he came up alongside the pickup. He grabbed the door handle before Justin had even come to a stop.

When the door opened, Aurelia flung herself out into Julio's strong arms. He swung her light body high off her feet and spun her in a circle with her skirt flying, then clutched her to him, his pelvis jutting into hers, his muscular shoulders hunched around her, his mouth claiming hers in a reunion kiss.

Justin had to look away. Now he did remember. Watching the lovers kiss, he remembered, all too clearly, what it felt like to be so young, so in love.

There was a small celebration in the old house that night. The kitchen was hardly up to sanitation standards, but Aurelia was used to far humbler conditions. She cooked a delicious Mexican feast for the men and Lorn's wife.

But as in the lives of all crossers, the peace didn't last long. "Someone comes,"

Juan Morales, who seemed to have a sixth sense about these things, announced the very next night.

Sure enough, Justin spotted moving shadows back in a thicket of live oaks.

Lorn went for his shotgun, but Justin restrained him. They would have to get used to the illegals approaching La Luz in all kinds of ways; from the jail in town to hiding in the woods to approaching the ranch in stealth.

"Come with me," he told Juan, and they went out to investigate.

The Ramos family consisted of a father, mother and two frightened little boys. The priest in town had directed them here. Hasty arrangements were made to feed and bed down the tired travelers.

Later that night, Justin walked out on the upstairs veranda to contemplate the starry sky and think about his mission. Below him the ranch land spread like a peaceful kingdom. Getting the Light at Five Points going was sure to be hard work, but already he had his first real family tucked in for the night.

His reverie was broken when he heard frantic arguing whispers on the porch below and then the sound of Aurelia hysterically crying, "Don't go!"

Justin hurried back inside and down the wide stone staircase.

"What's wrong?" he said as he emerged on the porch.

The Morales brothers stood there, with their shabby backpacks slung over their shoulders.

"We didn't have nothing to do with no fire," Juan said defensively. "The man paid us to go there for one night and make noise."

"What are you talking about?" Justin demanded. Were they talking about the barn fire that killed Danny Tellchick?

"The sheriff is asking a lot of questions. These bad hombres." Juan's Spanish was so rushed, Justin had trouble keeping up. "They will lay the blame on us."

"Shut up," Julio snapped. "We're leaving," he declared to Justin.

"No!" Aurelia wailed, clinging to him. She was wearing a simple shift nightgown, probably something Lorn's wife had given her.

"But why?" Justin asked. "Why now?" It was practically the middle of the night. What had happened to make them want to run?

"We are sorry, my friend," Julio said a little more calmly. "We thank you for your kindnesses, but you cannot help us. We have been tricked."

"Let's go *now.*" Juan looked frightened as he tugged on his brother's arm.

"But what about the stonework?" Justin argued as he followed them down the porch steps. "You're just getting started." He didn't care about the renovations so much as showing Julio and Juan that they could be of genuine value in their new country.

"Sorry, amigo," Julio called. "Someday I will try to finish it!" And then the two young men disappeared into the night.

CHAPTER FOUR

Tonight I figured out that when Justin's brows draw together in that frowny way of his, it doesn't mean he's mad or anything. He's just intense, sorta like his dad, only in a good way. I met the congressman finally. Yikes. He's even bigger than he looks in his pictures, a bull of a man with a tiny little pair of wire-rimmed glasses perched on his nose. I took a hard look at him. Then I took a look at Justin. Can they even be related? I wondered. Then I realized people could say the same thing about me and my mother. Nothing alike.

Anyway, I think that look just means Justin cares.

Actually, now that I think about it, it's the look he gets right before he's going to kiss me. His brows draw together that tiny bit,

like he's in pain or concentrating or something. His eyes squint up a bit, like he's
studying me real hard. Oh, I can't describe
it. All I know is, I love it when he looks at
me that way.

Except tonight I think he was frowning
because he really was kind of upset. We
took a couple of horses for a moonlight
ride out on his ranch, way out to the place
where that big flat outcropping of limestone
looks so pretty. Justin told me there are
caves under there, which I kind of knew, but
I've never actually been in them. He had a
flashlight and was going to take me down
into one, but right then we saw headlights
and this big Cadillac came rolling up. It just
drove right up on the limestone.

Justin stopped the horses back in the trees
and said that was weird, for his father to
be out here so late at night. And then we
saw a shadow get out and carry something into the cave.

It was really kind of creepy.

Justin was in a hurry to split, so we turned
the horses around and got out of there.

Later I told him about how my mom is

weird like that, too, sometimes, and later he really opened up and told me all about his dad. We're getting that close. When you love someone, you tell them every-thing, even about your crazy parents.

"ROBBIE AND THE BOYS WON'T be staying here," Markie announced without preamble as she bounded down the last few steps of the stairway leading from the attic.

She marched through her mother's gleam-ing green-and-white kitchen to the dinette table where her laptop and papers were spread out. The southwest sun was high in the sky now, creating a glaring backdrop at the bay window that cupped around the small table. How deceptively comfortable and se-rene her mother's fastidious decorating made the spot feel. The room was already filling with the savory aroma of roasting meat.

Marynell turned from the sink with a half-peeled potato in one hand and a potato peeler in the other. "What fool nonsense are you talking now?" She turned back to the sink and resumed her task. "Of course they're staying." Her mouth was pinched tighter than the clasp of a change purse as she proceeded to whack at the potato.

"The boys and Robbie are ready to go home." Markie proceeded to stack her papers. "I'll be going out to the farm with them."

Marynell's jaw dropped, then she quickly snapped it shut again. "I have already put a roast in the Crock-Pot and peeled a dozen potatoes for the boys' supper. They've been instructed to get off the bus down here at the road after school, just like always."

"Just like always?" Markie frowned. "It's only been a week since the funeral, mother. The boys only went back to school the day before yesterday. There is no *like always* in Robbie's boys' lives right now, nothing routine, unless it's the Tellchick farm, their home. That's where they belong. I'll be going out there to stay and help Robbie."

Marynell carefully placed the potato into a large pot at her elbow. She rinsed the slicer and propped the blade over the edge of the sink, just so. As she wiped her hands on a towel, she slowly crossed the room toward Markie. "You always do this," she started in a low, threatening tone. "You can't stand to be in this town two seconds without thinking you have to tear everything up. For once, Margaret, think of someone besides yourself. You can't seriously be considering taking those children back out there to that place, not after...not after seeing their father killed that way."

"Robbie has decided that's what she wants."

"*Robbie* decided? Robbie is not herself these days, and you know it." Marynell grabbed Markie's arm, gripping it somewhat viciously, but Markie was used to her mother acting this way. She stared, unblinking, while her mother demanded, "This is about that damned diary, isn't it?"

"You had no right to take it, Mother." Markie jerked her arm away. "And where the hell is my picture?"

"What picture? I have no idea what you are talking about."

"When did you take it?" Markie persisted. "How? Back when you and Daddy were moving me the last time? From Dallas?"

Marynell wrung the dish towel for an instant before she folded her arms across her chest and steadied herself. "I simply didn't want you to be reminded of that painful period of your life. I wanted you to have a fresh start in Austin."

Her gut wrenched as Markie realized that of course her mother had read the entire diary, every last word of it, the parts written after Markie had left Five Points and gone to live with Frankie in Austin—the parts after she moved to the Edith Phillips Home.

Which meant Marynell knew about Brandon. Well, she didn't know that was his name or where he lived or who his parents were. None of that was in the diary, thank goodness. And Markie would make sure this woman never did know those things.

"Does anyone else know?" she said, fully aware that her mother knew exactly what she was asking.

"No. And they're never going to, Margaret." Her mother seemed suddenly sincere. "As far as I'm concerned, the whole incident is in the past. I would think *you* would be glad to have all that in the past, too. Why do you want to stir up trouble now, when your sister's life has been practically destroyed?

You should never have taken that diary out of the box."

Markie sensed a subterfuge behind Marynell's persistent blaming. Turning things on the other person was the same old trick her mother always used to defend her actions, no matter how indefensible. What had she done now? Perhaps she had, in fact, told someone else about the baby. Or perhaps for some reason *the incident* was not really in the past as Marynell claimed.

"If it's all in the past, why didn't you simply destroy that diary?"

Marynell's face grew slightly flushed, the same way it had when she was up on the ladder. "You always insist on twisting the most innocent things," she hissed. "You do it in order to cast me in a bad light. If you must know the truth," she sniffed, "I simply forgot all about the silly thing. I didn't even know it was in that box with that other stuff. P.J. keeps so much old junk up there, anyway." Her eyes shifted sideways. "I intend to give him a good talking to about that room. That's nothing but a firetrap up there."

Markie studied her mother with growing

suspicion. "Why were you so anxious to get the diary back from me a while ago?"

"I told you, I don't see that there's any reason for you to relive your past mistakes. And I certainly didn't see any reason for Robbie to have to know what happened. I hope to goodness you haven't upset her. Where is she?"

Another deflection.

But Marynell's games didn't matter now. What mattered now was Brandon. Now that Marynell knew Markie had given her baby up for adoption, what would happen when Brandon Smith showed up in Five Points? Markie wondered if she should put a stop to that plan immediately. But how could she? The sound of Brandon's voice letting out a *yee-haw* when she told him he'd been chosen for the internship rang in her ears. How could she possibly disappoint a young man who had worked so hard for this opportunity?

"Markie," Marynell snapped, "I said, where is Robbie?"

"Upstairs. Packing her stuff." Markie turned away from her mother and started to cram her own things into a tote.

"Oh, this is just plain ridiculous. Robbie

has no business going back out to that farm in her condition after the shock she's had." Marynell strode back to the sink, picked up another potato and started peeling it as if the matter were decided. "You are making a mountain out a molehill, Margaret, same as you always do." She spoke with her back to Markie, dismissing her. "Getting in a snit about something that doesn't matter anymore."

But the way Marynell was attacking that potato told Markie that the diary, for some reason, did matter. It mattered very much. She quietly moved to the counter and gave Marynell's profile a wary once-over, wondering with increasing ire why *had* the woman kept that diary all this time?

Marynell continued to hack at the potato without looking at Markie, but when she said, "What did you do with it, by the way?" Markie's suspicions were confirmed.

"The diary?"

"Of course, the *diary,*" Marynell's voice became suddenly shrill as she turned on Markie. "What on earth have we been talking about here?"

"What does it matter what I did with it?"

Despite herself, the volume of Markie's voice rose to match her mother's. "The incident's in the *past,* remember?"

"You think this is all about *you,* don't you?" Marynell yelled, and tossed the unfinished potato into the pan with the others. "For your information, your sister is in an extremely vulnerable position right now and I am trying to protect her." Clearly flustered, she pawed in the sink for another potato.

Marynell had claimed the same about Markie upstairs earlier—that she was only trying to protect her. The woman, Markie thought with a healthy dose of skepticism, had become a regular Mother Teresa. "What has my diary got to do with protecting Robbie?"

Marynell whirled to face her daughter again, this time with a hard, meaningful stare, as if she held a gun and was tempted to pull the trigger. "All right, then. If it's the only way to make you give up that diary, then I'll tell you, you little—" Before Marynell could spit out whatever was stuck in her craw, from the mud porch attached to the kitchen a familiar Texas twang sang out, "What in tarnation is all this racket?"

Markie and Marynell both started at each other, slapped into an uneasy silence by the sound of P. J. McBride's voice. In the heat of their exchange, they hadn't heard the screen door open. Or close. Markie wondered how much her father had heard.

His slender, benign face appeared around the doorjamb. "I could hear you hens squawkin' all the way down to the barn." P.J. grinned as he awkwardly pulled off a knee-high mud boot, hopping on one foot to keep his balance.

"Oh, shut *up!*" Marynell snapped. "And stop slopping mud everywhere!"

"Mom," Markie chastised. Suddenly it occurred to her that she never called her mother *Mom* except when her father was being attacked like this.

"Well, honestly," Marynell huffed, "I can't stand it when he goes around talking in that hick way. It's so affected."

"Mom!" Markie scolded again. "Hi, Daddy." She stepped into the mudroom and gave P.J. a quick, conciliatory hug and a kiss on the cheek. "How's that low-water bridge looking?"

"Terrible. Still running high. Almost too high to drive across. What's going on in here?" His tone was more serious now, though he demonstrated his usual wry perspective. "Or am I already sorry I asked?"

"It was nothing," Markie explained while her mother presented her back to the two of them.

P.J. shrugged and removed his other boot. Markie went back to packing up at the table while the room grew so painfully quiet that the tick of the grandfather clock that had been passed down on Marynell's side could be heard from the living room.

"Heard a real interesting rumor in town today." P.J. spoke as if he were offering the distraction of a cookie to a couple of quarreling toddlers. He stepped into the kitchen and smiled. It broke Markie's heart the way he always strived for normality.

When neither woman responded to the comment, P.J. tried again. "Robbie's gonna have a new neighbor. Justin Kilgore's taking over a big hunk of the Kilgore Ranch, moving into the old mansion."

Markie's eyes went wide. Her head snapped

up to see her mother returning her stare with similar shock. But Marynell's expression quickly congealed into a mask of fury. "Now, that *is* interesting." Her voice dripped sarcasm as her gaze bored into Markie's.

P.J. seemed oblivious to the undercurrent between the two women. He had gone to the refrigerator and retrieved a pitcher of iced tea. "Rumor is he's decided to restore the old ranch house. Got some kind of project going with the Mexicans. I always liked that old house—solid limestone. And I always liked Justin."

Her father turned and gave Markie a bright look as if something had just occurred to him. "As I recall, you and him was pretty good buddies that summer back when you was volunteering on his father's campaign."

"I—" Markie started but found she couldn't speak.

She swallowed against a thickening in her throat that threatened to choke her. She could feel her cheeks beginning to burn and was relieved when her mother turned her back to them again and resumed working on the potatoes with a renewed vengeance.

Justin was coming to Five Points? *To live?*

Right next door to Robbie? This was impossible, the cruelest blow fate could render. What kind of wormhole of fate had she been sucked into? If she hadn't promised her sister she would stay until the baby came, she'd high-tail it back to Austin *right now*.

"Maybe you two should get together, while you're both here in Five Points and all. Bill Keenan over at the barbershop said the guy's single again. It wouldn't hurt you to be social. Kilgore's a decent fella, good-looking, kind of in your league, I reckon."

"I…" Markie finally found her voice, "I'm afraid I won't have time for any socializing. I'll be too busy at Robbie's place."

Marynell's thin arms jerked with three vicious swipes of the slicer before she spoke. "Your daughter has some fool idea about taking Robbie and the boys back to their farm."

"Oh, really?" P.J. poured his tea. His manner remained evenhanded and accepting, as always. "Is that what Robbie wants?"

"Yes. She said so. I'm sorry, Daddy. I know you were looking forward to having the boys here with you for a while. But Robbie's got to do what's right for her." *And I do, too,* Markie thought. She would protect her heart. After all these years, the thought that she still needed to made her incredibly sad.

"Well, it's her choice. I guess that means you and Justin Kilgore will be neighbors, too, at least for a while." P.J. smiled as if this was a dandy idea. "What can I do to help you get settled?"

"Oh, that's typical. You go and take her part." Marynell jerked her head at Markie, though her gaze remained fixed on the potatoes. "Isn't that the way it's always been?"

P.J. extended his well-honed farmer's arms toward his thin wife. "Now, Marynell. Hon."

She shrugged him away. "Leave me alone. Nobody cares that I've done all this work, getting things ready for the boys. Now it's just— pfft!" She flipped a hand and water droplets sparkled in the sunlit air. "Change of plans!"

"Now, Mother," Markie said sadly.

P.J. tried again. "Come on now, sugar," he coaxed. "We're all just trying to do what's best for Robbie here. She's got a lot to cope with. While I was in town I talked to Mac Hughes and the farm situation is not good."

Mac Hughes was the local banker who handled the loan on the Tellchick farm.

"What did he say?" Markie asked quietly, casting an eye at the stairs. If the news was really awful, they'd have to break it to Robbie carefully.

"Danny was way behind on his payments, Mac wouldn't say how far. He said he can wait a few weeks until Robbie gets over the funeral and all, but he's going to have to have some kind of payment soon."

Marynell flew across the room at Markie, flapping the dish towel like the wings of an angry hen defending her chick. "See? I told you it would be better if they were here. And didn't I tell you not to upset Robbie! Well, if I have anything to say about it, we are not going to lose that land! Now, go upstairs and get me that diary!" She punctuated the last four words with four pokes of a bony finger to Markie's shoulder.

"Mother!" Markie yelped. "Cut it out!"

"Marynell." P.J.'s level voice stopped the women's bickering. "Just calm down now and tell me what this is all about."

"It's all her fault." Marynell's hurt-filled

eyes were now brimming with tears. "After all she's put me through. Now this!" She pressed the wadded dish towel to her mouth. "Now she's trying to take Robbie and the boys away from me!"

"Mother," Markie repeated, more quietly this time, though she was undeterred by Marynell's emotional display. She decided to get back to what her mother had been ready to blurt when P.J. came in. "What does my diary have to do with Robbie's land?"

"Your diary?" P.J. said. "You mean that old pink diary I stuck in the box with your other things? Is that what this is about?"

Markie and Marynell stared at P.J. Just as Markie hadn't needed to ask her mother if she *had* read the diary, she did not need to confirm that her father *hadn't*. And so she realized that not only was he unaware of her teenage pregnancy, he knew none of the other things that had happened eighteen years ago. He certainly had no idea he had a grown grandson on his way to Five Points.

"*You* put that diary in that box?" Marynell asked. Anger flared again, quickly replacing her self-pity.

"Well, I figured *you* wouldn't want it. You don't even want to keep my family diaries that are a hundred years old. It was on a shelf way up in your closet. I found it back there when I was putting some Christmas stuff up. Long time ago. I just figured Markie left it there…did I do something wrong?"

"It's all right, Dad. Mother and I will talk about this later, after she's had a chance to calm down." It was clearly a threat, a warning that Markie would somehow get to the bottom of this deal.

For her father's sake Markie patted Marynell, even though what she really wanted to do was strangle her. But she had to get her dad out of here. Marynell would make him suffer for this trespass.

"Right now I've got to go upstairs and help Robbie get packed," she said. "We could use a little help getting the heavy bags downstairs." Her fingers tightened ever so slightly on her mother's shoulder. "We are going back to Tellchick Farm. You understand that now, don't you, Mother?"

Marynell gave her a bitter look, but nodded when P.J.'s head turned.

"You female-types." P.J. took a sip of his tea. "If it isn't one drama around here, it's another."

OVER THE NEXT TWO WEEKS, Markie became progressively more fatigued. The move to Robbie's farm had cost her dearly, not only in time and money, but in a hidden emotional toll that couldn't be calculated.

And it had cost her plenty of plain old sleep. To the point where she was having weird dreams again. Dreams where she was kissing Justin Kilgore. Dreams where the two of them admired their newborn together. She chalked it up to being in this place, to knowing that he was near.

Every night, after Robbie and the boys had hit the sack, she went downstairs and soundlessly went about the task of plugging her laptop into Robbie's phone jack in the kitchen and setting to work at the sturdy oak table.

She knew she couldn't last like this—working until 2:00 or 3:00 a.m., answering e-mails, devising strategies, setting up schedules, just plain putting out fires for her client. It seemed as if she had her cell phone plastered to her ear all day, burning up the minutes. And at night her fingers were tethered to the Internet, a curse and a blessing it turned out, keeping her awake far too long into the night.

But every morning she was up early to fix breakfast for the boys and Robbie and help her sister sift through the wreckage of her life. These first two weeks had flown by in a blur of trips to negotiate payment schedules with the funeral home, the doctor, the bank. They'd sorted through Danny's clothes early in the first week because Robbie burst into tears every time she so much as glanced at a pair of his boots. They'd gone through the farm's books and bills and paperwork together and, together, had come to a sad conclusion. Danny and Robbie's debt was horrendous. Robbie admitted to Markie that it was far worse than Danny had let on.

"Sissy," Markie started gently, "I don't see how you can hold on to this farm."

They were sitting at the same oblong oak table where Markie had been working her late-night hours. Only it was midafternoon and the slanting southwest sunshine made the table, made the whole house, in fact, look dusty and stagnant. Several flies had slipped in when the boys had clamored out to play. The insects wasted no time in finding the smears of ketchup the boys had left on the worn countertop.

As Markie got up to swat the flies and wipe the table, she longed to be back in her sleek, new air-conditioned town house on the edge of Austin's urban sprawl. As penance for that selfish thought, she vowed to give her sister's kitchen a thorough cleaning…as soon as they confronted this financial mess.

Robbie moaned softly with her elbows propped on the table, her head cradled in her hands. "But what are Mother and Daddy going to say if I default on the note? They co-signed on this place."

"Let's not worry about them. Let's try to decide what's best for you and the boys. If you file for bankruptcy, I believe you can stay on the place as a homestead."

"Bankruptcy?" Robbie lifted her pale face. "I can't do that. Danny would never do that. I'd rather sell out."

Once Robbie had made up her mind, they'd gone to a Realtor in town, arranged for the sale of the place, and Markie had taken on the task of riding and walking the property with the appraiser.

"He said it might take months to find a buyer for a farm of more than a thousand acres," Markie told her sister when she got back.

"Then the sooner I list the place, the better."

"He thinks you should fix it up first."

"Oh, *really*?" Robbie's voice rose sarcastically. "Now, there's an idea! Oh. But wait. I'm flat broke, pregnant as a pea, with three kids pulling at me all day long. Well, *shoot*."

Markie had just stood there, flabbergasted. This was not her nicey-nice sister talking.

The work and stress had been going on like this for a few weeks when one night in the wee hours, right after she'd unplugged the laptop and jacked Robbie's phone back in, the thing let out its jangling ring, as if it had been waiting. Markie snatched up the receiver.

"Hello?" She kept her voice down. A farm could be so eerily quiet. Noise carried especially far in the wee hours. Down by the remaining outbuildings one of the dogs set to barking.

"Markie?" The resonant baritone voice was unmistakably like the one she'd heard on the phone from Dallas recently. "This is you, isn't it?"

"Yes." She swallowed and had to remind herself to breathe.

"I hope I'm not calling at a bad time. Well, I realize it's a bad time for your family. I guess I mean to say…" This resonant voice sounded older, of course, more seasoned and mellow than Brandon's had. Twenty-one years older, to be exact. Her heart started to pound as Markie sank back against the edge of the counter. She was feeling genuinely light-headed.

She had not expected to ever hear from him again. Not here. Not now. Not like this. For eighteen years they hadn't spoken, and now this—hearing his voice on a greasy black farmhouse phone, ringing in the middle of the night.

CHAPTER FIVE

"THIS IS JUSTIN KILGORE," the familiar voice finally blurted.

"Yes?" Why couldn't she force out anything more than that one stupid breathless syllable? At least Markie had not said the word expectantly, encouragingly. At least now, with the maturity of some years, she could disguise the old euphoria that overtook her every time she heard the sound of his voice. At least she had said that *yes* calmly, as if to indicate, *And? So*?

Justin Kilgore no longer had any kind of hold on her, she repeated to herself, like a mantra. They were no longer *bonded,* or whatever the hell had happened to her that summer. And now she would give him nothing. Nothing. Nothing of herself. Nothing about Brandon. Civility. Aloofness. That's what he would get.

These were the decisions she had made long ago, while her labor-flushed cheeks were pressed against a tear-sodden pillow in a birthing room. She wasn't going to back down from those decisions now. No looking back.

She heard a sigh of frustration over the phone line, as if he sensed her coolness and felt deflated by it. And well he should be.

"I'm sorry," he apologized again. "I guess this is a bad time. Markie, I...uh. It's sure been a long time, hasn't it?" His voice shifted, trying for kindness. "How are you? How have you been?"

"Fine. But my sister could be better." Markie frowned at a chipped nail as if to fortify herself with an air of detachment. "How did you find me here?"

"Your mom. She told me what happened to your sister's husband. That's so awful, Markie. I'm so sorry."

"You talked to Mother?" Markie could only imagine how *that* conversation had gone. Marynell would have been by turns apoplectic and hostile. Markie had to hand it to Justin Kilgore. The man had guts.

"She said you would probably be up working late."

"I am."

Another uncomfortable pause told her that Justin was taking her clipped responses for what they were—subtle rebuffs. What in the hell was he doing calling her, here, at Robbie's, *now,* right before Brandon was due to arrive? Before she could ask, he said, "I'm sorry to be disturbing you in the middle of the night like this. But the reason I'm calling is kind of important, kind of timely. Can you talk?"

"Yes." She swallowed, hard and dry, croaking out that one, lone syllable again, then her will took ascendance. "But I don't want to disturb my sister. She hasn't been doing too well lately—" Markie brought herself up short because that was none of Justin Kilgore's business. "Hold on."

She stretched the spiraling cord on the wall phone, hoping it would reach as far as the mud porch where she could pull the door closed, but it wasn't quite long enough. She opted to duck inside the small pantry closet beside the refrigerator.

She found the pull chain on the single bare

bulb and yanked it. The aroma of spices hit her nose and a sense of the surreal hit as she realized that, surrounded by her sister's extensive stock of canned goods and cereal boxes, she was about to have a conversation with Justin Kilgore.

"What's this about?" Markie was used to being direct, good at cutting to the chase.

"I'm in the area—"

"You're in town? Here? In Five Points?" *Already?*

"Well, at the moment I'm out on the old Kilgore place, actually."

"Are you working for your father's campaign or what?" Wouldn't that be the height of irony? The two of them squaring off in opposing campaigns.

"Hardly. That's why I called. I understand your sister is planning to sell her farm?"

Now, Markie thought, I see why Mother talked to him. She would have bit that hook, because she hadn't dropped her agenda to get her grandsons moved onto the McBride farm. Selling Danny and Robbie's place must fit in with her plans. "Mother told you that?"

"No. I found out in town, before I called

to get Robbie's number. I found out through my father, actually. He wants to reclaim that property."

"Whatever for?" What would Congressman Kilgore want with a thousand overgrown acres, a ramshackle house, a bunch of outbuildings in sad disrepair and a scorched barn lot?

Danny Tellchick had been cute. Funny. Sweet. But underneath the cuteness and the sweetness, the man had been nothing but a big overgrown, incompetent child. Markie eyed the jars of pickles and jelly that marched along Robbie's pantry shelves in precise rows. There was a freezer on the mud porch packed with cuts of pork and beef, another full of corn and green beans and squash from the garden. All of it a testament to her sister's heroic efforts to keep their ever-multiplying family well fed.

"My best guess is to spite me. You see, I've started a project that he doesn't exactly approve of. After my parents divorced last year—"

Markie knew all about that. Her research had uncovered the congressman's Washington mistress. A brittle younger woman who was gifted at conducting polls and flinging herself into the arms of powerful politicians.

"My stepmother arranged it so that her portion of the Kilgore lands would go directly to me," Justin was saying with no small amount of enthusiasm. "You see, Mom wants no part of that land. So, I've finally got a place to start up my humanitarian effort. We're calling it the Light at Five Points. Have you heard of it?"

He waited for her answer while Markie was thinking, *How can he be talking to me like this? Like we were old prep-school chums instead of lovers who had produced a child?* But, of course, Justin knew nothing about the child.

"I hadn't heard it called that," she answered mildly, "but I did hear that you were doing some kind of rescue work, or whatever you want to call it, with Mexican illegals."

"Undocumented immigrants," Justin corrected gently. "People who are willing to work for a better life, but in the meantime they have desperate needs. Medical care, legal guidance, financial support. It can be complicated. Anyway, I'm planning to use

Kilgore Ranch as my home base. I'll convert the mansion into housing for families and women with children, refurbish the two bunk houses for singles. I'm planning to run a small herd of cattle on my part of the lands.

"The whole thing's an expansion of a service organization I've been developing for several years. At one time I thought I might set it up on the Mexico side of the river, but this will actually be better. We help Mexican immigrants and their families acclimate to life in the States. Our goal is to help them overcome obstacles to citizenship, learn English, develop marketable agricultural skills, stuff like that."

"Sounds worthy. Ambitious, but worthy."

"Yeah. Well. I'm afraid my father doesn't think so."

Markie was well aware of her opponent's rigid stand on this issue. Close the border! Save Texas! The congressman's approach was designed to pander to ranchers, not address the problem of what to do when the richest nation on earth shared a four-thousand-mile border with one of the poorest. She liked Justin's realistic approach better.

"What has my sister's farm got to do with this?"

"I've only got a few people now, but eventually, I'll need additional land suitable for the farming aspect of it. The Tellchick Farm is the part of Kilgore Ranch that was originally farmed. It's closest to the Blue River. The rest of the ranch is too high and rocky for good farming. We'll run cattle out there."

"Yes, I recall." They had ridden practically the whole of the place on horseback that summer. Markie couldn't begin to remember what it was like to be that young and carefree.

"When I heard that your sister's property was going on the market, I started looking into it. It would be ideal for our purposes. It's already a working farm."

I wouldn't say the place works, *exactly,* Markie thought ruefully. She picked at a label stuck on a jar of Robbie's home-canned peaches while Justin went on, "And Danny Tellchick had accumulated a lot of equipment."

The equipment doesn't exactly *work,* either, Markie thought, but loyalty kept her from mentioning it.

"My preference would be to buy the place

outright before my father gets his hands on it. But—" Justin heaved a dispirited sigh "—there's a problem. The Light at Five Points has very little operating cash. We have to depend on charitable donations. I'd like to meet with you, and your sister, and try to work out an arrangement."

"An arrangement?"

"Something where she could continue to live on her farm. My plan is to bring in Mexican laborers to repair the place, then farm it."

"Mexican laborers? You have got to be kidding."

"No. I'm not. These guys work hard. On land that fertile they could produce crops like you wouldn't believe. I'm thinking we'll start with cantalopes and corn. They'll be learning about modern farming methods and they'll help Robbie get her place in shape while they work toward their citizenship. It's long a drive around on the ranch road, of course, so that would cut into their productivity. They're staying over in the big ranch house with me for now."

A vivid memory of the massive three-story limestone ranch house that Justin's great-grandfather had built more than a hundred years ago flashed into Markie's mind. The place had been all but abandoned for decades while Kurt Kilgore, the heir, did his thing in Washington.

There, she and Justin had made love for one long, stormy night on top of a nest of sleeping bags before a blazing fire that Justin had built in the giant fireplace. The fragrant smell of burning mesquite came back to her now, and the sound of his throaty voice saying, *I love you, Markie…and I will always love you.*

"I'd like Robbie's permission to quarry some limestone from that outcropping by the caves. The point is, with hard work and luck, I believe this can work," Justin was saying in a more upbeat, businesslike tone now. "Would you and your sister be willing to meet with me to discuss the details?"

"I don't know," Markie hedged. The prospect of being in the same room with Justin Kilgore, even with Robbie there as a go-between, made her palms go all sweaty. "I'll have to ask her. She's asleep now, of course. Um." *Be cool,* she reminded herself. "How soon do you want to meet?"

"Right away. Tomorrow."

"Tomorrow?"

"The sooner the better. There's another problem here. Maybe your sister doesn't realize it, but my father holds the mortgage on her land."

"What?"

"He backed it with an anonymous signature loan at the bank. My stepmother found out during the divorce proceedings. That's why your sister's interest rate, as I understand it, is so low."

Markie hadn't really thought about those kind of details while helping her sister with the farm's finances. "Why would he do such a thing?"

"It's kind of odd. I only found out about it myself yesterday. But you can bet it wasn't out of charity. The point is, to get his hands on that land, he doesn't have to buy your sister out. All he has to do is call in the note. Please. The sooner we talk, the better."

"Where?"

"How about the Hungry Aggie café? Early, if possible."

Markie looked at the oven clock. It was

now 1:00 a.m. and she still had work to do. But the boys caught the bus at seven-thirty and after that she could get free. "Okay. Eight o'clock."

"I'll see you there. And Markie?"

"Yes." One more flat monosyllable, though her heart was beating like a rabbit's.

"It'll be nice to get together again."

"Uh. Yeah. Yeah, it will be." *Pure hell, that is.*

CHAPTER SIX

Justin Kilgore showed up in the back of the church, just like he said he would. I think Mother was suspicious when me and Robbie left the house. Robbie always gets fixed up for stuff like choir practice, because she knows she's gonna see Danny practically everywhere she goes, but I don't usually bother. Ponytail. Sneakers. I'm good to go.

But tonight, I could hardly eat my dinner, could hardly get upstairs fast enough so I could change clothes and borrow some of Robbie's makeup. Wow. I look so different with mascara and lipstick! But I think it was the little flowered skirt and peasant blouse that set off Mother's alarm bells. That's my blouse, Robbie informed anybody who'd listen. Like I didn't know that.

Mother said, Where on earth are your

own clothes? If Robbie wanted me to take the blouse off, I knew Mother would make me. She always takes Robbie's side.

Please, Robbie? I said, and gave her my best I'm-your-baby-sister look. I needed that blouse! I was hoping it would disguise my puny bust.

Robbie said, Just don't get hot fudge on it, and headed for the car. The gang was going to Braum's after choir practice like always. Why hadn't I thought to tell Justin Kilgore about that?

But guess what? He was already slumping in a back pew when we slipped in the side door, like usual. He sat up on the edge of his seat when he saw me.

Would you please excuse me for a minute? I said to my sister, like a real adult.

Woo-hoo! Hottie alert! she said like a real juvenile.

He stood up as I walked down the side aisle. He said I looked nice! He wanted to know if it was okay if he watched. His teeth are so white, I could see that flash of his smile even in the dim church. He wore jeans and boots and a white T-shirt. There was only a little light from a stained-glass window back there. But there was sure enough light to make out his muscles bulging in that shirt.

You look nice. A compliment like that could completely undo a girl like me, coming from an older guy who looks the way he does. I think my whole body was blushing.

But at least I had the presence of mind to say thank you.

Robbie was waiting for me, watching us. Go on up to the altar! I telegraphed to her with my eyes, but she just stood there like a dunce.

He said he wanted to watch and promised to be real good. Quiet as a little church mouse. He looked anything but a little mouse, sitting back there with his muscles bulging and one big boot propped up on the kneeler.

Sister Beatrice actually squinted at him and wanted to know who that strange young man was. I swear. I cannot stand this small town.

Robbie blabbed that he was Congressman Kilgore's son.

I'm sure I was singing off key the whole

time. Every time I looked Justin's way my throat felt as if Daddy had attacked it with his eighty-grit sandpaper.

After practice, he came along with us to Braum's.

Robbie was with Danny, so they sat over in another booth ignoring us. I've gotta work on Robbie so she doesn't tell. It's not like I'm not allowed to date. I'm seventeen, after all. It's just that my parents kind of have this rule about dating college guys. Which I am *so-o-o* breaking.

I ordered a cherry limeade instead of my usual sundae. I didn't want to take a chance on getting hot fudge all over Robbie's top.

But when he saw me eyeing his banana split, he grinned and raised one eyebrow while he aimed a spoonful at my mouth. When I rolled my eyes after I took it, he gave me another bite. And another. In no time, it felt like he had me eating right out of his hand! When a little caramel stuck to the corner of my mouth, he licked his thumb and wiped it off. S-l-o-w-l-y. S-o-f-t-l-y. Thought I was going to die.

He said, You sure are pretty.

I'm afraid I did a lot of jabbering. About Five Points, no less. Like it was the most interesting place on the planet.

Justin has spent a lot of time in Washington and in boarding schools and off at college. He said he doesn't even feel like a Texan anymore, much less like he's from Five Points. But someday he wants to come back and live on his family's ranch, the Kilgore, and make it a real working ranch again, the way it was when his grandfather had it.

Oh, cool! What if he ends up living in Five Points someday? What if we fall in love? Get married? Have beautiful babies? Struggle to make a go of his ranch? Build a big house and fight over exactly what it should look like? Get old and fat and retire?

The way he kissed me when we said goodbye, Diary, made me believe it could actually happen. It really did.

MARKIE WAS LATE, and with good reason, but even so, her tardiness made her tense, especially since she was meeting *him*.

She had over-thought her clothes, then ended up looking like she hadn't given her apparel any thought at all. Her white long-sleeved split-neck T, slim jeans and simple sandals had seemed right for the May weather, but the plain outfit did nothing to convey her professionalism or her financial status, which was very healthy, she was proud to acknowledge.

Yet somehow, whenever she was back in Five Points, she never wore her sleeker, more expensive urban clothes, instead always reverting to the relaxed style of the country. The only thing that hinted at her status was her Rolex watch and a high-quality black leather satchel purse, which she habitually wore strapped across her body to free up her hands.

She'd even toned down her makeup, which was usually fairly sophisticated. Today it was little more than lip gloss, sheer foundation and featherings of a rich sable eye shadow and mascara that somehow made her blue eyes look bluer.

She had fussed overmuch with her hair, she realized, first getting the long layers too tightly curled with the round brush, then pulling a damp comb through in an effort to get it more relaxed. As she tucked one side behind her ear, she imagined the effect had ended up more limp than sleek. For a brunette, a very fine line.

All this obsessing about her looks irritated her. Justin Kilgore had left her pregnant and alone. Why was she trying to look nonthreatening, nice, feminine even? Why did she give a flying flip what he thought?

She resisted the urge to check her reflection in the visor mirror and bolted out of her Jeep. Her chin went up as she walked away from the vehicle. It was a Liberty Renegade in the perfect shade of silvery green, brand spanking new, and she was proud of it. Justin Kilgore had been handed life's little luxuries on a silver platter. She had earned all of hers.

The Hungry Aggie café hadn't changed one jot in three decades. Surely, Markie thought as she pushed open the glass door and felt the rush of refrigerated air, they'd repainted the walls somewhere along the way, but they looked to be the same bilious green as they always had, decade in, decade out. The booths and bar stools, still the same neon-red vinyl, had surely needed recovering at some point. Over the pass-through window at the back, a glittery silver garland was unevenly looped, festooned with tiny flags in honor of the upcoming Memorial Day. But even the flags didn't keep the overall impression of the place from being like Christmas in May.

An air of bustling purpose reigned inside the narrow storefront shop that stretched to a loud, pot-banging kitchen at the rear. A hum of chatter assaulted Markie as her eyes swept the length of the room for Justin's face. Would he look the same? She saw that practically every seat was taken. Farmers, downtown businessmen, retirees. The same old butts on the same old bar stools, as her father would say.

Markie had to admit that she secretly enjoyed frequenting such greasy-spoon establishments in her political wanderings, but she marveled that Justin Kilgore would condescend to even sip a cup of coffee here. Then she remembered that he had once harbored the same secret craving for hand-cut French fries as she did.

They'd had a lot of little things like that in common in their youth. She wondered if they still did, then slapped away the thought.

There he was, sitting in a booth near the back, facing her. When he spotted her his eyes registered the same intense interest they had from the first time he'd seen her. Markie bit her lower lip, then squelched that reflex, too. He did look the same, only better, more handsome, better built. My gosh. Did the man lift weights or something?

As she approached, he rolled out of the booth to stand and face her. Her heart had already set up a struggle in her chest. *Damn.* She shouldn't have come here. But someone had to speak up for Robbie.

She had wanted him to look bad. Faded. Pasty, maybe. Balding with yellowing teeth. Atrophied muscles and a disgusting paunch would have been a nice touch.

But he looked good. Too good. He looked like Justin still, just like she thought he might look someday as a vibrant, virile, thirtysomething man. Which was what he obviously was.

He was wearing a dusky blue Henley-style knit shirt with the placket unbuttoned, which accentuated his tan and showed off the fact that he was meatier in the shoulders now, but still trim around the middle. He looked at ease in his clothes, with the shirt tucked into a pair of well-worn Levi's that fit snugly down to some broken-in-looking black cowboy boots.

"Hi," he said, and smiled. White teeth. Still those perfect white teeth. A hint of a five o'clock shadow, even though it was morning. A few laugh lines that gave his intense dark eyes a sexy, knowing quality.

"Hi," she said back. But she found she was way too nervous to feign a smile.

This was exactly the way they had started, saying hi and looking into each other's eyes.

Markie broke the gaze first and slid into the booth. Her heart was drumming so hard she fumbled her purse strap as she slid it over her head. The buckle caught in her hair and she felt her cheeks developing an annoying blush as she worked to untangle it.

She stole a glance through wisps of her hair, abashed, and saw that he was staring.

"I'm sorry." He cleared his throat uncomfortably. "I don't mean to stare. It's just...it's kind of a…it's so amazing, seeing you after all these years. Your hair." Justin smiled at her as he eased back onto the bench across from her. "It looks…wow. Just the same." His eyes studied the shape of it intently. "I mean, the style's a little different, but it's…you always did have the most beautiful hair."

Right away, before Justin was even fully settled back on his side, Nattie Rose Neuberger swooped over. "Why, Markie McBride," she cooed happily while she cut a glance at Justin and refilled his coffee cup. "I haven't seen you in an absolute coon's age. Where have you been keeping yourself all these years?"

"Hi, Nattie Rose." No one around Five Points ever called Natalie Neuberger *Natalie,* or even just plain, "Nattie." It had always been both names, Nattie Rose.

Nattie Rose, a sweet girl in high school, was undoubtedly even sweeter now, Markie thought, as she looked up into her old friend's plump rosy face and smiling brown eyes. Tempered by time and maturity. By motherhood, too. Nearly all of the girls Markie had gone to high school with had children now.

It was the kind of thing on which Markie had checked.

Nattie Rose Neuberger, now Kline, had two daughters, Markie recalled. She wondered if they were as softhearted as their mother. Nattie Rose had always tried to draw Markie out even while Markie retreated into her own private hell during their senior year. "I'm living in Austin now," she answered simply.

"Ah. Big-city girl, huh?" Nattie Rose was wearing a lime-green 4-H T-shirt, loose-fitting Levi's and white Nikes with red laces. The ensemble was topped off by a tightly lashed white butcher's apron. Markie was pretty sure it was unintentional, but the waitress's outfit matched the faux Christmas atmosphere the diner owner had created with the tinsel and the garish red-and-green color scheme.

"Are you kidding?" Markie smiled. "They'll never make a big-city girl out of me. You can't find fries like the ones they make here in a big city." It was surprising how easily she fell right back into this easy small town chitchat. As successful as she was in Austin, a part of her always yearned to return to the country, always felt at home here. In fact, if Justin Kilgore hadn't been sitting across from her right now, she would have been as relaxed as a cat in this humble restaurant, sipping coffee from a heavy white mug and ordering eggs over easy.

Nattie Rose topped off Justin's coffee and he thanked her with a smile.

"What about you?" Nattie Rose waggled the coffeepot in front of Markie.

"Please." Markie smiled again.

"And to what do we owe the honor of your visit?" Nattie Rose asked pleasantly as she poured.

"Uh, well…" Markie's smile faded. "Maybe you haven't heard. I'm staying out at my sister Robbie's. Helping her get back on her feet and all. You know…after…"

Nattie Rose looked suddenly stricken. "Oh, honey, please forgive me! How could I forget such a thing as that? I just get so distracted when we are busy with the breakfast crowd like this. And since I always think of Robbie as a Tellchick now…"

"It's okay," Markie mumbled automatically.

"No, it's not. And I am really so sorry. That was such a terrible thing. Nobody can quite get over it. Especially that man over there." Nattie Rose inclined her head toward a booth up front where a large man sat with two others. All three wore firefighter's uniforms.

"Zack Trueblood," Nattie Rose said in a low voice. "The one with his back to us. And what a back that is," she muttered to herself. "I tell you, if Miss Nattie Rose was a single girl—well, anyway." She dragged her eyes away from Trueblood's physique and back to Markie. "Zack was one of the guys that answered the call. He was the one that pulled Danny out of that barn."

Nattie Rose had always had a tendency to gossip, but never maliciously. She seemed, in fact, to consider it her mission to make people aware of good doings or to spread sympathy for their neighbors' plight if the doings were not so good.

As one, Justin and Markie both leaned toward each other and inclined their heads, trying to check out Trueblood.

Markie caught a glimpse of one long leg clad in navy gabardine angling out of a booth across the room. A dark head ducked before a massive shoulder. Big hands wrapped around a coffee mug.

Justin cleared his throat and their eyes met before Markie quickly looked down, then glanced back up again. Both had seemed caught off guard by a charge of connection as they leaned in close.

"I've never met him, I guess," Justin said while he continued to look into Markie's eyes.

"Me, neither." Markie couldn't seem to drag her gaze away from Justin's. "But I think I saw him at the funeral."

"Yeah. It would be like Zack to do something like that," Nattie Rose jabbered on, oblivious to the eye contact taking place at the table. "To go to the funeral after he tried to save the guy. I hear he's taking it real hard. On account of your sister's expecting and all."

Justin's eyebrows shot up and a new tension tightened the air between them.

Nattie Rose's gaze swiveled from Justin to Markie. "What are y'all doing in here this morning, anyway…getting back together?"

"Starving." Justin shot the waitress a wry grin and grabbed a menu from behind the napkin holder. When he realized there was only one, he offered it to Markie. "I'll have the ham and eggs." He smiled up at Nattie Rose. "Scrambled. And some of those home fries."

Markie took the menu and pretended to peruse it while she internally winced over Nattie Rose's question. Despite her chagrin, she studied Justin, finding his looks as fascinating as ever. Over the top of the menu, their eyes met again.

Markie closed it. "Nothing but coffee for me, I think. I ate oatmeal with the boys and Robbie."

"I take it she's not coming," Justin said quietly.

Their eyes locked again. Markie swallowed. How much to tell? Certainly not the part where Robbie had said she wouldn't even want to breathe the same air as Justin Kilgore after the way he did her baby sister wrong. Sister loyalty—who could top it? That's why she had to be cautious, telling him only enough about Robbie's situation to get whatever information she could out of him in return. "There's a complication," she said just as quietly.

"Okey dokey." Nattie Rose chirped as she flipped her pad shut. "Y'all need some OJ or anything like that?" But the two staring at each other across the table seemed to hardly notice the waitress now.

"Be back in a sec, then." Nattie Rose shot off.

When she was out of earshot, Justin said, "Your sister is pregnant?"

Markie sighed, covering the fact that just hearing that word coming out of Justin's mouth set her insides fluttering. "Yes. Almost five months along. Baby's due in October."

"Is that the…complication?"

"I wish it was that simple." Markie sighed again and looked at her hands, wrapped around the mug. She stared outside at the quaint, old-fashioned buildings of downtown Five Points, dreading this confrontation.

Justin, always long on patience, waited, but she could feel him looking her over.

"The latest word is," Markie said without looking at him in turn, "there's some possibility Danny's death might not have been an accident."

"Really? You mean like the fire was some kind of…"

Before he could say the ugly word *arson,* Markie interjected, "The fire marshal is still investigating it." She omitted the part about Danny's debts and how collecting after a fire might have seemed easier to a guy like Danny than the hard work of salvaging his farm. She omitted the part about the autopsy, too. About how the results seemed awfully slow in coming and how that, too, could mean bad news.

"Don't tell me," Justin said without missing a beat, "that they suspect the immigrants of having something to do with that barn fire."

Markie's eyes widened. She turned her head and stared at him. "How did you know that? I mean about the immigrants. The sheriff only came out to question Robbie about that incident this morning. That's why I was late. Because the sheriff showed up and I didn't want to leave my sister to deal with him alone."

"I see." Now she could see that it was Justin who was deciding how much to reveal. "I'm aware that some Mexicans were seen on the farm, in the vicinity of the caves that run underground from the Kilgore north forty. I'm aware that Danny ran them off his land a few days before the fire."

"And the next thing we know, my brother-in-law is dead. You have to go to the sheriff with whatever you know. At the very least—" Markie leaned forward "—those people were trespassing."

"Crossers trespass practically everywhere they go. What if they were merely lost, trying to find their way to the Light at Five Points? Word has spread quickly about it. New people are arriving every day. What if they were just in the wrong place at the wrong time?"

"Wait a minute." Markie gave his face a shrewd once-over. "You *know* these guys?"

Justin looked away. How could it be that after more than eighteen years of absolutely no contact, this girl—correction, this *woman*—could still read him like a book? Despite himself, his lips compressed, his mouth turned down at the corners, his brow furrowed. He was thinking of how the Moraleses looked, scared to death, when they had returned to La Luz, grabbed their meager belongings and disappeared into the night.

"Even if I did know who the sheriff is looking for," he dissembled, "I could never find them once they realized the authorities are after them."

"What were those Mexicans doing on my sister's land?"

"I really can't say."

It wasn't a lie, exactly. Aurelia had sworn him to secrecy after Julio and Juan left. The story she told would sound like a bigger lie than the small one he'd just told. Aurelia claimed Juan and Julio Morales had been looking for a lost Mayan artifact in those caves. Days later a man had paid them a lot of money to go back to the Tellchick farm and intentionally get caught trespassing again. But then the brothers had found out about a fire, a bad fire in which the man who caught them died. Afraid they were being set up, they ran. Now Justin felt caught between winning the trust of the crossers and answering Markie's questions.

Justin hated to withhold anything from Markie, of all people. What he wanted between them was the total honestly, the authenticity, the unconditional acceptance and trust they had shared one beautiful summer. What he wanted was the—there was no other word for it—what'd they'd had was intimacy. Again he marveled that they had shared something so deep and genuine, even though they were so young. But from the vantage point of his thirties, he couldn't deny it now. What they'd had was rare. It was true love. His experiences since that time had taught him that the hard way.

"I don't… I don't like secrets," Markie said, and Justin thought he detected something strange in her tone.

At the worst possible moment, Nattie Rose showed up with a crockery platter heaped with home fries, eggs and a slab of ham the size of Texas. "Anything else?" she said as she plunked down a bottle of ketchup and scribbled the total at the bottom of the check.

"Everything looks fine." Justin shook out some ketchup.

"Enjoy." Nattie Rose dropped the tab on Justin's side, then shot off again to refill coffee mugs around the room.

Glad for the distraction, Justin forked in his first bite of home fries, swallowed and rolled his eyes heavenward, hoping to break the tension. "Bliss. Sure you don't want a bite?" He tried a grin as he held a forkful of hot, crispy potatoes toward Markie.

She shook her head. "I ate with Robbie's boys. I'm still full."

Justin made a face. "Did I understand you to say you made those poor children eat oatmeal? That's just plain cruel." He popped in another forkful of buttery potatoes.

Markie might have smiled, she thought gloomily, if she weren't so dead set on acting like a stiff. Too many things weighed on her right now to give in to Justin Kilgore's charm. Though, she had to admit his smile was as sexy as ever. Chemistry. Such a mystery. And so annoying. Once upon a time, *chemistry* had nearly ruined her life. Never again.

She tore her gaze from Justin's attractive grin and frowned at Nattie Rose across the room, as if the waitress's activities were terribly interesting. When Nattie Rose stopped at Zack Trueblood's table, Markie didn't have to feign interest.

At something Nattie Rose said, the big man turned, looking at Markie over his shoulder. He was also drop-dead handsome, but in a rougher way than Justin, with deeper-set eyes and a more chiseled jaw.

Justin forked in a couple of more bites before he spoke again. "Listen. I can understand if your sister got upset about Mexicans out on her farm. But accusing these people of having anything to do with Danny Tellchick's death, when there's nothing but circumstantial evidence…I always thought you had a stronger sense of justice than that, Markie."

But before Markie could answer, Zack Trueblood started across the room with heavy-booted footfalls.

He approached their booth and nodded at Markie, then at Justin. "I hope I'm not disturbing you folks, but Nattie Rose says you're Robbie Tellchick's sister."

"Yes. I'm Markie." Markie smiled up at the man and extended her hand. He took hers in his for an instant, then released it and extended the hand to Justin. "Zack Trueblood." He had the relaxed, unpretentious mien of a Texan raised on the farm.

"Justin Kilgore," Justin supplied, equally relaxed.

The men shook hands.

"You're Markie's husband?" Zack said it as if verifying an assumption.

"Uh. No." Justin felt his face warming up. He kept his gaze trained upward toward the firefighter, so he didn't have to look across at Markie, though out of the corner of his eye, he thought he saw her making a wry face. So it was there, then. Some old unspoken bitterness about how things had turned out between them. Justin didn't understand it to this day.

He had *wanted* to be her husband, once upon a time. That was for sure. But she hadn't waited. She hadn't *wanted* to wait, apparently. And that was that. Though in the ensuing years, no matter how hard he tried, he couldn't quite shake his fascination with Markie McBride.

"I'm the *single* sister," Markie said, Justin thought somewhat pointedly. Was she attracted to this guy? Was she attached back in Austin? What had she been doing with herself all these years? Who had she been with?

"I remember you from the funeral." Zack gave his full attention to Markie now, and

Justin wondered, was this guy attracted to *her*? But the way he asked the next question made Justin think something else might be going on here. "How is…" Trueblood swallowed. "How is Mrs. Tellchick doing?" The look in his eyes became unspeakably sad.

"She could be better, naturally. It's rough. Up and down, you know?"

Trueblood nodded. "I was wondering. I… do you think it'd be okay—I mean, do you think she'd mind if I came out and checked on her sometime?"

"I think she might like that, seeing someone familiar. Robbie and Zack went to high school together," Markie explained to Justin.

"Ah. You went to Five Points High?" Justin said, making an effort to be cordial to the guy.

"Yeah." Trueblood narrowed his eyes as if trying to place Justin. "Did you?" The two men were about the same age.

"Justin attended prep schools back east," Markie put in. Again, her words had the barest edge of resentment. "He's the *congressman's* son."

"Oh, *right*." Zack aimed an index finger.

"Kilgore. I should have made the connection. And this is an election year, isn't it?"

"Yes. But I'm not in town because of my father," Justin said. "I'm here to start up a humanitarian operation out on our family land."

"The Light at Five Points," Markie chimed in again. "You've heard of it?"

"Oh, you're *that* guy," Zack said. "I read about that deal in the paper." Justin couldn't tell if the firefighter approved of his mission or not. People leaned strongly both ways. "Well, somebody needs to do something—"

"Has the sheriff talked to you?" Markie interrupted abruptly.

"As a matter of fact, he did. My buddies and I were questioned again last night about what the fire marshal found. But I'm afraid we already told him everything we know." Trueblood gave Justin a look that indicated he knew about the Morales brothers being on the Tellchick farm. "Well. I'll let you two get back to your food. Markie, would you please tell your sister I asked about her?" he added quietly. "And tell her I'll do anything I can to help her. Anything. It was nice to meet you both."

"Likewise." Justin nodded.

When Trueblood was gone, Markie said, "Listen, I came here for one reason. To tell you that under no circumstances will my sister sell her land or lease her land or make any kind of deal with you."

"Even if it means she goes bankrupt and my father takes the farm?" His gut told him something would be very wrong with that picture, though he hadn't quite put his finger on why. Or maybe—and he hated to admit this—it was just that he didn't want his father's shadow squatting on land right next to the Light at Five Points.

"I'm doing my best to see that that doesn't happen. In the meantime, if you decide you're ready to tell me or the sheriff whatever it is you obviously know about these illegals, give me a call. This is my cell number." She snapped a business card on the table.

Justin picked it up.

This standoff was not what he wanted. "Let me help your sister," he said. "Let me bring some of my people over to help her work her farm." The words had just flown out of his mouth, but he really meant them.

Markie's cheeks suddenly looked like two dollops of the ketchup had been smeared there.

"Robbie would never agree to that. Not with all this suspicion hanging in the air. You'd better just tell those people to stay clear of Robbie's place."

"What if I came with them? What if I supervised them? I spent my childhood working on a ranch, when I wasn't being coddled at a prep school, that is."

Her color rose higher. He couldn't tell if she was flustered because of his offer or angry because of his stupid crack about prep school. He shouldn't have done that. His background had always come between them, and he wasn't going to win this woman's affection by being a sarcastic prick about it now.

"You don't owe Robbie anything," she said. "You hardly know her."

"I know *you*." He cupped a hand over Markie's wrist, all will to resist touching her gone. "And I remember how it was between us."

Markie jerked her wrist away and looked around the crowded restaurant with an expression so incensed he might as well have thrown cold water in her face in front of everybody. "I remember a lot of things, too, Justin," she hissed in a voice that was obviously meant to be confidential but that rose in spite of her efforts, "and for that reason you will stay away from me. And you will absolutely stay away from my sister."

She fumbled at her side for a moment, then slapped the long purse strap across her body and hurled her slim frame out of the booth. Before he could make a move to stop her, she was across the room, banging open the glass door with too much force. "I mean it," she said, again too loud, right before she went out, "stay away…from all of us."

The whole diner grew hushed, suspended in the wake of Markie's dramatic exit. Then Nattie Rose and her regular customers stared Justin's way.

Justin swept them all with a look that said, *Mind your own business,* an unheard-of concept in a town like Five Points.

When the casual chatter started up again, Justin quickly shoveled in the last of his food, fully aware that across the restaurant, wearing an expression that was none too friendly, Zack Trueblood was the only patron who had continued to watch him.

CHAPTER SEVEN

IT TOOK ALL OF HER self-control for Markie not to break into a fevered run as she hurried to her Jeep. But she held her pace to a determined stride.

The way she'd just left the restaurant had been nothing short of mortifying. People had stared. She plowed down the sidewalk, past a procession of pickups and SUVs canted to the curb, toward Ardella Brown's flower and gift shop where she'd parked.

The last thing she wanted to do was draw more attention.

Even now, Sam Landsaw, one of her father's nosy old buddies, was waving down at her cheerfully from the bucket of a cherry picker. From high up on the streetlight poles, Sam was removing Lone Star-shaped flags with lupine blue flowers stamped at the centers. The Bluebonnet festival had been this past weekend. With a wave of sadness Markie realized that in the past, Robbie had always designed an elaborate float for the parade, but hadn't this year, of course.

"Hey there, Miss Markie McBride!" Sam sang out loud enough for folks down at the lumberyard to hear. "You tell your old man to get himself into town and help the brother Elks decorate once in a while."

"I'll tell him, Sam, but you know he won't listen!" Not a great comeback, but at least she managed to sing it out as if nothing at all were wrong on this sunny May morning.

Once the bluebonnet stuff was packed away, Five Points would get all gussied up for the Firemen's Barbecue at the end of May. Then came the Flag Day festivities in June. Then the Fourth of July. It was forever *something* around here. With the tourist season soon to reach its peak, both congressional candidates would be signed up to speak or cut ribbons or wave the Lone Star or the Stars and Stripes at every little silly do.

But at that moment Markie couldn't have cared if the president himself were rolling down Main Street and waving from the back of Sam Landsaw's pickup. She scrambled into her Jeep and slammed the door.

She gripped the steering wheel while she drew and released two shaky openmouthed breaths. She flipped down the visor mirror and examined her face. Was this what he'd seen? Cheeks blazing with the high red of embarrassment. Eyes plainly troubled with pain and confusion.

"You'll be okay," she vowed aloud to the mirror, but saw her features pinch as she fought back the tears.

The possibility of her mother finding out about Brandon was one thing. But now that she'd seen Justin, she realized that the prospect of him finding out was a thousand times more horrifying.

It had all started so innocently. She had been the brainy brunette who hardly ever got a call from a boy, thrilled to have a guy as good-looking as Justin Kilgore pursuing her.

She stared at Ardella's storefront, remembering the afternoon Robbie was on her way to Ardella's to pick out the flowers for her wedding.

"I need to get some flowers, too," Justin had said on the phone.

She gripped the steering wheel of her Jeep. Daddy had never let her drive his brand new 1986 Ford Taurus into town. He always said the whole thing like that: Nineteen-eighty-six-Ford-Taurus. Robbie they trusted. Robbie drove her to town.

He had been waiting out on the sidewalk, looking so-o-o sexy in a black Harley-Davidson T-shirt. She still remembered reading the inscription: Rolling Thunder, and thinking, *Thunder and lightning is more like it.*

He was holding a rose! When he handed it to her she took a second to smell it appreciatively, then asked him if he was into Harleys and they were off and running.

They walked uptown and had a cherry Coke at the Hungry Aggie.

They could talk about everything, right from the start. He asked her if she liked movies. If she'd seen *Out of Africa* yet. She asked him if he'd seen *Platoon.*

She had to smile ruefully when she remembered how she tried to sound grown-up, asking him if he was planning on attending any of the Texas Sesquicentennial events.

"Planning on attending?" He had imitated her prissy wording. "When I can't even pronounce it?"

That made her laugh. He made her laugh so many times.

But she loved the way he could be serious, too. Even back then, he was all into some act of Congress that had just passed having to do with immigration reform. And he could be so...passionate. His dark eyes were snapping like fire when he said, So now the government thinks it's fixed things—you can give these people a job, but it's illegal for them to cross over to get those jobs!

He walked her back to the car and asked her if she wanted to go see *Top Gun* that weekend, holding her hand right in front of her nosy sister.

She remembered her silly answer—Does the pope wear a beanie?—and how excited she'd been. How she'd climbed into the car and hugged herself.

And she also remembered how Robbie had

said, "What in the Sam hill do you think you are doing?"

"I'm going out with a congressman's son! Somebody slap me awake!"

"I refuse to help you sneak around like this," Robbie had said. "That guy's too old for you."

And Robbie, unfortunately, had been all too right.

Ardella Brown emerged from her shop and gave the entranced Markie a funny look. Ardella had halfheartedly cashed in on the tourism craze with the rest of Five Points, hawking the same bluebonnet paraphernalia in the same window year after year. But Ardella's heart wasn't really into the latest festival. Her real passion was weddings, the gaudier the better. For years, she had cozied up to Markie's mother, anticipating the weddings of her three daughters. Frankie had dashed Ardella's hopes by marrying down in Austin in a courthouse near the campus. Robbie hadn't been much better. Though Marynell had ordered the flowers from Ardella, resourceful Robbie had done most of her wedding decorations herself.

That left Markie.

And Markie knew that in Ardella's mind she would forever be consigned to the role of the weird sister who had little hope of getting married. It didn't matter how much success, how many candidates she vaulted into the House or the Senate or even the gubernatorial mansion, from grade school on Markie had been branded as the lanky daughter who would not conform. Even if their weddings had been a disappointment, Ardella respected Frankie as organized and responsible, and everyone in town thought of Robbie as sweet and reliable.

But Markie was the dissident. The one that Ardella and Marynell rolled their eyes about in whispered conversations in the produce aisle. And in the end Markie had obliged by doing a fine job of proving Ardella and her mother right, hadn't she?

Ardella busied herself hanging a sidewalk display of fluttering wind socks. She looked over her shoulder at Markie, flashing a mincing smile each time she put up one of the garish things shaped like elongated armadillos, cowboy boots and six-shooters. *Gee, I wonder why those things don't sell?* Markie thought sarcastically.

The third time Ardella gave her a look it was more searching, so she fired up the engine and backed out onto Main Street. She didn't want to hang around until Justin came out of the restaurant, anyway.

The countryside on the drive back to Robbie's farm was beautiful, and the glorious summer scenery should have soothed Markie's spirit, but it did not.

The glimpses of rushing rivers in small canyons, the gleaming limestone cliffs in the distance, the rolling cedar-dotted hills, only made her feel sadder, lonelier.

Why did Justin Kilgore have to look so good!

In all this time, in all these years, she had never met another man like him. What was it about him? He was handsome, for sure. Even more so now than as a younger man. More filled-out. More confident. More...*everything.*

If only she'd never made love to him, but even after all these years the memories of how wonderful he had been came flooding back.

What would life have been like if she had

married him? If they'd kept their son to raise? She imagined them living on one of the old places that scrolled by outside her window, imagined renovating it to suit them. Maybe they would have run a small herd since Justin had always seemed so taken with the notion of livestock.

Stop it, she told herself. Just stop it right now. None of that happened. It's never going to happen. Your life is one giant snafu, and the best you can hope for now is to protect the innocent. First and foremost among them Brandon Smith.

As Markie bumped up Robbie's long washboard of a drive, she wondered what she was going to tell her sister. Seeing Justin today had been every bit as difficult as she thought it would be. If she hadn't been going on behalf of her sister, she would have chickened out. And what now?

But even as she tried to concentrate, her thoughts turned to him again. His eyes. His mouth. Even his smell. She bit her lip and gripped the steering wheel. It seemed no amount of willpower could wrench her mind free of him for long. Here she was a thirty-five-year-old woman, a powerful, successful woman, hanging on to a cheap teenage diary and nursing a crush on a bygone love.

She knew the exact place where the entry that hurt the most was written. And she knew what it said. After that entry she'd stopped writing about him. After that entry she knew she would not find the name Justin Kilgore in those pages again. In fact, she'd never actually written the name Justin again, anywhere, ever, after that. Certainly not on that form that she was asked to fill out, giving the information for the birth certificate. On the blank where it said "Father," she had written "unknown."

But he wasn't unknown. He was Justin.

Justin.

Today he had looked the same and not the same. What experiences had shaped him through the years? What was in his heart? When he'd touched her in the café, she had thought her own heart was going to pound right out of her chest.

Although her mind remained stubbornly consumed for months, years, with thoughts of the boy who'd been her lover, who'd made her pregnant, it had almost seemed as if he'd ceased to exist at times. But when he touched her she realized he was as real as he'd ever been. And all this time he had been living a life somewhere. With *someone*.

The woman he had married—and according to the old men at her dad's barber shop, recently *divorced*—was an unknown to Markie. She had tried to look up Michelle Kilgore on the Internet once and found nothing but a one-liner in an article about the congressman that mentioned his son and daughter-in-law "in the audience," having recently returned from a mission trip to Mexico.

And yet, she couldn't blame Justin for everything that had happened, could she? He hadn't even known she was pregnant when he left for college. She hadn't included him in her stubborn plans. She hadn't included anyone.

Unfortunately, that had become her life pattern. Independent to a fault. To a *fault*.

Maybe that had always been her problem, even before a teenage pregnancy tilted her life off its axis.

She parked her Jeep and trotted into Robbie's house.

A note on the table read: Gone to town to buy groceries.

Markie hoped Robbie had enough money to buy everything they needed. She made a mental note to find some tactful way to ask Robbie about it.

She went back through the mud porch to the cramped room she occupied at Robbie's and slid the diary out of the top drawer of the little dresser in the corner. She closed the drawer soundlessly, as if she were some sort of cat burglar committing a crime.

She stared at the diary for a second, then sat down on the bed next to her briefcase. Looking back at the past wouldn't help her make this decision. She pulled a pile of applications from her briefcase and set them on her lap. She pressed a palm over them, closing her eyes like a television preacher praying over a pile of petitioners' letters.

This felt like the hardest decision she had ever made in her life. No, it was the second hardest.

And just like eighteen years ago, she had to think, *what was she going to do?* The right thing? Or the expedient thing?

They were not the same. In fact, in this case her two choices seemed diametrically opposed, like forks of a road that led off in wildly different directions. That road was her life, and until today she had kept it on the straight and narrow. No chance for detours. Certainly no chance for anything as messy as love. No. Not love. She had found out early that love could mess your life up but good.

Ever since that disastrous mistake, she had always trusted her core values to anchor her when making decisions. Especially when mental clarity and time were in short supply. And both were running pretty short right now.

She pressed her palm down harder on the papers, over her son's picture in the stack. All grown-up. A young man. A worthy young man. The right young man for this internship, it turned out.

Brandon Smith had earned the opportunity to work on Doug Curry's campaign for the summer. Yet she had to protect him, didn't she? Or was it herself she was protecting?

Reviewing the past had only made her decision in the present more difficult. It seemed impossible, looking back from the distance of eighteen years, that she'd done the things she'd done that summer. That she'd made love to a boy for the first time. Given the way she'd lived ever since, her affair with Justin Kilgore seemed nearly impossible. Unfathomable. And yet they had made love. That was an undeniable fact.

A child existed as living proof.

Not a child. A young man. She leafed through the stack until she came to the glossy photo she'd buried somewhere in the middle. She stared hard at it, trying to reconcile this youth's face with the tiny one of the baby she had touched all too briefly eighteen years ago.

She picked up her cell phone and tried to think what to say while putting on the headset and punching speed dial. "Lacy. Any messages?"

Her secretary's remote, tinny-sounding voice came back, "No, ma'am, but Curry will be checking in anytime, I expect."

"I won't be available for a little while." This call to Brandon would be difficult and she didn't want any chance of Lacy clicking in to page her.

"But the candidate—"

"Just leave a voice mail if he calls." Markie's tone was clipped. She was finding it hard to be calm, not like her. *Breathe,* she commanded herself. For the task ahead she would have to be beyond calm.

"Even if Doug's freaking out about something, tell him to hold on and that I'll get right back to him." She tried to sound unruffled, even as she separated the application from the rest of the stack and stared at the black-and-white picture of a smiling young man that looked so much like Justin it made her hand shake. *Just hold everything,* she wanted to shout. *Okay?* Hold everything for the rest of this terrible day. For the rest of the week. For the rest of the year.

"Okay, chief. You got it." Lacy clicked off.

In fact, just stop my life right here, Markie thought as she flipped the photo up so she could see the applicant's phone number.

Be strong, she told herself as her eyes focused on the numbers through a sudden blur of tears. *And remember that he has no idea.*

He picked up on the first ring. "Hello?" Even in that one word, a west Texas drawl and the quality of Justin's voice echoed. It was the same resonant public-speaking voice that had made Brandon's grandfather stand out in the halls of Congress.

She swallowed, then started again, "May I speak to Brandon Smith, please."

"This is Brandon."

Markie closed her eyes. She was talking to her very own son again. Just like the first time, it was scary, but also strangely intoxicating. Her heart pounded, and it took all of her will to suppress tears as her mind flashed back to the pages of her journal where she had made those promises to him so long ago. Would she keep them now? Or would she injure her child? Would she hold him back? Or let him go?

"Hello?" the youthful voice prompted.

She'd been silent too long. "Yes. Brandon, it's Markie McBride, from the Doug Curry for Congress campaign."

"Oh, hello!" His excitement was palpable, genuine. "I've been expecting your call." He chuckled. "Actually, I've been packed for days. Like a kid waiting to go to camp or something."

He had his father's unassuming humor.

Was that possible? To inherit a quality as intangible as that? Or was she just hearing things she wanted to hear? Assigning things to him from her memories of Justin?

Brandon said, "So, did everything go through? My stipend and all? Is everything cool?"

Right here she was supposed to say, she had planned to say, *I'm sorry. It turns out we won't have a place for you, after all.* Better luck next time and all that. She had to say that for his sake. To protect him. From her mother. From seeing Justin. Or was that merely the expedient thing? After that scene with her mother, she had been unable to make herself call and crush his hopes, but now she was determined to. The situation with Justin was untenable. But the kid was still talking.

"I found a blog on the Internet where lots of people were making comments about this election. The primary's going to be hot. Old man Kilgore—"

Your grandfather, Markie thought with a shudder.

"—is living in the Dark Ages, but we'll still have to beat him in the trenches. But once the primary's done, I think we should get a blog going for Doug. I know plenty of U.T. students who'd log on there. I could set it up. I've done one before. It got a lot of traffic."

As she listened to his confidence and enthusiasm, she didn't have the heart to turn the kid down flat. There had to be a way to do this. "Brandon, listen. I've been thinking about how to best use you, and I was thinking that if you went to Austin—"

"Austin?" The contempt in the kid's voice was unmistakable.

"You could work out of the party headquarters—"

"Believe it or not, Kilgore's campaign offered me a place at the party headquarters, too, but that's not really my thing, you know? I mean, you know I'm gonna support the guy who wins this primary either way, but—"

Markie's heart pounded so hard it made her ears buzz and she couldn't really absorb the rest of what he was saying. Kilgore's people had contacted Brandon? For one wild, irrational moment she feared the congressman knew. But how could he?

No one knew Brandon's birth origins but herself and his parents.

"No disrespect, ma'am—" Brandon sounded clearly disappointed "—but I want to be where the action is. And this thing's going to be duked out in the heart of the district, right there in Five Points. Not in some stuffy state party offices in Austin."

Despite her anxiety, Markie had to smile. He was *her* son, too. And, in the end, the craving to see him, to meet him, won out.

"Okay, Brandon," she relented, "when does school get out?" She would have to find a way to work around him.

"Next week."

"Then come down to Five Points as soon as you're done. You'll be staying in a house with a couple of college guys near a storefront headquarters downtown. Take down my cell number." She repeated it to him. "Call me when you get to town. We'll be expecting you to work your hind end off."

"Yes, ma'am!"

"And please don't call me *ma'am,* okay?" Under different circumstances, she might have said, *even if I am old enough to be your mother.* "Everybody around here calls me Markie."

"Okay. Everybody around here calls me Brandon."

That made her chuckle. "All right, Brandon. The guys on the campaign will be expecting you. How will you get down here?"

"I have a pickup."

"Good. We can put that to use."

"Yes, ma'am! I mean, Markie. I mean—"

Again she smiled. "The headquarters is right on Main Street. You can't miss it. The windows will be plastered with Curry signs. I'll show you around and introduce you to Benjamin and Chad."

"Yes, ma'am!" She could almost hear him biting his tongue at the reflexive response.

"You're going to have a great summer, Brandon. As long as you don't say 'yes, ma'am' again."

"Yes, ma'am." This time she could hear his teasing grin.

Somewhere in the center of herself, Markie knew she'd made the right decision. Maybe not the expedient one or the easy one, but the right one. It would be hard seeing him. It would be hard keeping him away from Justin and her mother, but if she could keep her cool, no one would know, she told herself. How could anyone possibly know?

CHAPTER EIGHT

I've only got a sec because the nurse is coming right back. Sister May has checked me into the hospital.

I think I'm in labor. This is so-o-o scary, although I'm not in any real pain—yet. At first I thought I just had some bad stomach cramps from CeCe's cooking. (That girl puts a ton of butter in everything!)

So I went in to lie down on the couch and watch the tube. Sister May came by and squinted at me. Are you okay, hon? she said in that velvety-smooth voice of hers.

I told her I just had a little stomachache, nothing serious.

Sister May just shook her head and said, Uh-huh. Is your bag packed, sweetie?

She said she'd go upstairs and get it

while I went to the phone in the kitchen and called my sister.

It was sad, leaving for the hospital without taking any baby stuff along, because it's the parents who will be taking the baby home, not me. It was sad, going to the hospital with a baby inside of me, knowing that I'd be coming home with empty arms.

Leaving without anybody going along with me but Sister May. No family. None of my friends from my high school.

No Justin.

Well, I won't think about him.

But how can I not think about him??? I'm having his baby! I swear, I can feel him with me. I try to tell myself not to think such crazy thoughts, but they keep on coming. Justin. Justin. Justin. His name. His face. Even the sound of his voice. It all came rushing back as Sister May and I rode to the hospital.

Sister May reached over and patted my hand with her warm one. Honey, she said, it will be all right.

But I don't know. I've never experienced anything like this in my life. I'm scared to death. I am going to have a baby, and all I can think about is Justin. Wishing he were here with me.

I feel so low. My poor baby just moved and I looked down at my huge stomach rolling with life, and I thought, My God, I don't even know you. Who are you? What do you look like?

And then I couldn't help myself from also thinking, Please, please don't hate me.

MARKIE'S HAND STILLED WITH the tube of lipstick an inch from her mouth. From the mirror, a stranger's eyes stared back at her, a frightened woman who did not know how she was going to get through the next couple of hours.

It was not every day that a woman met her grown son for the very first time. Well, not for the first time, technically. That nurse, the one who had brought the baby around the table and held his tiny face up near Markie's, who had let her stroke his tiny red cheek, that nurse had had mercy on her.

But somehow he'd gone from newborn to grown young man, all without Markie there.

She'd had no experience to compare this to. No way to be prepared for this meeting. All she had was his résumé picture. She looked at it again. Again, she saw the stamp of Justin in the eyes, in the handsome mouth. She tilted it and examined his features for aspects of her own father. That would be nice, to see some of P.J. in his unknown grandson.

Then it hit her. Wouldn't Marynell's dreadful genes be in the mix, too? And what about Justin's real mother? Markie knew little about her, except that she was of Hispanic descent. And the congressman? Thinking about this gave her a touch of anxiety.

Seeing Justin last week had brought into the foreground the hard reality that this young man was *his* offspring, too. Which made Brandon Smith the blood grandson of Kurt Kilgore.

No. She shook her head at the thought. Brandon was himself alone, his own person, with a unique set of life experiences that had developed far away from Five Points, with separate and distinct influences from his parents and a whole extended family that his mere genetic forebears were not a party to, thank goodness.

Markie had discovered, through the kind of digging that only a skilled, resourceful political consultant could pull off, that Brandon's parents were in the ministry. It was with great joy, and no small measure of guilt, that she discovered the couple had been missionaries in Mexico before they returned to pastor a large church in the Dallas area and start a family. Reverend and Mrs. Smith had love to spare, apparently, since Brandon was the second son they'd adopted. They'd also adopted two little-girl babies.

The whole family was apparently outstanding. Brilliant, talented, socially connected athletes and scholars. Markie had looked them up on the Web site of the huge church the father pastored. The photos of Brandon, always grouped with his parents and siblings, were more dated than the black-and-white one she'd been hauling around in her briefcase. He was a handsome kid, as were his brother and sisters. They all actually looked related. They looked, in fact, a lot like…their parents.

Although Markie knew this was largely the by-product of careful matching, it also gave her a kind of perverse hope. Maybe environment was the dominant influence, after all.

She finished applying her lipstick, then checked her overall appearance in the full-length mirror that hung on the back of Robbie's bedroom door one last time.

The trim black pantsuit—too severe?—made her look older, more dignified than her usual knit tops and belted chinos. And she would look totally out of place on the streets of Five Points where tourists, artsy types and country girls alike dashed around in blue jeans, but she needed the armor of professional attire.

Curry's campaign headquarters was smack in the middle of the historic district on Main Street.

Markie unlocked the tall oak door of the ancient storefront with trembling fingers. The air inside smelled of old wood and new paper. Freshly printed red-white-and-blue campaign signs leaned against one wall. Folding tables were stacked high with literature. No tangles of wiring for phones and equipment like in the old days, except for the snakes of cable for a couple of TVs in the back and the dangling connections for the computers. The laptops and cell phones, they took home. She flipped on the fluorescent lights and tossed Brandon's file on a table. She was early, but a civilized knock on the door told her Brandon was early, too. A chip off the old block, perhaps? *Stop it,* she told herself as she rushed to the door. Stop looking for yourself or Justin Kilgore in every breath the kid takes.

When she opened the door, her heart almost stopped. She was staring straight into her own blue eyes set in a Justin-like face. That vivid color hadn't shown up in his black-and-white headshot or in the tiny, grainy thumbnails she'd found on the Internet.

"Hi," he said shyly, sheepishly.

Markie stared at him while her heart threatened to thunder right out of her chest.

He was absolutely beautiful, everything anyone would ever want in a son. Handsome, clean-cut, strong-looking. His good looks were disarming enough, but as he peered past her into the headquarters, it was his youth, his obvious enthusiasm, that undid her even more.

He stood waiting, hands at sides.

Belatedly, she realized that etiquette dictated that a woman must offer her hand first, and she would bet he was well schooled in etiquette. "I'm Markie." She put out her hand, realizing they hadn't met in person.

He shook it confidently. "I know. I checked your Web site. And I was watching for you. Over in that gift shop across the street." He inclined his head in the direction. "I guess that makes me your typical eager beaver."

"Eagerness is…that's…that's good," she stammered dumbly, moving aside so he could come in the door.

"Wow," he enthused as he stepped inside the barren storefront. "You gotta love a place like this, don't you? A Texas campaign headquarters in full attack mode."

She followed him inside, trying not to be obvious as her eyes took in every aspect of his person. His impressive shoulders stretched a white T-shirt that had "And you shall know them by their T-shirts" stamped across the back. His was the back of a well-developed football player. Could this young man really be her baby?

He turned to her, eyes shining. "I think I'm gonna love Five Points. And being away from

Dallas all summer. My dad's a great guy, but he just doesn't get the politics stuff. He wants me to go into the ministry like him but, honest to Pete, I think this stuff's in my blood, you know what I mean?"

Markie did know what he meant. Again she found herself wondering, could such tendencies be inherited?

"I know you'll be an asset to us." She forced a smile and tried not to sound as wooden as she felt. "You'll be spending most of your time with Chad and Benjamin. Two eager beavers like yourself." *And not with me,* she vowed. *Because I couldn't take much of this.* Her eyes followed him as he explored the room.

"But you can call my cell number anytime you have a question." Her heels clicked sharply on the bare concrete floor as she crossed the room. Was she coming across as strident? She handed him her crisp, embossed business card. "I'm afraid I won't be working with you as closely as I'd hoped. I'll have to spend a lot of time out on my sister's farm. Family crisis."

"Oh, I'm sorry to hear that," he said as

he frowned at the card. "Nothing too serious I hope."

"Well, um." She turned to a card table. "Actually, we had a death in the family. My brother-in-law." She cleared her throat, which was rapidly closing up with unbidden emotion.

"Oh, wow. Well, it's good of you to take the time to mentor me when you've got so much on your plate and all. Don't worry about me. I'm sure I'll be fine. I'm pretty adaptable."

"I'm sure you are." She picked up his file and studied it, flipping the pages like a doctor reading a chart when she already knows what it says. "And I'm sure my family will be fine in the long run. It's just—" she dabbed at one eye before continuing "—kind of hard right now." She felt guilty, using Danny's death to cover her sudden swell of tears when the tears were really for the pride she felt for her son.

JUSTIN SPENT THE NEXT couple of weeks cutting cedar with his best friend and ranch foreman Lorn Hix, working with the new arrivals of Mexicans at the Light at Five Points.

Cutting cedar was hard, dirty work, physical in the extreme, battling heavy limbs, dragging the smaller trees up onto the bed of the trusty old faded orange pickup they'd kept out on Kilgore Ranch ever since he could remember. But it was necessary, and it gave the immigrants a sense of earning their room and board.

The familiar elements of the task—the sound of the gas-powered chain saw, the tangy smell of cedar chips and sawdust—reminded him of his grandfather as nothing else could. The old man had been the soul of integrity, a font of wisdom, a barrel of fun. Those sayings were cliches now, but hadn't been back when his Grandpa Kilgore had actually lived them. Even now that he was pushing forty, Justin found he still wanted to be just like the old man.

He sneezed.

"¡Jesús!" one of the Mexicans called out. It wasn't a foul curse. The saying amounted to *bless you!*

Justin smiled and scrubbed a sleeve across his nose. At least in one respect, he surely was exactly like Grandpa Kilgore. Before the cutting was done today, he'd have himself a roaring case of what his grandfather and the old-timers used to call "cedar fever," known these days as seasonal allergies. Only with Hill Country cedar, there didn't seem to be anything seasonal about it.

But even the discomfort and hard work didn't take his mind off Markie. Seeing her in the café had been a kick in the gut. She hadn't looked that different to him. A little smoother around the edges, maybe. There had always been something exotic, even ethereal about her looks. Maybe it was the contrast of her white skin, dark hair and pale blue eyes. He was absolutely haunted by her eyes. There was a light that shone from within their depths. But it was always her mouth he went back to in his dreams. Her mouth called to him without ever saying a word. He remembered her soft smile when he'd given her the locket.

Somewhere back in the ranch house was the locket that he'd once fastened around Markie McBride's throat. He'd brought it back here and left it on one of his trips home many years ago. He'd never even considered giving it to another woman.

The morning and the work wore on and the back of the pickup was filled with cuttings, and still he was thinking about her, thinking of ways he might see her, connect with her. After they took this load of brush out to the ravine and dumped it, he just might take the Mexicans over to Robbie Tellchick's fence line and clean it up for her. Markie might never know, but he'd know. Anything to make their lives a little easier.

"Let's wrap it!" he called out in Spanish to the Mexicans.

They started gathering up the tools, the shirts discarded in the heat. Aurelia, who had turned out to be a spectacular cook, would have chili on the stove and tortillas in the frying pan for lunch.

She also had a bun in the oven, Justin suspected. He'd overheard the girl, who couldn't be more than nineteen, telling Mrs. Ramos, the mother of that first family to arrive at the Light, that she wanted to stay in Texas until her baby came so that he or she would be born under the Lone Star. Lucky Julio. She seemed very taken with her man. Devoted.

Obviously they'd found a way to see each other even though Julio wasn't staying at the Light. He wondered if they'd found a way to get married yet.

Justin wondered if he would ever have a child. He wondered if he wasn't getting a little long in the tooth for fatherhood. Wondered if he'd missed his shot. Well, hell. It might help if he had a woman first. He'd once had a wife. But he hadn't loved her, not like he should have. And having seen Markie McBride again, he was more certain than ever of the reason why.

The Mexicans piled into the bed of the pickup, pushing down the cedar, and Justin climbed into the cab. They'd ride over to the fence where Lorn had been cutting smaller brush, and fetch him.

"Hey! Hey!" He heard Lorn's voice, booming with irritation over by the fence line. "This here's Kilgore property!" He was yelling at some boys, or rather, some young men, down in the bar ditch.

Justin sent the pickup bumping across the pasture to check it out.

The three young men were standing, talking to Lorn, with neon-fresh Doug Curry for Congress signs dangling in their hands.

"I'm sorry, but y'all will have to move on," he heard Lorn say as he pushed his hat back on his head. "This is the congressman's property, and we don't want none of them signs around here."

"This is the easement on a county road," one of the guys informed Lorn, his tone a bit snotty. Justin had heard plenty of that attitude when he'd lived back east, but Lorn was having none of it.

"The hell it is. The *county* don't mow this ditch. I do." Lorn Hix was big as an ox, a good guy, but he could be intimidating when he wanted to. And he was used to running the Kilgore in the congressman's absence without saying by-your-leave to anybody. He was also used to thinking of Justin as his sidekick and hunting buddy, not the owner and the boss.

Justin got out of the pickup and slammed the door. "Good morning," he called out as he strode up to the fence. "Justin Kilgore. This is my property." He'd said the last as much for Lorn's benefit as for the intruders'.

They were college-age, wearing red-white-

and-blue Curry for Congress T-shirts, all apparently full of fire-in-the-belly about their candidate.

"You're the congressman's son?" the youngest-looking among them said.

"Yep." Justin nodded, wondering if he should know this kid. He was wearing sunglasses, but there was something familiar about his face. He was a good-looking boy. Good-sized. Smiling, relaxed, while the other two were tense and scowling. That made him the smart one and the leader. So Justin addressed him.

"Let's say you guys go ahead and put your signs up."

In the middle of a nod the kid abruptly turned his head and sneezed. And sneezed again.

"¡Jesús!" one of the Mexican workers called from the bed of the pickup.

"We call that cedar fever." Justin smiled.

"Yes, sir. Pardon me. Go on."

"You put your signs up along here. And about five minutes after you're gone, I'll have Rigo and Carlos back there—" Justin indicated the Mexicans in the pickup "—pull them all up out of the ground. Or I could just let Lorn here chew 'em up with his big mower. I would do that, you know. Because if the congressman were your dad, would you let his opponent's signs be seen anywhere near your ranch?" Even if Justin disagreed with his father's politics, he wasn't going to do anything to disrespect the man.

A grudging twist of the mouth replaced the kid's smile. He looked down at the ground, then up at Justin. "You have a good day, sir. Come on, guys," he addressed his companions. "We wouldn't want to waste Doug's signs."

Justin was only a little surprised when the older-looking two followed the boy. As he watched him climb into the Suburban parked across the road, he thought how great it would be if his dad could attract a kid like that to work on one of his campaigns.

MARKIE KEPT UP HER RESOLVE to avoid Brandon Smith as much as possible, which wasn't hard since every contact with Brandon brought fresh waves of regret to her heart. She worked out of Robbie's farmhouse kitchen whenever she could, using the handy excuse that her sister needed her. When she did meet with Curry, she made sure it was in the back room of the headquarters with the door closed.

Whenever she asked how the interns were working out, she always got a positive report from the staff. Mostly the three younger guys stayed glued to the candidate, making the rounds of small-town speaking engagements with him, helping him canvas door to door and plastering the endless miles of Hill Country roads with Curry for Congress signs.

Chad and Ben were the kind of jaded young college turks who could roll from one adventure to another, and they dragged Brandon right along with them. She knew Brandon was getting the hands-on experience he longed for—she just hoped it was the right kind. She was very mindful of the fact that his parents were in the ministry and that they were trusting her to look out for their son. Or was she feeling overprotective because he was her baby? Had she felt this way about any other young person placed under her aegis? Other interns in other years had been bright boys and girls exactly like Brandon, and she hadn't stewed over the propriety of their activities this way.

"Where were you guys last night?" she couldn't keep herself from asking one morning after a staffer told her the boys were partying late.

Brandon turned. He was sitting on a folding chair in front of a laptop, scrolling through some newspaper archives. His blue eyes and dimpled smile were startling. Today, however, the blue eyes looked a bit bloodshot.

"At a dive. A watering hole." He pumped his eyebrows. "My dad would shit a longhorn steer if he knew I'd been there."

"Brandon. You are underage." Markie kept her tone level, but suspected she sounded like a Dutch aunt. "You have no business in a bar."

"Yes, ma'am." He grinned. "But wait till you hear what I found out."

"What?" She stepped up to his side to look at the screen.

"Dirt on Kurt the Jerk, that's what." Brandon smiled his fetching smile and turned back to his laptop.

Kurt the Jerk was what the staffers had labeled Kilgore ever since the congressman had lost his cool and morphed into a red-faced, snarling bulldog during a recent debate with Curry. "He's hiding something. I'm looking up anything I can find about his ranch now. Apparently there are some caves out there somewhere."

"Hiding something? In some caves?"

"Yeah. I heard two nice Mexican chaps discussing it in that hole last night."

"Brandon, listen to me."

"I bet I can get to the bottom of this." He was working his mouse, not listening to her. "I'm good at this stuff. You'll see. I wonder if there's a topographical map of the area."

The caves. Markie knew exactly where those caves were. And she remembered that she'd seen Kilgore, acting suspiciously at those caves, many years ago. Hadn't she written something about it in her diary? She'd have to look for that entry.

"Have you told anyone else about this?"

"No."

"Don't. Let me check into some things first."

"Wasn't Kilgore investigated for illegal campaign contributions once upon a time?"

Brandon's eyes were still avidly searching the screen.

"Brandon!" Markie's voice was sharp. This kid was giving her a headache in more ways than one. "I *said,* I'll handle this. Now, I want you to tell me exactly what you heard in that bar last night."

"THE STORE," AS LOCALS referred to it, with tongue in cheek, was plunked out on a remote gravel ranch road in the middle of nowhere. It was little more than a dusty tin shack with a gravel parking lot and a rolling marquee out front that read, 99C MARG. The margaritas served inside this hole were likely not even worth the ninety-nine cents, Justin observed wryly. Made, no doubt, with the kind of tequila that had a dead worm curled at the bottom of the bottle.

He went inside, was greeted with a nod by the solitary bartender to whom he said, "Just water," as he slid up onto a bar stool to wait.

Not another soul was there. No sign of Brandon Smith yet.

Whatever the kid had to say, Justin had resolved to hear it with an open mind. The kid was a crosser of a different type in this case. Justin had to give the guy credit for having guts. Moving between political camps in the heat of a race. Justin could only imagine what Curry would say about one of his volunteers meeting with the congressman's son.

He supposed that's why they were meeting in this long-lost watering hole. He checked his watch as the bartender plunked a glass in front of him and twisted a lime into it with a flourish.

"Gracias," Justin said, and stuffed a dollar in the tip jar. "I've always wondered," he said because the room was too quiet, "why do they call this place The Store?"

The bartender grinned. "Honey, I'm going to *The Store.*"

"Ah." Justin returned a wry grin.

The rusty door hinges creaked and Justin swiveled on the bar stool to look. Silhouetted in the stark sunshine was a young man. Justin couldn't be sure because of the sunglasses, but he was pretty certain this was the same kid he'd seen in the bar ditch a few days earlier. He was trim, but tall and muscular in snug jeans and a loose hoody sweat-shirt that had RELAX emblazoned in foot-high letters across the front. He had the hood up even though it was hot as hell outside. His physique made him look as if he'd be right at home playing football for Permian or some other powerhouse Texas team. Against the glare of afternoon sun, Justin couldn't see much else, and he could make out even less of the kid's features when the door slammed to, eclipsing the light.

His boots clunked heavily as he strode across the shadowy room. "Mr. Kilgore?" In the sleepy silence of the bar, his deep voice resonated. Justin thought he recognized that voice.

"Yes."

The kid slid up onto the stool next to Justin's. He didn't look directly at Justin. Instead he cocked his head at the bartender, now wiping the other end of the counter. "Sir. Could I have a Coke, please?"

Justin dug out some more bills. "What's this all about?"

The kid said nothing, waiting until the bartender tapped a Coke can down in front of him and took Justin's money. "Let's go over there." Brandon Smith jerked his head toward a booth in the corner.

They slid into the booth and the weak light winking through a crooked blind illuminated the kid's features. He was truly handsome. Clean-cut. When he dropped the hood, Justin decided there was something unsettlingly familiar about his features. He had the uncanny sensation one might experience when looking at an old photograph of an ancestor.

The kid took a long draw on his Coke, looked around, and said, "Thanks for meeting me way out here. I don't know this town very well yet and I couldn't think of anyplace else where nobody could spot us. Boy, it's a different joint in the daytime than at night."

"You were here at night?"

"Yeah. Me and my new friends. Ben and Chad. I call 'em the Two Suits."

Justin smiled as he eyed the kid's casual attire. "Curry's campaign aides. The ones with you the other day. So, you don't wear a suit to the headquarters?"

The kid pointed at himself. "Me? Yeah, *right*. They've got me out in the bar ditches, pushing signs into the mud."

"As I recall. I take it that's disappointing?"

"You tell me. I'm a whiz with numbers, good with computers." The kid stated these facts unapologetically. "Love research, and they send me out to work from the bed of a pickup, bouncing down some country road with the boys on the sign crew. I mean, I know everybody's gotta start somewhere, but I was hoping to at least get to keep the books. Or merge the mailing lists. Work on the press releases. Anything."

"You want a future in politics?" Justin could imagine it. Brandon Smith had a certain charisma. And he liked the boy's straightforward style, his obvious intelligence.

"I'm not ashamed to admit it. I wouldn't mind running for office someday. People act as if public service is some kind of *disease* these days, you know? I guess you'd know a lot about that, huh?"

"Politics? Absolutely. I've spent the better part of my life avoiding it."

"Yeah?" The kid smiled. "Well, I get that. My dad's in the ministry, but I kind of avoid that whole scene." He fidgeted as if now he was going to get down to it. "So, are you and your dad close?"

It was an odd question to open with, but Justin answered it. He had nothing to hide. "Not especially. I'm not closely involved with his campaign, if that's what you're getting at. I have my own life, my own work."

The kid squinted at him, sizing him up. "I heard about your place for immigrants. My dad would approve. Not that I have any plans to follow in *my* dad's footsteps. Sometimes I don't think we've got anything in common, but then, I'm adopted."

"I see." Justin wondered where this was going.

"Okay, then. Here's the deal." The kid took a piece of paper out of the pocket of his hoody. It was a bunged-up cocktail napkin with notes scribbled on it. "I had to write some stuff down last night. I was pretty lit. Should the opportunity ever arise, don't share that information with my parents." He gave Justin a crooked grin. "Remember, I'm a P.K."

"A P.K.?"

"Preacher's kid."

"Oh. Right." He wondered if it were as hard to be a minister's son as it was to be a congressman's.

Brandon unfolded the napkin. "Pass the pepper. 'Cause I'm gonna have to eat this dude when we're done."

Justin smiled.

"You have many illegals yet? Out at that place you've started? The Light at Five Points?"

"Quite a few. Several men. A couple of families already."

"Wow. Already?"

"Word spreads."

"How do you do it, if you don't mind my asking? I mean, financially."

Because the kid seemed sincerely interested, Justin answered candidly.

"I'm using my own funds to pay a very small staff for now. Donors are starting to materialize. Some of the larger churches and synagogues in metro Dallas and Houston areas see the need. And, of course, these people are not afraid of hard work. They've already started refurbishing the ranch house, clearing ground."

"Wow. Could I come out and have a look sometime? I'm actually into stuff like that. My parents have taken me and my brothers and sisters to Mexico almost every summer to work as missionaries down there."

Because of the kid's history, Justin said, "Sure. Come on out. But call my cell first. Some of the people don't want to be seen."

"Yeah. I will. Wouldn't want that big guy coming after me. So…" Brandon consulted the napkin. "You know some brothers named…Juan and Julio Morales?"

Justin frowned. "I might." What was this about?

"Well, see, I happen to speak Spanish."

"And?" Practically everybody in this part of the country did.

"Not the high school variety. I even understand Chiapan dialects. My two buddies are not that fluent."

"Ah." Justin nodded, impressed. He had yet to master those cadences himself.

"The point is, there were some guys in here last night, speaking in Chiapan dialects, or maybe they were from Jalisco. I couldn't really tell. Anyway, I could make out enough to know what they were saying, even though it was loud as hell and pretty crowded."

"The drinks are priced about right." Justin said dryly as he panned the dingy room.

"These guys were looking for these brothers."

"So is that why you're coming to me with this? My connection to the Light at Five Points?"

"There's more." Brandon took a nervous sip of his Coke. "What made me perk up and listen to Mutt and Jeff in the first place was the mention of your dad's name."

"My father?"

"They seemed to think the congressman— and I didn't mess up the translation—would know something about these caves, that they were located on his land or something. They even said he had some stuff hidden in there."

"Stuff? What kind of stuff?"

"That's all they said. That's the closest translation—stuff."

Justin frowned. "Have you told anybody else about this?"

Brandon Smith nodded. "A lady who works for Curry."

"Markie McBride?"

The kid looked surprised that Justin had

produced the name so quickly, but then he nodded. Justin felt a familiar tightening in his chest at the confirmation that Markie knew about this.

"I trust her," the kid was saying. "If it weren't for her, I wouldn't have this internship. She's got a lot on the ball. She's a nice lady."

"Yes." Justin knew well how nice Markie was. "What did she say?"

"She said it might explain a lot of things, about why the Moraleses were poking around in those caves. And why the sheriff can't find them. She figured we—Curry's people—could make trouble for the congressman with this if we could get to the bottom of it, since it's Kilgore land."

Justin sighed. "You could, I guess. But my father can take care of himself. I'm more worried about the Moraleses. Too bad they didn't trust me enough to come to me with the whole truth—that the congressman is connected to this. But then I suppose I *am* his son." He tried to keep the resentment out of his voice, but he was thinking, *And no matter how much humanitarian work I do, no matter how much trust I earn, I'll never escape his shadow.*

None of this concerned the boy, of course. He wasn't a Kilgore, he had no idea what a burden that name could be. Justin scrubbed a hand down his face. He took the napkin and turned it over. Nothing on the back.

"Ready to destroy this?"

"Sure."

As he ripped up the napkin, a foolish hope rose in Justin's chest. "She didn't tell you to come to me?"

"Markie? No. In fact, she specifically told me *not* to tell anybody. But because you're… well, because you're *you* I decided you might be able to help." The kid cocked one eyebrow as if nothing more need be said on that score. "I did some digging. Saw some old newspaper articles about you and your dad. I can read between the lines. And I remembered how cool you were about the sign deal. And my conscience started bugging me, about these brothers. Once a P.K., always a P.K., huh? Anyway, I'm thinking we might not have time to play political games. I mean, what if those guys find those Morales brothers? Sounded like they might be out to get rid of them.

"Those guys?" Brandon jerked a thumb toward the bar as if they were still there. "I think they could be coyotes. I was reading a book about that last year."

Coyotes. People smugglers from Mexico, who often engaged in illegal activities on this side of the border. The kid was sharp. "I think you might be right. You did the right thing, Brandon, calling me."

"Yeah. Let's hope so. I don't think Markie's gonna be too thrilled with me."

"You leave Markie McBride to me."

CHAPTER NINE

I don't know how much I can write in here. In my house, certain people read other people's private stuff that they have no business reading. But I have to pour out my heart somehow or I swear I'm gonna explode. I sure can't tell Robbie or Frankie about this. They're both such prudes.

We went back to that narrow place on the Blue River today. It's so beautiful there. The trees are huge. The rocks are huge. It's about the only spot in the Hill Country that isn't hot as an oven in July.

I really don't know exactly how it happened. That's part of what I'd really like to figure out, you know? Seems like we started out just having fun, just being normal, and in no time at all it gets so intense. Today it got really intense.

Oh, man. I really do not know how much I should write here.

Like usual, we spread out our sleeping bag—that ratty old one he keeps in that ratty old orange pickup he's so fond of—

I don't know. This part is hard. All I know is, when he nuzzled my neck, and his lips felt so warm, and his hands, too, I didn't want him to stop.

I didn't want any of it to stop. I wanted to give myself to him. All of me.

Maybe we went too far. (No *maybe* about it.)

What if I got pregnant? I said as he wrapped his shirt around me, after. I sure picked a fine time to think of that, *after* we—you know, after.

He pushed my hair behind one ear and said that even if that happened, he'd take care of me. He said next time we'll take precautions. His eyes got that squinty look I love and he said, unless you don't want a next time.

I told him I wasn't like that. I am not some silly girl. I wouldn't do this if I didn't mean it. I'm not shallow or fickle. I'm not gonna act like this was all some big accident, like oops! I wasn't thinking about giving my virginity to him, like it was all some big surprise. There are girls at my high school who've done everything but the actual act, and are still run around claiming they're virgins. As if.

He said he'd never met a girl like me.

I asked him if it was his first time. Seemed like I was thinking of a lot of things just a little too late. But I have a right to know that, you know?

He started helping me get into my jeans. He slid them onto my legs like I was little girl. It would have felt weird if it was any other guy zipping up my pants. But Justin makes everything seem so easy, so natural. When he was done, he propped himself up on one elbow above me and looked into my eyes and said yes.

That was his answer! *Yes*. It was his first time!

I couldn't believe it. He's been in college for two years and he's so good-looking, he's such a hunk, obviously he's had plenty of chances. Don't get me wrong. I'm glad.

And I told him so. But I also told him he was gonna have to explain that one to me. I mean, I just assumed all college guys had *done it.*

He said there was nothing to explain. He said plenty of people wait. He said he's had no trouble with willpower until he met me. He said he was waiting for the right girl, for the right time.

He said he was not sure I was really ready.

I told him I was plenty ready! He still insists on underestimating me. But I'm very mature for my age. Every high school boy I ever dated has just about bored me out of my mind. But Justin has been so exciting. The only way I can explain it is that he's a real man. I think I'm in love with him.

Then he gave me a little kiss on the lips and tried to tease me out of my scared mood.

He said considering the momentous event that just transpired here, we should give this place a special name so only the two of us will know what we're talking about.

I said, Like what?

Like Still Waters or Secret Cove. He was grinning.

I said, Oh, shut up! and rolled my eyes. Then I turned my head and grinned back at him and said, How about we call it The Rocks?

He grabbed me and fell back, laughing so hard I thought we were going to roll right off into the river.

"MARKIE? IT'S JUSTIN. Listen. We have got to talk. Right away. I may have discovered why my father wants your sister's land back. Is this a good time?"

No. No. This is not a good time, was all Markie could think while her heart beat out of control at the mere sound of his voice. *This is the worst of times.* "Okay. Talk."

"Not on a cell phone. And not in town where someone might see us together or overhear what I have to say."

"Where, then?"

"The Rocks."

"The Rocks?" Her mind screamed *no,* but her mouth managed to say, "Why there?" as calm as you please. Ever since she'd seen him in the café, she'd been determined to prove that she was *not* affected by their past.

But there wasn't any point in pretending that she'd forgotten it, that she didn't know exactly the spot he was talking about. How could she forget *The Rocks,* so named because of the huge jutting limestone formations there, and for other, less innocent reasons. It had been the kind of adolescent joke that had made Markie feel mature, when, of course, back then she was anything but.

"It's secluded," he was explaining. "No one will see us or our vehicles way out there. And it's easy to find. You remember where the river crosses Robbie's land, right?"

"Yes." The Rocks was only ten minutes down a winding ranch road from where she stood now, on her sister's back porch. "When?"

"Right now."

THE GURGLING WATER CREATED a pleasant backdrop of sound for the whole scene. On this quiet summer evening the narrow bend of the Blue River looked exactly the way it had back then. Serene. Remote. Mysterious.

The clear pools of green and blue and gold caught the reflection of sky and trees, of light bouncing off limestone. Those ochre-colored stones rose along the banks and out of the water like giant loaves of bread or, as Markie had imagined once, the thighs of giant gods. Towering above the rocks and providing seclusion and shade were dense cedar and cypress trees, dipping their knobby-kneed roots right down to the water's edge.

She climbed a rock that overlooked the water, their favorite one. The *very* one, in fact. Realizing this, she started to get back down, but then she saw Justin scrambling down a sloping path toward the water. The grace with which he moved arrested and disquieted her as she realized again that she was still attracted to him.

"Markie!" he called when he was within shouting distance. "I'm sorry," he said breathlessly when he got closer. "I couldn't think of any place else to meet you. I hope this isn't…uncomfortable for you." That was Justin. Straightforward as an arrow. Or more like a spear. Right to your heart.

"Don't worry about it." Markie shrugged, rubbing her arms and keeping her eyes on the water as he climbed up on the rock.

After a moment he stood facing her. "All I could think was…I… I knew we would both remember this spot."

She turned to him. "And the reason we couldn't meet in the restaurant in town again was…?" She wasn't going to get all sentimental and emotional. No looking back.

"I don't want to do anything to endanger Brandon Smith."

"What?" Markie tried to hide her shock, but not soon enough. He was eyeing her suspiciously.

He nodded. "I met with him in secret. He told me that he told you."

"Ah. And so I take it he told you…everything, as well."

"Yes."

"And?"

Justin scrubbed a hand over his face, unsuccessfully disguising his frustration. "Why do I feel like I'm playacting in some B-grade spy movie?"

Markie felt her mouth wanting to twitch into a grin. But instead she turned her face back to the water. "Meeting this way was *your* idea." She crossed her arms over her middle, pressing down a dangerous quavering sensation there. He had met with Brandon? Had seen him in person? Did he suspect anything?

He touched her arm. "Could we sit down? Please?"

Markie looked around. *On this very same rock?* The quavering gelled into a tiny knot of panic. "Um. Sure." She settled herself up higher on the gently sloping mound of limestone. It felt warm with afternoon sun. Glad she's worn a tank top and khaki capris, she arranged herself like a self-conscious schoolgirl at a church picnic. Hunched shoulders. Arms clutched around knees.

Justin settled himself below and to the right of her, so that he was looking up into her face as he braced himself on one palm, with one knee cocked up.

Markie did not care for looking down at his limbs arranged in such a relaxed, athletic pose, one that highlighted his masculinity. His body hadn't changed much at all, it turned out. She fixed her eyes outward, on a glittering patch of the water, lazily coiling in the sunlight.

Justin turned his head toward the water, as well. "Man. Don't you love the Blue River as it comes around that bend?" It was as if he was reading her mind. "The way it's sheltered by those high rocks." He stretched an arm forth. "Those little pools that swirl like they've been stirred by a magic wand or something."

Despite herself, she nodded.

"Do you remember when we used to go down to the water and goof off?" he said.

Again, she nodded.

"Do you remember when we were crossing on those stepping stones down there and fell in? You acted as if you were drowning, even though the water's only waist-high."

"I was a silly girl," she said automatically.

"No. You were a beautiful girl." He looked up at her, regarding her face seriously. "You still are."

"A tall girl," she countered, avoiding the look in his eyes. She did not want the mood to get all intense, but he wasn't letting the memories die.

"You came up sputtering. But you were laughing so hard I knew you were okay." He had scooped her up in his arms and whirled her around in the waist-high water. "Do you remember what you said to me?"

"That no guy had ever scooped me up like that before," she murmured before she realized she'd answered out loud.

Suddenly Markie was was remembering how he had looked, smiling down at her and then how he had kissed her. How it had felt like an electric flood, as if somebody had flipped a switch. Suddenly she wanted nothing so badly as to feel that intensity again. His strength, holding her up in the water, kissing her like there was no tomorrow. She had never felt anything like it in her life. The water so cold. His mouth so hot. She hadn't been able to tell if she was dizzy from the spinning, the water, the kiss or what.

"I guess you never forget your first time," he said quietly. He ducked his head, making sure she was looking into his eyes. "Markie. What if we… I've been thinking…do you think it would be possible for us to start up again?"

Markie stared down at him. He had no idea! After all these years she realized how wrong that was. She had to tell him, but how? Her pulse raced. Her ears started to buzz. Her whole body flushed. Despite her resolve, sudden tears filled her eyes.

He had been smiling up at her as he waited on her reply, but now his expression grew concerned with that tiny frown line she'd once loved to see forming between his brows. His eyes were so gorgeous! His lashes were so long and dark and thick, they actually cast shadows on his cheeks. He had the sexiest eyes she had ever seen. As Markie stared at him she realized she loved him still, but he had no idea what she would have to over-come to let herself be loved by him in return. Even though there had never been, and never would be, another man like Justin Kilgore, she couldn't see how she could ever go back and undo all the damage that had been done.

"Markie?" he said, his voice gentle, wor-ried. "I didn't mean to dredge up old memo-ries and make you sad." He scooted up the rock, near to her, not quite touching. "Why the tears?"

She swiped at her cheeks, remembering how she had started to shiver in the water, how he had carried her over to the bank and helped her climb up onto the biggest rock, into the sunshine, where it was warmer. Almost the exact spot where she was sitting now. How he took off her tennis shoes and poured the water out of them, pulled the laces loose and the tongues up. How he wrapped the sleeping bag and then himself around her. How they had ended up making love. Oh, she should have told him! No matter what it might have cost her in humiliation or rejection, she should have told him about his child!

She bit back an incoherent sob and bent her head to her knees, hiding her face, her shame.

He was swift to wrap his arms around her. The press of his solid body was fierce and she could feel the thrum of his strong heartbeat against her shoulder. "Sweetheart—" he reverted to the endearment all too naturally "—what is it?" There was fear, alarm, in his voice. "Tell me what's wrong," he urged.

As she gulped for air, the scent of him filled her nose and mouth and lungs—the same clean and virile scent he'd exuded a young man. *Oh, Justin. I should never have let you get this close to me again.*

But aloud she managed to say, "I've had an emotional day. It's…let's just…let's not look back, all right?"

"All right," he said warily. "We won't. Not if it upsets you." She could tell he was confused. He hugged her tight, as if it was all he knew how to do. He even kissed her hair.

Markie sank against him. *God.* Justin had always been so sweet, so giving and generous and pure of heart. How could she have lied to him, cheated him the way she did?

He pressed a warm palm to her cheek and thumbed a tear away. "It was stupid of me to bring up the past. I know this is a really difficult time for you and your family."

"Yes, it is." She felt dishonest for latching onto that excuse. Her guilt caused her to stiffen in his embrace. "Maybe you should just tell me why you wanted to meet me out here."

"Okay." He loosened his hold. "It's about this thing with my father and the caves. I wanted to ask you not to go public with this."

Instantly, something in her bristled. "And why shouldn't we try to expose that? Obviously he's hiding something."

"Think of your sister. My father will retaliate. And think of Brandon Smith."

"Brandon?" Markie's heart hammered. "What about him?"

"My father will find out who leaked this, and any political future Brandon hopes for will be over before it starts. I know how Dad operates."

"Then what do you suggest?"

"There's got to be another way to flush out my father, a way to find out why he would be after the Mexicans who trespassed on your sister's land."

"And why he would want the land back so bad."

"Right. And what he's got hidden in those caves. But finding out all of that might take some real digging."

"And in the meantime, Curry loses. That's convenient."

"You know I'm not trying to get my father reelected. And you're sharp enough to know that the outcome of this election will be the same no matter what you and I do. Curry doesn't have what it takes to evict an incumbent."

Markie knew it was true, but still she admired Curry for trying. Kurt Kilgore had been imbedded in office for twenty-four long years, and he doubtlessly expected to reign for twenty-four more. Despite her protestations to her sister that her involvement in this campaign was not a personal vendetta, Markie had to admit that she at least wanted to see to it that Kurt Kilgore never enjoyed the honor of running unopposed.

But Justin was right. Curry was doomed to lose, no matter what. Protecting Brandon was more important. "What do you have in mind?" If they had to work together, for Brandon's sake, then they had to work together.

"I guess Brandon told you he overheard some of my father's men in a bar. They were looking for some brothers called Morales." Justin sighed.

"Yes." Markie nodded. "Could these people be a threat to Brandon?" As soon as she said it, she wondered if Justin would get suspicious of her overprotectiveness toward the boy. But she had to keep reminding herself that Justin had no idea what had happened eighteen years ago.

"He didn't think they really noticed him. They were tossing down bad tequila, and Brandon stuck to Cuba libres."

At her concerned look, Justin amended, "Heavy on the Coke, I'm sure. He seems like a levelheaded kid."

"I think we can safely assume these men will be up to no good if they find the Moraleses," he continued. "And for some reason—Brandon couldn't figure out why—they assume the brothers will return to the caves eventually. I've already alerted the sheriff to keep a lookout on that area of your sister's farm."

"The sheriff? He hasn't got enough deputies to watch the Tellchick farm."

"That's where you and I come in."

Markie knew her squint did nothing to disguise her turmoil at the words *you and I.*

"I want to come out to the farm and keep watch over those caves myself."

"What?" She stiffened.

He put up a palm. "It'll be cool. I'll stay in the old rock house. A person can see forever from up there." *The old rock house* was what everybody called a turn-of-the century limestone cottage built by an early Kilgore. The place was a one-room shell with rotting roof and cracked foundation. Perched on the highest hill on the Tellchick farm, it offered a clear view in all four directions from its hollowed-out windows. But the structure was so dilapidated that even the Five Points Historical Society wouldn't touch it.

"The Morales boys are likely in the vicinity somewhere. One of them is involved with a girl staying out at the Light. I figure they might make a try at the caves again soon, but I'm thinking it'll only be at night—because of the way your sister has already complained about trespassers and because of the way the mounded rock formations over the caves are so bare and exposed in the daylight. I can't speak for what my father or his henchmen might do. It's pretty clear to me now that he wants to call in the note on the land so he can control it. You know, take care of any trespassers in his own way. Or maybe it's so he can get at whatever is hidden in those caves."

"Drugs? Stolen goods, maybe," Markie mused. "Years ago your father was investigated for irregularities in his campaign funds.

He had to have some way to bring in big money that would be hard to trace."

Justin winced. "Good old dad." That had been the summer he met Markie. He wondered if she knew that.

"Why can't we just go into the caves and try to find whatever it is ourselves?" Markie reasoned.

"That could takes days, weeks, and we might still come up empty-handed. Those caves go on forever, one twisting passageway after another."

"So, what are you going to do if you see somebody out there? Follow them in?"

"If it's the Moraleses, I'm going to try to get them to cooperate with the authorities. Even if they try to run again, they should be easy enough to catch out there."

"I suppose. Given that there's only one ranch road out of here."

"In the meantime, I'll appear to be supervising the Mexicans working on Robbie's farm during the day. We'll actually help Robbie, just as I suggested before."

Markie gave her head a shake. "Robbie will nev—"

He put a palm up as if he knew what she was going to say—that her sister would never allow illegals near her farm after they'd been suspected of starting the fire that killed Danny. "I have to have a reason for being up there. Once she knows the deal, don't you think Robbie will want to cooperate?"

"I suppose I can talk her into it, as long as she knows you'll watch those men every minute."

"I give you my word."

They fell quiet then. Markie scooped up a few pebbles and started tossing them one by one in high arcs out over the sparkling water.

"What are you thinking?"

"Nothing." But the rippling sound of water as it bubbled over stones punctuated an uneasy silence that said she *was* thinking of something important.

Justin studied her, wondering if she was remembering again, same as he was.

But he didn't need to ask and she didn't need to volunteer. He could tell by looking at her that she was, and that she'd suffered the same as he over the loss of their relationship. All these years. But why? It all seemed so senseless. He had to ask. "What happened to us?"

Without taking her eyes off the hypnotic water, she slowly shook her head.

"You know, you are even more beautiful now than you were then."

When she still wouldn't look at him, his frustration mounted. He wanted to blurt out, Why did you send the locket back?

Too clearly now, he remembered the day he gave his mother's locket to her.

They'd been right here at the river, lying in the shade at that wide place. He could see it now if he just turned his head, where the bank was flat and grassy and the high rocks blocked the view from the road.

They had shared a can of Coke and talked about his dad for a while.

As always, he hadn't been able to resist kissing her and he couldn't help wondering what would happen when he went away to college. He'd been carrying the locket around for weeks, waiting for the right moment.

Markie, he heard his own voice saying as if it echoed in this very spot, *are you going to miss me when summer's over?*

His old fear that Emily Conners had interposed herself in the situation reared up now.

After he'd broken it off with Emily upon his return to Brown, he'd always worried that she would retaliate.

There was nothing dignified about their breakup scene. He was the blunt-spoken young bachelor trying to pry a clingy female's hands off himself and run. And Emily was the stereotypical hysterical chick, denying and crying and making it all ten times harder. She'd screeched at him at first, then collapsed on his dorm bed, keening, crying and salivating over the pillow she hugged to her bosom.

"It's another girl, isn't it?" she had howled.

"No," he'd lied. Because Emily, he had decided after spending his summer in the calm company of the warm, genuine and solidly happy Markie McBride, was a manipulative and unstable young woman, to say the least. As high-strung and temperamental as any of the Thoroughbred horses her father raised. "It's just not working between us."

He didn't add that she had been his father's choice all along, not his. Just as Justin had been her father's choice for a son-in-law.

Later, Emily had had the gall to contact his

mother. He couldn't begin to guess what Emily might have been capable of telling an innocent girl like Markie, should she have found a way to contact her. Which was another reason he had decided Emily didn't really need to know that he'd met someone else when he was away from her on that long hot summer in Texas.

But Emily must have found out somehow, must have made trouble. Because when he called Markie's home the next day her mother had shrilly announced that he was never to contact her daughter again.

The next time he called, the woman came on stronger. "My daughter is still in *high school*," she had hissed, "and her father and I have decided that she has no business with a man who is way too old for her, especially one who has a fiancé. I'm warning you, young man, do *not* call here again."

The next time she advised him to take it up with his father. And the next time, the woman simply hung up on him.

So he had bided his time and waited.

Markie McBride would not be in high school forever.

But then the locket had arrived in the mail with no note of explanation, not one word. And to this day Justin did not know what had happened, but now he intended to find out.

"We need to talk about what happened back then."

Markie flushed so fast her face looked sunburned. "About what happened?"

"I know you remember. Just as clearly as I do."

She turned her head, looking downstream, away from him.

He was suddenly in no mood to play games. "Don't do that." He grabbed her wrist.

She turned on him. Her eyes grew huge, as if he had no right to touch her.

"Don't pretend it didn't mean anything when we made love. When we said 'I love you' to each other. I don't know about you, but those words mean something to me. I thought we had decided, at least in our hearts, that we had a future together. Do you think I'd give my dead mother's locket to a girl I wasn't serious about? And then two weeks after I went back to Brown, my locket shows up and I find out you're with some other guy."

"What?" The shock in her eyes was real. "I was never with *some other guy.* It was *you* who abandoned *me.*" She twisted her wrist free of his grasp. "You went back to your fancy fiancé and forgot all about your little summer fling in Texas."

"No." Justin frowned. "No, I did not." He said it slowly, sadly. "Look at me, Markie."

She spared him a distrustful glance.

"Okay. Maybe I should have told you about Emily. I wanted to so many times. It's just that she seemed...irrelevant."

"Being engaged to someone is irrelevant?"

"No. It's *not.* But we were *never* engaged. I don't know where you got that idea. Your mother seemed to think that, too. I guess there were a lot of assumptions about me and Emily. Our families have known one another for decades. We were paired up at all kinds of social occasions. But I never asked Emily to marry me. I never loved her. As soon as I went back east I broke it off with her for good."

"And promptly proceeded to never contact me again," Markie pointed out bitterly.

"No! I called and called. Your mother refused to let me talk to you. She said you were still in high school and they would not allow their daughter to be involved with an older guy. I understood that. But then I found out from my father that you were dating another guy. Apparently your feelings were not all that deep, despite what had happened…out here."

Markie stared at Justin, recalling those weeks when, heartsick for him, she had holed up in the attic room, shunning even the company of her sisters. And all the while Marynell was downstairs, standing guard over the wall phone in the kitchen. And in the meantime, the congressman was making sure Justin had the wrong impression about her.

Her mother and Kurt Kilgore.

With a jolt, Markie realized what must have happened. Now she knew for sure that she had to tell Justin the truth, even after all these years, perhaps especially after all these years. She looked into his eyes. He was waiting for her to say something. It was going to be so hard. She covered her mouth with her hand as fresh tears sprang to her eyes and her courage plummeted. "Oh, God," she cried as she bent forward to her knees again.

"Markie!" Justin grabbed her again, with

his arms around her so tight she couldn't pull away this time. "What is it? What's the matter with you?"

"Oh, God." Markie bent forward until her forehead touched her knees. She should have told him.

He bowed himself into a protective cover over her, his warm breath near her ear. "Sweetheart—" again, the endearment came so naturally to him "—please tell me." He kissed her hair, her temple, the same old tender gesture that came so naturally to him. It undid her.

For one crazy instant Markie wanted to throw herself at him, to sink into his arms and feel the beat of his strong heart against her breasts again. Oh, his strength would help her now, she was sure. It would heal her in an instant. But she had no right. Not until she told the man the truth.

"They lied to us." She breathed into the mask of her palms. But it was her own lie she needed desperately to confess. She straightened, bracing herself to face it.

"They lied to us," she repeated, looking him in the eye with such steeliness that Justin sank back from her. "My mother. Your father. I don't know why they were so dead set on keeping us apart, but they were. They told me you had a fiancé and they told you I was going out with other guys. Don't you see?"

Justin's brown eyes took on a stricken look. "They...? Why would they do that?"

"I don't know. Well, I do know one reason." Markie grasped for his hand, for the next part would be hard. So hard. "You see, Justin, I lied, too. To everyone. But especially to you."

He looked down at their joined hands, then frowned up at her, seeming to sense that something terrible was coming. He had never been a man given to excessive talk, but now Markie desperately wanted him to do something besides look at her like that. When he didn't, she felt forced to go on.

"Justin. That summer, right after you left, actually, I found out..." She swallowed and squeezed his hand. Hard. He squeezed it back while his gaze studied hers, searching. His grip felt so manly, so warm. So full of life. The feel of it convinced her more strongly than ever that she was about to harm him, about to kill a part of him.

"I found out that I was…I was pregnant."

His gaze froze on hers for an instant, then he blinked. "You were…" He frowned, blinked again. "You were pregnant? With my baby?" He splayed a palm on his chest.

"Yes. Just barely."

"Just *barely*?" When he slid his hand away she thought her heart would stop.

"Why didn't you tell me?" His tone was suddenly cold.

"Because I only discovered it after you left, and then I thought…" Her voice grew small, weak. "I thought you were engaged."

He stared at her hard for some seconds. Then his gaze traveled around the trees, the rocks, the river, as if some answer, some relief, were imbedded there. When his eyes came back to hers, they were filled with comprehension and pain.

All these years she had sealed herself off from him, had almost hated him at times, and suddenly, faster than a glimmer of light reflecting off the rippling water, she yearned for nothing so much as his forgiveness, his understanding, his love.

"I don't care if you thought I was *married*." He rose up higher on his knees, straddling them wide on the rock. "A man has a right to know something like that." He bent forward over her, then jabbed a finger into his chest. "We're talking about *my* child."

Markie twisted around, rising to her knees to face him, to plead with him. "Justin, please. You don't understand—" She tried to reach for his hand again.

But he jerked away and stood abruptly, looming over her. "You're damned right I don't! What happened? What did you do with it?" he demanded.

"The baby?"

"Of course the baby!"

She sank back on her heels. "My mother found out about the pregnancy right away. Foolishly, so foolishly, I had written about it in a diary. She…she read it. She—and your father was involved, I think—she wanted me to have an abortion."

Justin closed his eyes and tilted his face up to the sky. After a long moment, he said, "So did you?"

"No. I faked it and then I hid my pregnancy. When it became impossible to hide it any longer, I went to Austin. My sister lived there."

Justin bent and grabbed her shoulders. "Are you telling me that you—that *we*—have a child back in Austin?"

"No. Not in Austin." She wrenched free of his grip.

"What?" Justin didn't seem to comprehend.

"I gave him away!" Markie blurted. "I went to a home for unwed mothers in secret. I gave him up for adoption there." Miserably, Markie sank back on her heels and fixed her eyes on the river below. This was the very place where Brandon was conceived, a peaceful place, now growing golden in the setting sun. But there was to be no peace for her. No forgiveness.

From above her, she heard Justin's voice, very quietly say, *"Him?"*

She looked up and he was staring at her with the eyes of a stranger. But stubbornly, she held his angry gaze. She owed him that much.

"Yes. A boy. We had a son, Justin."

"You don't even know where he is?"

It was the most terrible of moments for Markie. She did know where Brandon was. And Justin was right. A man had rights. But so did the child. "I…" But she stopped herself before telling him the whole truth about Brandon. Her old instinct to protect the child, no matter what, won out. She didn't know Justin Kilgore, not the Justin Kilgore of today. Not this stranger staring at her with such fierce eyes. She only knew a sweet, sincere, passionate young man who had made her pregnant one summer long ago. A young man who had loved her. With all his heart.

But the Justin Kilgore of today continued to stare at her with stone-cold eyes. "So he's gone, then," he said with a finality that chilled her to the bone. "You felt you had a right to give my only son away," he accused, "before I ever knew he existed, before I ever had a chance to see him, even once."

Markie was shaking her head in protest, ready to defend herself now, but Justin was already stepping away.

"Justin!" She jumped up. "Wait!"

But he turned his back on her, scrambling down the slope of the rock as if he were bolting from a rattlesnake. He left her standing there, alone. Alone again, she thought, just as she had always been.

CHAPTER TEN

It's so odd, how your life can change almost overnight. Only a few short months ago mine used to be about my friends and my silly social life and somehow managing to get myself off that godforsaken farm at Five Points. Now I'd give anything to go back there.

I guess.

I do know one thing. Carrying a baby is not easy. Especially when you go to bed at night all alone, and when you know that you're still going to be all alone when it's over. Some of the girls here have family supporting them.

But not me. That's so weird. Everybody in Five Points pretends the McBrides are like, this perfect little family. But the perfect little family is not here when I need them.

Well, I'm not technically alone. There's Sister May, bless her fluffy heart in her fluffy chest. Sister May is not a nun. She's just one of those hyper-religious black ladies who likes to call herself Sister. She wears a lot of leopard prints and earrings the size of canning-jar lids. She runs a tight ship here at the home, brooks no foolishness.

But at least she can be trusted with my secret, old Sister May can. It's pretty scary when you are keeping a secret from your nosy mother, let me tell you. Like maybe I shouldn't be writing about it here.

But Sister May is up to the task. That's because she has walked the walk. She still has a tiny picture of her own newborn baby, the one she had and gave up for adoption when she was sixteen. She keeps it inside a locket tucked down between her big bosoms. She'll take it out at night and show it to you when you go to her office to ask something or if you're in a bad way, or when she comes to tuck you into bed. (Yes, she tucks us in if we really need it, just like we were her little girls or something.)

I wish there weren't this terrible need for secrecy.

I wish, more than anything, that I could tell Justin about this baby. Maybe I'll tell Sister May about that when she makes it to my door. I can hear her heavy tread on the stairs, the low rumble of her soothing voice, talking to one of the girls on the way up. It's Jillsie, I think. She's nineteen, was in her first semester of college when her birth control failed. Doesn't believe in abortion. Very pretty. Very sweet. Very sad.

If it weren't for all the heartache, I'd like it here, especially at bedtime when it's all hushed and quiet like this and everybody's settling in for the night. Sister May insists that we all get our beauty rest. I don't have trouble sleeping, even if there are fourteen of us girls crammed into eleven bedrooms. (I don't have a roommate, which has its good points and bad points.) My room is quiet and clean. White woodwork. Even a tiny marble fireplace. You'd think this place was still a sorority house, except the girls who live in this house are all out to here.

Especially yours truly. Sister May said I

look like a toothpick with a bowling ball glued to the front of it. I can't help it if I'm tall and thin. I eat as much as my two curvy sisters and never gain an ounce. It's not my fault. I guess I get it from my mom, who's, like, skinny as a rail. Boy. I sure hope I'm not like her in any other way. Like, for example, on the inside. I'm keeping this a secret from her, too. That hypocritical witch. I can't figure her out. Trying to make me get an abortion when she's always prissing around down there at the biggest church on Main Street.

Well, I'm a hypocrite, too, I guess. Worse than her. I should have told Justin. I should have told him. This is all going to come back to haunt me someday. I just know it.

THE CABIN OF THE PRIVATE plane vibrated with the claustrophobic hum of a hospital room full of equipment. The drone of the engine outside his window, the serene colors of the decors and a stiff Bloody Mary were all conspiring to lull Congressman Kurt Kilgore into the first real sleep he'd enjoyed in days. Even as he dozed off, some part of him hated the fact that he had fallen into this despicable little habit—nodding off into stuporous "power naps" in front of anybody who might be watching, once even on the House floor. He knew it had to stop. If only he could sleep adequately at night. The pills weren't even working anymore.

But once again he was succumbing to sleepiness as, for the moment, only for the moment, he wanted to push the pressures of the campaign down under the fog.

It was not the prospect of a spirited campaign back in Texas that was keeping him awake nights. He had skillfully bludgeoned many an opponent over the years. Speaking with ginned up passion in auditoriums where the empty seats up front spoke louder than the hecklers in back. Tramping around in the blasted Texas heat wearing cowboy boots as if he preferred the damned things. Smothering little grass fires of gossip about his divorce or his foreign contributors or his bleeding-heart son. Always with an eye to keeping a grip on power. Power and secrets. His head lolled and he jerked it up.

Across the aisle, one of his aides sipped

nonchalantly at a Diet Coke. She was young, pretty, even if her face was perpetually furrowed with worry these days. It was a long, droning flight from Washington to Austin, one he and his entourage had endured many times.

It promised to be a long old summer in Texas, with nothing to console him—not even an occasional evening sitting in the cool shade of the old limestone porch in the calming presence of his wife, Vivian. Ex-wife. Vivian picked a fine time to pull up stakes. And now Justin had the house with his part of the land, the congressman thought hazily as another aide popped into the cabin, aiming a cell phone in his direction. "Sir, it's your son."

"Justin?" Kilgore snapped awake. He straightened and took the phone, instantly alert. Justin never called when they were in flight. Justin never called, period.

"Justin!" he sang out, then bit his lip. His voice had been too loud, too bright.

"Dad." Always the same one-word greeting. The same level baritone.

"What…what are you… Where are you, boy?" Kilgore could never get his bearings, could never feel in control, when it came to Justin. He loved the boy. He truly did. Just hearing the only person who had the right to do so calling him *Dad* caused something to stir in his insides. But at the same time, a familiar annoyance tensed the muscles at the back of his neck. Justin did not make the relationship easy. Unfortunately, his son would never call just to say, Hey, Dad, how ya doing? That was not the nature of their relationship. Year after year, he waited. But year after year, Justin kept his distance.

"I'm in Five Points, Dad. Is this a good time to talk?"

"Sure. I'm in the air. Nothin' happening up here but clouds." Even as he chuckled with that forced cheer he tried not to adopt with Justin, but somehow always did, he winced at his stupid joke.

He looked across the aisle at the aide, who sipped the canned soda and stared out her little window. Her ears were working overtime. Everyone knew of the troubled waters that swirled around the congressman and his only son. And women of all ages could not suppress an avid interest in Justin. The boy was a mighty good-looking specimen, all right.

"What can I do for you?" At other times the congressman might say, What do you need? But the implication was always the same—that Justin only called when he needed a favor.

"I want to talk to you about the Kilgore land."

"What about it?"

"I guess you know Vivian deeded me her part of the ranch."

"She's already done it?" Kilgore imagined Vivian, serene in the knowledge that she had done the right thing throughout the divorce, resolute in her decision never to set foot on the ranch—or in Washington, D.C.—ever again. Where was she now? And who was she with? "That gal has a lot of class." He knew he dare not criticize Justin's stepmother to the boy. "How is she?" he asked in a lower tone, lest the aide across the aisle overhear his needy query.

"She's fine. Very happy, I think. Some of her paintings are on display in a prominent restaurant in San Antonio and she's planning a trip to Spain with a group of other artists next fall."

"That's great," Kilgore said. *But he was*

thinking, Even if she has a lot of class, the woman picked a fine time to turn heel and run off and humiliate me, she sure as hell did. What did she care that he was fighting for his life in a dirty race just when he needed her, and her family money, the most.

"The deal is, Dad," Justin went on, "the house is on my part of the land."

"You can have it," Kilgore said without hesitation. "Free and clear."

"I appreciate that. There's something else. I was told, by someone in Five Points, that you are planning to repossess the property next to the ranch. The Tellchick farm? I guess you know that the widow who owns it has put it up for sale."

"Yes. That poor young woman. Now, tell me again, exactly how did her man die?"

"He was trapped in a burning barn. Why are you doing this, Dad?"

"Why am I doing what?" Kilgore had a moment of panic as he thought surely he must have missed something, what with the noise of the plane. His son couldn't possibly have connected him to that Tellchick man's death, not in a million years.

"Why are you taking back that land? Isn't it enough that you've got almost 80,000 acres down here that you never even see? Why are you causing more trouble for that poor widow? She's got enough problems. Illegal aliens keep trespassing on her property. I think they're using those caves as hideouts."

Kilgore rolled the muscles of one shoulder, ending with a crank of his neck. Not good. How much did Justin know about the caves? But he wasn't going to probe Justin about it, not on this plane, not with an aide listening in. The very aide who was taking a too-long pull on her Coke. Turning his face away, removing his wire-rimmed spectacles with a swift, practiced motion, Kilgore lowered his voice. "I'm just wanting to make the Kilgore ranch all of a piece again," he said mildly. "That land was originally mine and now I want it back. The woman can't keep it up. It's a pretty place. The Blue River runs through there—lots of limestone formations. What does it matter to you? You've got your part of the property now. You suddenly turned big rancher or something? I thought you were busy being a reformer, off doing your humanitarian work, whatever it is."

Justin tilted the front legs of the bentwood chair in which he sat back down to the porch boards, bristling at his father's words. He ground his jaw and squinted hard out at the Kilgore lands, choosing what to say. His father knew very well what Justin's work was. They'd had words about it. More than once. In fact, more than once, his father had called him a fool for getting involved with "those people." Never mind that "those people" were the people of Justin's mother. But this time Justin had to ignore the bait. He focused on what Brandon Smith had told him. "Right now, I'm doing my best to keep those people out of the caves. That's why I called to ask you about the old house. I need a place to house them until I can get some family shelters built. Maybe we'll put in some trailers or something. I'm planning on expanding—"

"Trailers?" There was the old unmistakable note of contempt for anything foreign to the Kilgores.

Justin thought of his mother, of how Kurt hadn't respected her cultured heritage. If you didn't love her, Justin always wanted to ask, why'd you marry her in the first place? But there was no need ask that. The congressman's track record with women was all the answer Justin needed. Rosa Martinez, Justin's real mother, had been nothing but another conquest to the congressman. A quiet, serene, cultured young woman of Hispanic heritage whom Kurt Kilgore could not bed until he'd married her. And so he did. And got ten thousand more acres of Hill Country land in the process.

"An alpha male," Kurt had once said in the only man-to-man talk about sex father and son had ever managed, "has got to meet his needs. You'll soon see."

They had been deer hunting on the ranch in celebration of Justin's sixteenth birthday, and had spotted a twelve-point buck standing sovereign over a herd of does. Even as an appetent teenager, Justin recalled how he had been mildly put off, being compared to an animal. Or was it from being compared to his father? But who was he to point fingers at his wandering father? Look how his life had turned out. Divorced. Finding out he'd fathered a child he knew nothing about.

Images, as vivid as if they were playing on

a movie screen, flashed into his mind. The steamed-up cab of Kilgore Ranch's battered old pickup. He and Markie parked high on the granite cliffs overlooking Marble Falls, facing a low golden moon. With headlights doused and only the glow of the radio dial— what was that song? "Stairway to Heaven"?—illuminating the milky glow of Markie McBride's beautiful skin. A petite breast, one smooth hip—all exposed to his ravenous eyes for the first time. When his mind drifted to a later, more explicit scene at the Rocks, he doused the memories.

He *was* different from his father. And he'd spent more than a decade proving it. Helping the very people his father disdained. His own people.

"What kind of operation is this?" his father's voice demanded again.

"It's a place for illegal immigrants to get their bearings," Justin explained with forced patience, "to learn English and up-to-date agricultural skills—"

"Nobody," his father's voice interrupted with a blast in his ear, "is bringing a bunch of Mexicans to live in trailers out on the Kilgore!"

"Dad—"

"Have you gone loco? What do you think something like that will do to my campaign?"

"I have no idea. But I don't need your blessing. It's already in the works. And I don't need your permission to buy that farm, either."

"You can't possibly raise the money to buy that loan before I foreclose on it."

"No, but I can make sure Mrs. Tellchick keeps up her payments." It was a bluff, of sorts. Money was tight enough, what with trying to get the Light at Five Points off the ground. But the idea was to prod his father into making a move on the caves. "You can't foreclose on her as long as she does."

"She'll default once she and those boys get tired of scraping by out there."

Justin sighed. "Look, Dad. I simply wanted to do this amicably, if possible."

"Amicably? Now you sound like your mother."

Which one? Justin wanted to say, but he decided that in either case his answer would have to be the same. "There are certainly worse insults."

"Ya know," his father started in testily, "you have just called me and interrupted a perfectly good nap so you could ruin my day. I have never insisted that you have to help me on my campaigns, like any other grateful son might. I know we don't camp on the same side of the aisle, but would it be too much to ask you to lay low until I get past the primary? And for God's sake, can't you leave the damned Mexicans out of it?"

"I'm not doing it to spite you, Dad. I'm doing what I think I've been called to do. Look, I think we'd better hang up now, okay?"

"Fine." The connection went dead.

Justin hung up, hoping the bit about illegals in the caves had been sandwiched in carefully enough that his father wouldn't see it as a plant. Kurt was a sly old fox. And apparently a lying one. Justin hoped his anger over what his father had done to himself and Markie McBride hadn't leaked out in his voice.

In all honesty, he didn't know who he felt more angry with, Markie or his father. He only knew that he had felt nothing but this burning anger ever since Markie had told him the shocking truth.

And now he'd have to see her, undoubtedly more than once, out on the Tellchick Farm. Perhaps even every day.

What would he say when they came upon each other? Good morning? How are you today? Is there anything else you'd like to tell me about my son?

CHAPTER ELEVEN

THE MEXICANS JUSTIN HAD brought to work on Robbie's farm were quiet. They were polite. *Humble* was the word Markie had heard used most often when referring to the hardworking cleaning ladies and yardmen and construction workers who had risked illegal immigration in the hope of a better life.

The ones Justin had brought with him to Tellchick Farm—hand-picked, she was sure—proved no exception. They put their backs to their assigned task and kept their gazes carefully averted whenever they encountered Markie or Robbie. Markie's three boys had quickly learned to josh with the immigrants, making jokes in broken Spanish. But Robbie had a fit when one of the *pollos* offered her twelve-year-old son a cigarette.

There were four of them. All wiry young

men, thin from too much physical labor and not enough to eat. They slept on simple cots, staying with Justin up on the hill in the little rock house. They ate simple meals made from provisions kept in an ice chest, cooking over a camping stove.

Markie had no fear of them, but she watched her sister carefully for signs of stress.

"What are...those guys supposed to do today?" Markie knew their names, but Robbie seemed more comfortable calling the workers *those guys*.

"They're tilling the ashes." Robbie was loading the dishwasher with breakfast dishes, wearing that same ratty pink robe, a constant for her these days. When she did shower and dress, she emerged with her tummy bulging in a pair of Danny's old overalls. No makeup. Her curly red hair straining back into a ponytail.

Along with everything else eating at Markie these days, she worried that her sister was sliding into depression. Damn that Frankie and her selfish ways. She had been here exactly one weekend—*one measly weekend*—since Danny's death. She'd flown up the highway in her Mercedes, bought the boys pizza in town, attended church with Robbie and Mother and Daddy, and basically acted like an ass the entire three days. Straightening Robbie's house as if it was too messy for her persnickety tastes. Making lots of noises about what a pain it was to move Dr. Kyle and company into their fancy new offices. Eyeballing Robbie's growing middle with plain-to-see envy. Markie predicted that turning forty would be hard, hard, hard for Miss Frankie. Two miscarriages this year. Another the year before. Her efforts to carry a child to term had become almost frantic.

Markie went to the coffeemaker and poured herself a second cup. "Grab some tea and sit down with me a second, okay? I'll finish cleaning this up later."

They could take a little time out now that there was help on the farm. Sit. Have tea. Talk. A rest from the constant strain of the last few weeks.

Tilling the ashes. What a sad way to put it, Markie thought while Robbie made her tea. The insurance company had cleared the charred debris of the barn and the ruined farm implements. But the coverage did not include doing anything that would reclaim the empty lot. The crust of ashes on top needed to be tilled into the soil, left to absorb, until Robbie could make a decision about what to do with the site. Markie would be relieved to see fallow earth in place of the constant blackened reminder of Danny's death.

"Is this setup bothering you at all?" Markie sipped her coffee as Robbie lumbered into a chair.

"It's fine." Robbie's expression was noncommittal as she lifted her mug to her lips and blew on the steaming tea. "I know they're not the same Mexicans who started the fire. They weren't even in the country then."

"Robbie—" Markie set her cup on the table, gripping the handle "—the fire marshal hasn't determined anything conclusively yet. Just because some Mexicans were seen around the caves, that doesn't mean they started the fire."

"Well, Danny sure didn't do it! He wouldn't set fire to his own barn!" Robbie's normally soft voice was loud and shrill. Just like Marynell's, Markie thought, then censored her criticism. Her sister had been through a lot. But in the last few weeks Robbie had been raising her voice plenty, especially when this topic came up. Was Robbie going to end up bitter like their mother? Was Frankie turning bitter because she couldn't have a baby? Was Markie bitter because she *had?* Was it something in the blood? Was anyone besides her even a teensy-weensy bit aware that their family was not exactly the American Gothic? Come to think of it, their mother did sort of resemble the sour old lady in that painting. Still, Markie preferred her sister's flashes of anger to her former moods of chilling sadness.

"Let's just take it one day at a time, okay? Right now Alonso and Carlos and Rigo—*those guys*—are doing a lot of good around this place."

Robbie slumped. "I probably seem ungrateful for all of this free labor. I'm not. It's just hard, you know? All of it is so hard." Robbie sat there, lifeless as a sack of feed, nursing her despair, and Markie didn't have any idea how to rouse her out it. She was getting exhausted just from seeing her sister this way day after day.

She reached over and gripped the back of

Robbie's hand. "I know it's hard, sweetie. But those men are really helping and Justin needs to be here to watch the caves."

Anger flashed in Robbie's eyes again. "*Justin Kilgore.* He's another thing. I don't know how you can stand being around him every day. You are a very forgiving person, Markie."

How could Markie explain that it was herself who needed to be forgiven? How could she tell her sister the truth without the risk of exposing Brandon Smith's true identity?

"I told him about the baby," she blurted.

Robbie nearly choked on her tea. "You didn't?"

"Yes. When we were talking about the caves. I decided he had a right to know."

"Oh, my gosh." Robbie's cheeks pinkened up a bit. "Well, what did he do?" She sat up and leaned forward, suddenly over her funk. "I mean, what did he say? Tell me everything!"

Markie was not about to tell *everything*.

One time, Robbie, Miss Holier Than Thou, had announced that she was determined to live her whole life by the book or die trying. When she was engaged, she had gone on and on about how she and Danny were saving themselves for marriage. Markie had said, Don't tell me your problems.

"He's very angry at me, I think."

"Angry!" Robbie's colored heightened some more. "What the devil has he got to be angry about? He's the one who was diddling around with you when he was already engaged."

Markie bit her lip. "Turns out he wasn't."

"What?"

"He was never engaged. That was a lie. And I can't figure out why Kurt Kilgore fabricated that story. Except, of course, that he didn't think I was good enough for Justin."

"Kurt Kilgore!" Robbie spat. "That dirty old donkey. He tried to buy me out, you know."

"He did what?" This was news to Markie.

"Old Man Hughes called from the bank. Said there was an offer on the farm that would get me out from under the loan. When I pressed him for details—"

Markie couldn't imagine her sister *pressing* anybody for anything. Her sister was definitely changing.

"—he said none other than Kurt Kilgore

was willing to take it off my hands. Forgive what's left on the land note and buy the rest. Lock, stock and barrel. All the livestock, equipment, tools, feed, chemicals, the house, the whole kit 'n' caboodle."

"What did you say?" Markie's palms started to sweat around the coffee mug. This was surely some indication that Kilgore had something hidden in the caves. In its current condition, Tellchick Farm was hardly worth the dirt it stood on.

"I said no. I think I can do better selling it outright, then maybe pay off the note and have a little to start over with. But in a way, I'm sort of sorry I put the farm up for sale so fast. I've been thinking…maybe with the help of these Mexican laborers I can hang on. I don't want to move the boys—"

The whine of an engine shifting gears interrupted Robbie's speech. Markie went to the kitchen window that looked out on the long gravel driveway. A navy-blue pickup rounded into view, bouncing over the ruts.

"It's Zack Trueblood," Markie said.

"Oh, my gosh." Robbie looked down at

her ratty pink robe. "I can't talk to him looking like this."

"I'll go see what he wants." She stepped outside onto the porch.

When he got out of his truck, Trueblood greeted her, then said, "Is Mrs. Tellchick home?"

"She doesn't much feel like company today," Markie explained with an apologetic smile.

He looked disappointed before his expression turned concerned. "Is your sister okay? Last time I saw her, she didn't look so good."

"She's taking this hard. But I think she'll do better once she knows the truth. I think she suspects something was not right about that fire. Even for a barn fire, it went up so fast."

Trueblood nodded. "I found out from the fire marshal that there were traces of an accelerant. The tractor gasoline, most likely."

"There's no implication that Danny did this himself?" Markie was thinking of how bad the farm's books looked when Robbie finally let her see them, of how Danny might have been desperate to get rid of a rotten barn for the insurance money.

"I can't speculate while the fire marshall is

investigating it. But I will say it's a good thing none of the rest of the family was hurt."

"I agree."

"Well, let me know if I can do anything for her." He looked beyond her shoulder to the door. "I run a little handyman business on the side. I could fix things up around here…if she'd let me. I really want to help."

"I will keep you in mind," Markie promised. "There's plenty to do around here."

Trueblood turned in the direction of the high hill where the pointed roof of the old stone house peeked up. "These locals she has working for her. They're illegals. Am I right?"

Why was he so interested in all of this? Markie wondered. "Justin Kilgore is sponsoring them through the Light at Five Points. But they didn't start working here until *after* Danny's death."

"Yes, ma'am. I know. Where is Justin?"

"He's supervising them. Over at the barn site. They're cleaning up the grounds."

"I'd like to go have a talk with them, and with Justin."

"I need to get back to my sister, but the barn is—was—" Markie started to point.

"I know where it was." There was an unmistakable note of sorrow in his voice.

Markie went back into the kitchen. "He just wanted to check on you and he came out here to talk to Justin."

"Why?"

"I don't know. But after he's gone, I'll make it my business to find out." Markie started cleaning up the breakfast dishes. "I think Zack is genuinely concerned about you. Maybe even interested in you in other ways."

Robbie gave Markie a look that would have curdled milk. "I hope to goodness you are listening to yourself." Suddenly Robbie had a little color in her cheeks, a little life in her voice. "My husband has been dead all of two months. If Zack Trueblood had that kind of interest in me, he would have to be the kind that preys upon widows. Does he strike you as that kind? I mean, *look* at him."

Robbie crossed to the window that faced the barn site and squinted. "A guy like that can have any woman he wants, and probably does. I imagine he just feels sorry for me because here I am, pregnant as a cow, and no husband. If he's interested in anything, it's this land. When the banker called he also told me that Zack Trueblood expressed an interest in the farm."

"Really? What kind of interest?"

"Inquiring about the asking price. But he doesn't have the money for the down payment. So don't get all impressed if he wants to come out and fix the place up."

"Oh. I see. Do you remember him from high school?"

"Not at all."

But Robbie was still staring toward the barnyard. Markie peered past her sister's shoulder and saw that the object of her intense interest was the form of Zack Trueblood as he strode out to the men working near the tractor.

"I'll go see Justin after dinner," Markie promised, "and find out what they talked about." She decided to wait and go up to the rock house once the men had called it a night. She'd have to go unannounced since cell phones were worthless out here. And she was already dreading the encounter.

CHAPTER TWELVE

THAT EVENING MARKIE TRIED, unsuccessfully, to concentrate on her work, finally moving the laptop out onto the back porch. But out there it seemed, paradoxically, too quiet without the boys' voices or TV news or even her ubiquitous talk-radio station to accompany her work. Finally she gave up, content to listen to the evening quiet, punctuated only by intermittent birdsong, as she watched the colors of the landscape transform from golden greens to hushed purples while the sun departed over the rim of the hills.

When it was nearly dark, she decided she'd put it off long enough. She would have to go talk to him. Alone.

But as she drove to the crest of the hill she could see the silhouettes of five men arranged around a small campfire. The open fire didn't concern her since the Hill Country had just experienced an unusually long rainy season and the top of this particular hill consisted of little more than a rocky patch of bare ground.

And Markie had no apprehension about approaching the gentle, diffident workers. It was Justin she feared as she parked at the end of the rutted, weeded lane that climbed to the top of the hill.

As Markie climbed out of her Jeep, the four Mexicans stood and quickly rolled down their sleeves and buttoned their collars high—a sign of respect.

As she walked up to the cluster of men she detected the lingering aroma of corn tortillas grilled over an open fire. Smoke still curled from the embers, and by the light of a flashlight Justin flicked on, she could see that they had just finished eating.

One of the men said something in Spanish to Justin, and after picking up the ice chest and the remains of their meal, they all disappeared into the shadows with polite nods, moving in the direction of the house, which sat higher up on the hill, dark as a tomb.

"They're beat. Turning in," Justin explained. But Markie knew that it was more likely they'd rather take a beating than talk to a gringa woman they perceived as privileged, possibly even arrogant.

"They're doing a good job out here."

"Yes. I hope it's okay that I let them build the fire tonight. They prefer to cook their tortillas over an open flame." He looked toward the thin ribbon of sun, narrowing fast in the west. "I'll have to douse it soon so I can keep watch."

Markie looked toward the pink-tinged limestone mounds at some distance far below them. "This really is a clear view."

"Yes. And there's the road." Justin positioned himself behind her, stretching an arm out toward it. The winding blacktop that led past Tellchick Farm and then twisted on toward the remaining Kilgore lands was clearly visible, pocked by pale highway lights reflecting off roadside scrub and low live oak trees.

With him standing so close behind her, Markie felt an immediate magnetism that caused her to step away and fold her arms over her middle.

"No sign of the brothers?" she said.

He shook his head. "And no sign of the my father's guys, either. Looks like this could take a while."

Markie nodded. They were being so civil. It disturbed her. Was he still angry? What had he thought about, felt, since that day at the river? Since he'd arrived at the farm, all of their exchanges had taken place in the presence of Robbie or the Mexicans. This was the first time they'd been alone. She did not know where to begin.

Fortunately, Justin took the bull by the horns. "Want to have a seat?" he said.

They arranged themselves cross-legged on the woven Mexican *zarape* blankets that the men had left there. Justin had an open bottle of Corona beer propped against a rock. "A treat for the guys," he said as he reached for it. "Want one?"

"Why not?"

Justin twisted on the blanket. "Oh, wait. The guys took the ice chest. Want to share?" He aimed the longneck at her.

She nodded, accepted the bottle, took a sip. It tasted tart, refreshing, just right.

"Thanks," she said, and handed it back.

"What did Zack Trueblood want to talk to you about?"

"He wanted to know if I knew the guys that were trespassing out here before the barn burned. Seems he's taken it upon himself to do some digging about Danny's death." Justin took a sip of beer and stared into the fire.

"What are you thinking?" Markie asked.

"I'm thinking I agree with Trueblood. Something's really wrong with this whole picture. First, the Morales boys, or, at least I assume it was them, were seen poking around the entrance to the caves. Then Danny's death. Then the guys in the bar."

"The ones Brandon overheard talking about finding the Mexicans?" She found that merely saying Brandon's name in front of Justin made her throat tighten up a little. She helped herself to the beer and took another drink.

"Yes. The ones who work for my father." He looked out over the undulating landscape that resembled a Dalhart Windberg painting as it turned shades of dark purple and deep emerald in the waning light, while low in the east, a yellow moon suddenly materialized. "God knows what will happen if they find the Moraleses before I do. The immigrants don't trust anybody, on either side of the border. They've been beaten, arrested, robbed. They know the ropes, where to go, how to hide, but they don't always know how to protect themselves."

"We have to get this cleared up for their sake, and for Robbie's sake. Justin, listen. I don't think I've thanked y—"

"Don't thank me. I want to get to the bottom of this as badly as your sister does. He's my father."

"Not really. No real father would do what he did. His interference harmed you, Justin. Irreparably."

"And it harmed you. And your family." Justin sighed. "I'm so very sorry for the way all of this has impacted your family."

She was astonished, and relieved, that he could say this. "Why are *you* sorry?" After all, he hadn't lied.

"Like I said, he's my father. None of this would have happened if I weren't a Kilgore."

She looked up. "You should be proud of your family. And you don't have any control over Kurt. You're not like him. You're a good man, Justin. I always thought so."

From the way the firelight caught the sudden flash of emotion in his eyes, she knew that what he had said before was true, that in all these years his feelings for her had not changed. Not in all these years. With a rush of equally strong emotion, she admitted to herself that if by some miracle she could have him back, she would fly to his arms in an instant.

And then he said it.

"Markie…I still love you."

Markie's breath caught and her lips parted. They stared into each other's eyes as the firelight softened their countenances with its wavering glow. They could have been teenagers again, sitting atop a high hill with the moon rising over the landscape. Facing each other, cross-legged, knees nearly touching, eyes examining mouths that were ready to kiss and be kissed.

"All I've wanted to do since I saw you again is touch you, kiss you." His voice was deep, thick with emotion, as he admitted this. "It's all I've thought about since I saw you in town and then at the river. Some things just never change. And when you say stuff like…that you believe in me in spite of everything that's happened—it makes me want—"

He didn't get to finish because she threw her arms around his neck and plastered her mouth to his.

Their kiss this time was just as passionate as the ones of their youth, but far more joyous. Because now they *knew*. And as this kiss lingered on, it communicated, as no words could, that nothing could come between them now. Nothing could change this. Not parents. Not lies. Not time. Nothing.

But Markie had to know one thing. When they broke off the kiss, she said, "Do you forgive me?"

He pressed his lips to her hair. "There's nothing to forgive, princess. It's all a bad nightmare, and I want to put it behind us."

"I wish it were that simple." Markie's gut tightened with the knowledge that there was still one more secret standing between them. She still hadn't told Justin about Brandon Smith.

"Let's make it that simple." Gently he turned her shoulders and settled her, her back to his front, situating her in the shelter of his legs, just as he'd done when they were young. And just like when they were teenagers, she could clearly feel the press of his already-full arousal. But Justin showed restraint. He folded his arms across her front, clasping his hands around hers, his fingertips grazing the backs of her wrists, while his warm breath caressed her temple, her neck.

"Because it *is* that simple." His voice rumbled near her ear. "That is, it is if you still love me."

She turned her head and kissed his cheek. The taste of him, identical, incredibly identical, to the taste of the young man she'd fallen so hard for so long ago, sent tiny tremors of longing to her core.

"*Do* you?" he insisted, as if he needed to hear some things, too.

"You know I do," she admitted. "I'll always love you." Her lips were still barely touching his skin as she breathed in his scent.

"You love me. I love you." He tilted his face and looked down at her, his jaw firm with emotion, his eyes dilated with desire as they glinted in the waning firelight. "We're right back where we started. Right where we should have been all these years."

"I do love you." She angled her body away from his a bit. "But you and I both know love isn't enough."

"We do? It isn't?" He seemed deprived by even the little bit of distance, his arms reaching to pull her back to him.

But Markie resisted, ever so gently, with a palm pressed to his chest. "No, it isn't. And you know it. If I loved you back then, and you loved me, what good did that do us? It got us into a lot of trouble, as a matter of fact. So, what possible difference does love make?"

"None. It makes no difference," he said flatly, but already she detected a disingenuous note. "Love is just a feeling. Unless you back it up with action." He turned her and scooped her up into his lap, tilting her back to hold her like a baby with one arm supporting her shoulders and the fingers of the other hand pressed around her thigh. "Unless you're willing to forgive yourself and me even when that's hard. But if you *are* willing—" He swallowed and tightened his hold. "If you *are* willing… Markie, don't you think we can put the past behind us? If you can forgive me, then—"

"That's not the question," she said in a small voice. "The question is, do you…forgive me?" she added in a whisper.

"No. Do *you* forgive *me?*" His voice grew huskier as his hand rode up, pressing into her flesh. He bent to brush her temple with soft lips and hot breath.

Markie almost tilted her mouth up to kiss him again, but she still desperately needed absolution. "You didn't do anything that needs forgiving," she whispered. "But I did. I lied to you."

"No." His hand stopped moving. "*I* got you pregnant. Protecting you was *my* responsibility." He pressed his mouth firmly to her temple again, then brought it down in a series of slow, deliberate kisses. "I've thought about it ever since you told me about the baby…." He spoke between each kiss. "And if I could… I'd change…the past…but I can't." The emotion in his voice was building with each kiss, "And I'm so…sorry…that I hurt you." He ended with his mouth resting, completely still, at the hollow of her neck.

His eyes were closed and he was breathing against her skin. The way his hands were gripping her told her how deeply he had meant every word.

She couldn't bring herself to look at him as his hot mouth began to press further down her body. If she looked at him now and saw that crease of passion between his brows, she'd be undone. But despite herself she arched into the feel of his lips.

"We were so young," she choked out in a whisper. "I'm not the same person now."

"But you *are* you. And I am me. And part of us will always will be young, Markie. At least to each other, deep down inside where it counts." At last he planted a kiss over her heart. "And I will always love you."

He brought his head up and they kissed again, and this one was more tender, more passionate, than any they'd had before.

When it was over, he said, "Don't you see? It wouldn't matter if I'd met you when I was twelve years old or if I met you when I was ninety, I'd still feel the same. I'd still love you. I loved you then. I love you now. I always will."

She heard his throat contract with a tight swallow before he said, "And, I hope, you'll always love me, too."

All she could get out was a choked "Of course."

He kissed her more fiercely. But when he reached up under her shirt to cup her softest flesh, she automatically turned her face toward the rock house, which stood quiet and utterly dark.

"Don't worry. Those guys know how to mind their own business. But we're not going to give them anything to talk about, anyway." With his boot, Justin shoved dirt and gravel onto the fire. The flames died, leaving them enveloped in darkness.

She turned into his arms, into his touch. Her breasts were fuller now, more mature and developed. Changed by one pregnancy and many years. But his hands on them felt the same. Just as warm. Just as urgent. Just as tender. Just as exciting. "I love you," she said as she let him touch her freely.

"And I love you." He kissed her again, with one hand on one breast, as he laid her back on the blanket.

"Just keep kissing me like this, okay?" she said as she went down.

He did. Again. And again. When her urges became excruciating, she broke off and said, "This is so crazy! We're making out just like we did back then, like a couple of tenth graders on ecstasy or something."

That made him sputter a laugh. "You always had a way with words. And just for the record, back then you *were* a teenager. I, on the other hand—" his voice dropped to a growl "—was a *much* older man who knew exactly what he wanted."

"Which was?" She made a teasing circle with her finger at the notch of his throat.

"You." His eyes grew serious, glimmering with moonlight as he studied hers. "Only you." He pulled her head to his shoulder and ran his hand from her jaw to her neck to her breast. "Always, always you."

"I never forgot about you."

"I never forgot about you, either. Even while I was married, I'm ashamed to say."

"Oh, that's so sad."

"Yes, it is. But I never let her know it. She was a sweet woman, in her way. Smart. Genteel. We were just very poorly matched. There was no fire. I started looking at living the rest of my life that way and I had to let her go. I hope she finds true love now."

"You honestly believe in true love, don't you?"

"Absolutely. Don't you?"

"I don't know. I want to. Tell me, is that why you came back here, in the hope of finding true love again?"

"Subconsciously, anything's possible, I guess. I don't think you can manipulate your heart. You feel what you feel. You are drawn to certain places, to certain people." He stroked her cheek, then slid his hand down to rest intimately at the base of her throat. "But I'm also committed to making a go of the Light. It's important."

"I agree."

"And I'd like to share that dream with somebody. No, not with somebody, not with just anybody. I'd like to share it with *you*. I'd like to share so many things with you." His hands slid down her body and she felt whole, alive, in a way she hadn't in all these years apart from him.

The fact that they were going to make love now seemed inevitable. The question was, where? Markie had already begun to consider the problem, never guessing what Justin was going to say next.

"Marry me."

She leaned away, trying to bring his face into focus in the dark. "Are you serious? I don't even know you."

He propped himself up on one elbow. "You know me. You love me. We had a child together, Markie. Marry me. Anywhere, anytime, any way you want. But the sooner the better."

She sat up abruptly, struggling to get her bearings. The moon had risen high. A million stars were out. The night air was thick with the earthy smells of summer. Beside her, Justin Kilgore lay stretched out on the blanket, warm and real. And he would be all hers if she wanted him. But she had waited too long, tacitly said no too many times to too many guys, to marry in haste now, even to Justin Kilgore.

She eyed him as he slowly stretched out a muscular arm to pull her back.

"Marriage is a huge step," she said, trying for a light tone. "You know the drill. Honor. Obey. All that stuff."

"Okay. If that's what it takes, I'll honor. I'll even obey you." Justin reached for her waist again.

"Come on, Justin." She eased his hand back. "I think your body's talking here and we're not kids anymore."

"Well, if I'd let my *body* do a little more talking back then, and let my head do a little less, maybe all this wouldn't have happened."

She twisted to peer at him in the dark.

"I'm serious," he said. "Did you know that? I wanted to marry you even back then."

She shook her head side to side, very slowly.

"Of course you didn't. Because I never said a word about it. I was too reasonable. Too rational. I told myself we were too young, that we hadn't known each other long enough, that there would be plenty of time. I'm not going to make that mistake again. I want you. I love you. And I'm not going to lose you a second time."

"You think getting married will seal the

deal? That it will fix the mistakes of the past somehow?"

"Something like that."

"Justin. No. We have to get to know each other first. We have to find out if we're compatible *now,* if we really have anything in common besides—"

"Oh, I get it. You want the courtship."

"The *what?*"

"The courtship. Okay. If that's what it takes to win you over, I'm game. But you have to agree to stay right here in Five Points and give me a fair chance. No long-distance relationship. No running back to Austin when the primary's over."

The primary would take place in one month, and the minute the results came in, Markie's professional life would explode. If Curry won, she'd be at the helm of a full press congressional race against the opposing party. If he lost, other candidates in lesser races were waiting in line to snap her up. A Cattlemen's Association had even been after her to do some lobbying for them in Washington. "Justin. In case you hadn't noticed, we're grown-ups now. I have a *job* back in

Austin, a life. We are perfectly capable of doing the long-distance relationship thing until we know whether this is right for both of us."

But it seemed like Justin hadn't even heard her reasoning.

"It's going to be a real challenge," he was muttering to himself, though it was clearly for Markie's benefit, "winning you over in such a short period of time, especially with everything else that's going on. You, with your sister and your election. Me, with the Light and my ranch. Ah, well. We must work with what we are given. Time for a little field expedience."

"A little what?"

"Field expedience. Making do with what you've got. It's the cowboy way. But I have to say, it's these Mexicans who are the real experts at it."

"It sounds like some kind of science experiment." Markie rolled her eyes, but her heart was already feeling strangely light.

"We'll start right away. Tomorrow night. Will you meet me back up here at sundown?"

"You are *insane.*" Markie said precisely, as

if he really was deranged. But even as she said it, she knew she would return up to this hill, to his arms, tomorrow night.

CHAPTER THIRTEEN

All that stuff I wrote about how my mother was being so understanding and how she'd helped me solve my problem and how everything was going to be okay and how I couldn't wait to get back to being a normal teenager?

Lies.

All lies. Written for the benefit of my mother's eyes, because she was still reading every word I wrote. For a while there I stuffed this diary in my backpack every day and took it to school, where I guarded it with my life. It wouldn't do to have Mrs. Beachum reading about my messy little mistakes. Nattie Rose says Beachum needs to get a life. I say all she needs is a little therapy. As in, psychotherapy. Psycho. Therapy.

But I digress.

Not being able to find the diary frustrated mother but good, I'm so sure. I could tell she'd been upstairs pawing through my stuff while I was at school. Everything was refolded just a tad too neatly, you know? So I determined to keep merrily toting this diary off to school.

But then I thought, wait! Why not fake her out?

Now for the truth: I am keeping my baby.

Mother wanted me to have an ab—chee! I can't even write the word, much less do it. So I'm in Austin now. Under the thumb of big sister Frankie, which is not much better than being under Mother's thumb, except that Frankie's got too much class to snoop around in my diary.

I can hear Frankie on the phone with Mother in the evenings, telling her how I'm studying hard and feeling better and my glands are less swollen. During these conversations, Kyle prowls around the apartment giving me the fish eye.

You see the story is, I've supposedly got mono, and Kyle helped us fake that deal. He says doing that could cause him problems in the future on account of ethics. Ethics, schmethics. Who am I gonna tell that Kyle faked my diagnosis? I mean, I've got bigger problems here. I'm getting ready to have a *baby,* or doesn't anybody get that?

Actually, Frankie does get it. One of the girls in her nursing class turned up pee-gee so she knows about a place, a home. I came around the corner of their little hallway-like kitchen and caught the happy couple whispering about it.

In my loudest, most annoying Texas twang I told them if they were talking about me and *my* future, and the future of *my* baby, then they could just stop it.

But Kyle crossed his arms over his chest like some warlord and said maybe it was time for an honest discussion.

I squeezed my pumpkin self into a chair at their tiny kitchen table and steeled myself for the worst.

We whapped all our cards down on the table faster than a blackjack dealer.

Whap! Kyle wants me outta there.

Whap! Frankie wants to facilitate an adoption in a safe facility. (Guess who learned the word *facilitate* at nursing school?)

Whap! I am seventeen, uneducated, without a husband or a job.

By the end of that civilized adult conversation, I was a blubbering, but totally resigned, bowl of Jell-O.

I mean, what real choice do I have? Going back to Five Points?

And I'd just as soon slit my wrists as go back to Mother.

MARYNELL WAS NOT GOING to make this phone call in the daylight, and certainly not from her kitchen wall phone. She waited for the sound of P.J.'s measured snoring to begin beside her, then she slid out of the bed.

She changed into a windbreaker and sweatpants in their cramped bathroom, then flushed the commode and clanked the lid. If that didn't wake her husband up, nothing would. She flicked off the light, then eased open the door, which creaked on its hinges like always. How she despised this old farmhouse.

Her sister-in-law, Roberta, and husband, Don, had last year built a pristine white stucco monstrosity on the crest of a hill outside Austin. Plumbing fixtures that shone like mirrors. Acres of fresh taupe carpet. No creaky doors. Marynell's envy had been colossal.

Out in the moonlit bedroom, P.J.'s pose was unchanged from when she left. He snored on as she crept across threadbare carpet in stockinged feet and closed another creaky door with a quiet click.

She tied on athletic shoes in the kitchen, fumbling with the laces in the eerie light cast from the yard pole. That afternoon, while there was still daylight and P.J. had still been out in the field, she had moved her minivan, pointing it downhill at the top of the driveway, making sure P.J. had gassed it up the day before like she told him to.

Releasing the brake, she put the van in neutral and let it roll down the drive. She intended to get to the highway before firing up the engine. The slope was gentle but challenging for her skinny arms to steer without power. The effort plus the lack of headlights and the quiet crunch of the tires on gravel made Marynell feel tense, clandestine. What if, she worried, she had a flat tire or hit an an-

imal? It happened all the time on these dam-
nable Hill Country roads. What if someone
spotted her van in town?

She started the engine. She'd never noticed
how eerie the dashlights alone could be.
When she got to the main highway, she was
relieved to turn on the headlights.

The drive to town seemed to take forever,
but she knew of a pay phone outside Ardella's
flower shop. Ardella had so much clutter and
what-not left out on the sidewalk, Marynell
figured she could slip in among the junk and
talk on that pay phone undetected. Main
Street would be dead at this hour.

She rolled into a parking place in the alley
around the corner from Ardella's, then scur-
ried to the drive-up phone box on the sidewalk. She had committed the cell phone
number to memory. She pumped in coins,
punched the buttons and pulled the phone
around on its metallic cord until at least part
of her was hidden behind a large hideously
decorated pot holding a fake ficus tree.

"Congressman Kilgore, please… Marynell McBride." A female voice had answered
and Marynell thought, *huh,* glad that she was

not married to one of these good-looking lady-killers.

To her satisfaction the congressman's voice, as rich and sonorous as it sounded on TV, came on the line almost immediately. "Mrs. McBride? It's been a long time."

"Yes. It has. I need to talk to you, sir. In person."

"About what?"

"It's a sensitive matter. One I don't think you'd want to discuss on a telephone." Marynell was beginning to feel exposed out here, with the near-full moon shining down at the end of Main Street like a spotlight.

"Very well," he said warily. "Do you mean now? It's almost eleven o'clock."

"No. Tomorrow would be soon enough, I suppose."

"Then come to my campaign headquarters in Five Points at, shall we say seven?"

"Absolutely not." She had meant she would not show her face in that place, but she was also wondering if it was a sign of disrespect to schedule a meeting so early in the morning. "It needs to be away from Five Points, in another town. You pick one." There were several small towns strung along the five highways that radiated out of Five Points.

She heard him cover the receiver and have a muffled exchange with the woman. "All right. I'm speaking at a town meeting in Fredericksburg tomorrow night. Can you meet me there?"

"No. A town meeting is too public. Meet me in Twin Sisters on your way. Beforehand." Marynell felt a certain headiness. There was power in this, making a United States congressman do your bidding.

"Twin Sisters?" The congressman did not sound particularly cooperative. "That's a bit out of the way."

That was the point, as far as Marynell was concerned. No one would see them together. Twin Sisters was but a wide place in the road. "I assure you, you will want to hear what I have to say. And you will want privacy when you hear it. There is a little store at the crossroads just before you get into town."

After a gravid pause, he said. "All right, Mrs. McBride. I can only imagine that this has something to do with one of your lovely daughters."

"It certainly does. What time?" If he set the meeting terribly late she would have to lie to P.J., not something she enjoyed doing.

"Four o'clock."

"Fine."

THE TINY STORE AT THE intersection of two roads near Twin Sisters was listing to one side, crouched down in a hollow. Peeling paint, clouded windows and a badly sagging moss-covered roof bespoke decades of neglect. Two old-time gas pumps stood sentry. *Rusty,* Marynell thought as she rolled past them. The whole place was rusty and dusty and brown. Certain tourists, she supposed, would find this little emporium quaint, a throwback to simpler times when folks came to this crossroads to buy moonshine out back, but Marynell would as soon see this shack burn to the ground. She parked under the giant tree out front and went inside.

An ancient-looking woman sat watch in a sunken chair while her ancient-looking man tended an ancient-looking cash register, behind which hung the most enormous Texas flag Marynell had ever seen outside of the state capital. The only other thing of note was a jumbled collection of old Dr Pepper memorabilia above the chest-style coolers. Bottle caps, posters, roadsigns. An upright cooler dispensing the actual beverage tempted Marynell. She loved her Dr Pepper, the real kind, made with real sugar, sold in real bottles, like they made up in Dublin, Texas.

The rest of the place was dim, dusty and ill kept, with one or two of each stock item lined up on eye-level shelves in no particular order. Business was not brisk. Nodding a hello at the couple, Marynell wondered if she'd made a mistake. If these two got a look at the congressman, they would doubtlessly talk about his appearance at this outpost for the rest of their lives.

She quickly bought a bottle of the Dr Pepper and went outside so she could intercept him. Before long a nondescript black Ford Explorer, a rental perhaps, rolled into the dusty parking lot and pulled up next to her van.

Marynell went right up to the driver's window as it glided down. She was startled to see a lovely young woman driving. The congressman leaned forward from the passenger seat.

"We should talk in my van," Marynell said as she spared the woman a cool-ish glance, "if you don't mind."

When the congressman was settled in her van she wasted no time. "What is the meaning of trying to take my daughter's farm away from her?"

The congressman didn't even blink at her attack. "It's nothing personal against Mrs. Tellchick," he said smoothly, "but unfortunately, your daughter is unable to meet her financial obligations. As I understand it, she had already decided to sell."

"Way back when, you promised Robbie could have that farm for good, no strings, no worries."

"I didn't mean they could live on it without making the mortgage payments. I've been very generous. Besides, that was all a long time ago."

"Eighteen years, to be exact," Marynell said, deciding to just go ahead and drop her bomb. "That is how old your grandson is now."

"My *grandson*?" Behind his designer spectacles, Kurt Kilgore's eyes flared, then narrowed. "I think you'd better say what you came here to say, Mrs. McBride."

"You have a grandson, congressman. And so do I."

"You have no proof of that." For a moment Marynell was surprised that he seemed to comprehend the situation so fully. But then she supposed one didn't ascend to his level of power without a certain shrewdness. She had been afraid she might be forced to spell things out, which she was perfectly prepared to do. But she wasn't looking forward to explaining Markie's foolish bullheadedness to him. So, fine. Now they could cut to the chase.

"Oh, but I do have proof." Marynell was proud of the way she kept her voice calm, cool. "I actually have a picture of the baby. And I have a diary that my daughter kept at the time." Marynell was lying just a little bit here. She had torn the picture to bits years ago in a fit of pique. And technically, Markie now had the diary in her possession, but she would get it back from her if need be. "And it's full of details. All kinds of details. The girl even wrote the name of the maternity home where she had the baby. I'm sure I could come up with the records if I had to. This would be terribly messy, would it not? Between you and your son? Especially if I tell him how you and I kept him and my daughter apart? Especially if I reveal how you promised us the land if we would agree to an abortion, and then took it back from my recently widowed daughter."

"You would never be so reckless as to do that." He was sizing her up so coldly that Marynell was suddenly glad the young woman was sitting there, in the vehicle right next to them. Marynell hadn't really considered the possibility that he might be capable of greater evil, but now she could see the potential for it in the malicious squint of those handsome eyes behind the glasses.

"I'm afraid I would. Telling the story to the media would expose an illegitimate grandson for me, but in the long run that is my foolish daughter's burden to bear. I think, from what I've read in the papers about your son, it would be worse for you. I think you might lose your son for good if he were to learn how you deceived him. And the diary has one other very interesting entry. My daughter and your son used to go to the caves, the ones out under that big limestone formation? But one night they went out there and turned back. Seems they saw *you* out there, unloading some boxes. Markie wrote about it—how your big old Cadillac was parked way out on the limestone like that. Seems odd to me, Congressman."

"Odd? That my own car would be parked out on my own ranch?" His voice was mocking, but Marynell didn't buy it. Even in the dim light, she could see a wash of telltale red climbing up his fat neck.

"Let that be your concern. As for me, my only concern is for my middle daughter. She has been badly hurt by her husband's recent tragic death and she needs to stay on her farm. She needs to be near her mother."

"What do you want?"

"The farm, of course. I want you to sign that farm over, free and clear, to my daughter Robbie."

Again, he didn't hesitate. Tough decisions came that easily to him, she supposed. "Give me a few days to get the paperwork done and to set up a spin on this. It will have to appear to be some kind of magnanimous gesture on my part. Certain reporters dig into everything I do and they will find the change in deed. Only you and I must know the truth."

"All right. Until then, you keep that diary in mind. It spells out everything, all too clearly. I will take it to your son and I will tell him what we did. I can even imagine copies of those handwritten pages appearing all over the media."

"I'll want that diary."

She gave her adversary a malignant smile. "And you shall have it, Congressman, just as soon as *I* have the deed to that land."

CHAPTER FOURTEEN

MARKIE HAD SPENT THE DAY in town at Curry's headquarters, organizing the phone-bank workers and stamping out a couple of ridiculous little PR fires because Curry simply could not keep his foot out of his mouth. Then she'd come home to find Robbie decked out in her best denim maternity dress and the boys in clean T-shirts and their good jeans. The house, especially the kitchen, looked hideously clean. Almost as if Mother had attacked it.

"We're going to the movies in Cedarville," Robbie announced brightly. Her glum mood seemed to have magically lifted.

Markie didn't say, But where'd you get the money? though the thought popped up.

As usual, sensitive Robbie seemed to read her sister's mind. "Justin gave us the cash. He gave me plenty to spare, if you want to go along with us."

"Sounds good," Markie said, though it didn't, exactly. The theater in Cedarville was a metal barnlike structure with seats bolted to the concrete floor, crackling speakers and a screen that sometimes wavered. "But I've still got work to do."

"You work too hard, you know that?" Robbie said gaily as she dug her keys out of her oversize tote. "Guys!" she stepped to the door of the living room where the TV was blaring. "Turn that thing off, and if you've gotta use the bathroom, do it now." She smiled back at Markie, who was shuffling through mail at the table. "You should get a social life. Go on a date once in a while, you know?"

Markie smiled. She didn't want to tell her that it looked like that's exactly what she was going to be doing this evening. Over the last week or so, Robbie had grudgingly admitted that Justin was not such a bad guy. He was at the very least, she said, hardworking. And now Justin had ensured their privacy and made Robbie's family happy in the process. Markie wondered what he'd done to get rid of the workers.

Markie was ashamed she hadn't thought of movie money herself. She sometimes forgot that not everybody on earth lived out their lives at warp speed in campaign mode.

"Oh. I almost forgot. Justin said to give you this." Robbie snatched an envelope off the counter and thrust it at Markie. "Guys! If you want pizza first, get a move on! The movie starts at seven-thirty."

Markie waited until the boys had tumbled out the door before she opened her envelope—a smooth, cool-feeling pale gray vellum. Inside a heavy notecard had the Kilgore brand embossed at the center top. Justin's angular handwriting read:

Markie, Would you share a late dinner with me? You don't have to do anything but show up. I know you've got work to finish, but when you're done, maybe you can take a nice, hot bubble bath and put on something pretty. I'll be waiting for you at the top of the hill, say about eight-ish. Justin.

Suddenly as excited as a kid at Christmas, Markie pressed the card to her lips, then she

threw herself into a chair, opened her laptop
and ripped through her e-mails. She tuned in
to the local news, standing in front of the TV
only long enough to make sure Curry's com-
mercial spots ran okay, made three calls to key
donors in Austin, checked on the latest polls.

Then she took that bubble bath.

Markie had nice clothes back in Austin.
Really nice clothes. But everything she'd
brought to Five Points seemed suddenly too
utilitarian for this all-important date. She
pawed through the stuff crammed into the
small closet of the tiny bedroom off the mud
porch that she currently occupied. Her casual stuff all looked too "farm girl" and her
business clothes looked too…well, businesslike. She grabbed the brown stretch jeans,
the sleekest pants she had. At least they
hugged her figure in the right places. But her
tops! Woefully plain. Downright drab. She
needed something with a little pizzazz, something a little more feminine for this night.

Robbie!

Surely her prissy sister had something…
how had Justin put it in the note? *Pretty.*

As young women, the three McBride sisters had borrowed one another's clothes shamelessly, but that was a long time ago and Markie felt just a tiny bit guilty, rifling through her sister's closet and drawers like a cat burglar. She told herself that this was a fashion emergency and Robbie would have to understand. And Robbie was restricted to maternity wear now, anyway.

"Aha!" Markie snatched a white top out of a bottom drawer, where it had been consigned to storage, no doubt. It was gauzy, soft, deeply V-necked, and had delicate crocheted detailing along the neck and sleeves. It was slightly reminiscent of the peasant blouse— also Robbie's—that Markie had worn the first time she'd been with Justin after choir practice. She held it up to her front before Robbie's dresser mirror. Perfect.

She allowed herself to filch a pair of Robbie's strappy red sandals, too, justifying the pilfering because Robbie's feet had become too puffy to wear them.

After she took extra care with her makeup and spritzed on a whiff of perfume, she was ready. She placed a hand on her belly as she looked in the mirror one last time. "You're a big girl now," she said solemnly to her reflection, having no idea why she felt compelled to say that.

THE LITTLE ROCK HOUSE at the top of the hill looked enchanting to Markie as she drove her Jeep up the narrow rutted road to the top. Tonight the bare windows appeared lit from within with a faint yellow glow that beckoned.

Undoubtedly she felt this way because Justin was waiting for her up there. In the west, to her back, the sun was almost gone. On the eastern horizon, the third full moon to make its appearance since she'd come home to help her sister rose up like the yearnings inside of her.

It was amazing how the little details of the Hill Country had seeped into her soul again, how this place had been laying its familiar images and peaceful rhythms indelibly upon her heart ever since she'd moved out to Robbie's. The billowing banks of high thunderclouds that rolled in on spring evenings. The cleansing susurrus of water over the little low water bridge on the county road after a sudden storm. The way a lone twisted live oak looked at the top of a hill at sunrise.

When she parked and got out, there was no sign of the Mexican workers. Had he sent them to the movies, too? And the little rock house was indeed softly lit. There had never been electricity up here, so Markie was curious.

As she pulled up and parked, Justin stepped out, looking spiffed up in a trim-cut white cowboy shirt and fresh-starched Levi's. His dark hair was slicked back.

"Hi." He smiled at her as she got out of the Jeep. "You look nice." His eyes appeared to sparkle in the dim twilight.

"So do you," she replied, returning the compliment.

"Come inside. I've got some wine." He put his hand to her back as he guided her through the open doorway.

The pale light emanated from a fire in the fireplace. The house only had two rooms, front and back, and the one with the fireplace looked bare. Where had they moved the cots?

"You cleaned up the place," she said, although, truth be told, it was too dark to tell much.

"Not really, but I made a place for us to sit and have our wine."

There were two straight-backed oak chairs before the fire. Between them sat the ice chest with the wine bottle and two crystal glasses atop it, reflecting the firelight.

They sat down and a sense of the surreal came over Markie. The scene looked like some old western painting, with the rough stone walls closing in, and the flickering fire and the planes of Justin's serious face glowing golden and the shadows of his hands looking so very masculine as he poured the dark burgundy wine. Even the folds of her white blouse looked softer. More timeless or something.

He handed her a wineglass, and without speaking or toasting or any other such silliness, they sipped, holding each other's gazes over the rims as they swallowed.

"Excellent wine. And these are nice glasses," she commented, for lack of anything else to say.

"They were my grandmother's. I've kept a few family things, but otherwise, I don't have a lot of stuff. In fact, I feel like I should apologize," he confessed as he stared into the fire. "Not even having a private place to invite you to tonight. But with two families living in my ranch house we can't go there, so this—" he raised a hand to the bare, dark room "—is the best I could do."

"Yes, we're a pair, aren't we?" She grinned and sipped her wine again. "I'm living in the back room of my sister's house, and you're camped up here with a bunch of illegals. Where are the guys, by the way?"

"Movie. I have a poor imagination."

"I think it was sweet of you to pay for everybody to go to the movies just so we could be alone. And Justin?"

He looked up, one eyebrow arched. "Yeah?"

"I think you are incredibly generous to open up your house to the immigrants that way."

He looked back at the fire. "It's a big house. I don't need all that room."

She nodded as if she understood, but she didn't, not completely. Markie had grown up in fairly humble circumstances. She couldn't really fathom having the kind of family money Justin had. And she was almost moved to tears by his generous willingness to give it all away.

"I had a place in Austin at one time," he said. "A condo. But I sold it because I spent so much time in Mexico. You should see how most of the people live down there."

"I've seen."

"You have?" His eyes met hers, bright with interest.

"Yes. And not just as a tourist. I went down with a senator once. A fact-finding trip. I was the interpreter."

"Fascinating. There's so much about you I don't know. But I want to, Markie. I want to know it all. I want to make up for all those lost years."

She was not ready to get into the subject of their past again, not yet, so she sipped her wine.

"So you speak Spanish?"

"*Sí.*"

He smiled. "I wish I had you out at the Light. I need somebody to teach some English classes to the immigrants. The more English they know, the better their chances of holding a steady job. Lorn and his wife are too busy getting the livestock going and their Spanish is spotty, anyway."

"I wouldn't mind giving it a try." Markie was surprised to hear herself say that. "Once the heat of the campaign is over." The idea of teaching little classes out at La Luz pleased her. Doing something simple and straight-forward for people who would appreciate it for a change.

"Come on." He downed the rest of the wine and stood up abruptly. "We'd better eat before the food gets cold."

"The food?" She looked around the dim room and saw nothing but rock walls.

"Come, my lady." He held a hand out to her, and when he'd raised her to her feet, he surprised her by hefting up both chairs and carrying them to the door. "Would you get the wine?" he called over his shoulder as he headed outside.

Out there, on the crest of the hill, in the very last traces of daylight, Markie saw a table set up with a white cloth. She had thought the furnishings by the fireplace were to be the setting for their date. But here it was, the real surprise. Some lumps on the table were covered with a large checkered dish towel.

He positioned the chairs facing each other and then held her elbow to make sure she didn't trip on the rocks because of the little sandals. He guided her in a dancing semicircle around the table to light upon a seat. Markie was grinning like a kid. "What have you done?" she said as she set the wine and glasses at the edge of the table.

"I paid Aurelia, who is an amazing cook, to fix us something special."

He whisked the cover away. There was china, crystal, place settings of silver, cloth napkins and three covered dishes. A small carafe of water. A candle in a glass globe. Justin proceeded to light it.

"What have you done?" Markie repeated.

"I hope what I've done is make you happy."

"You have made me…" She wanted to say something light and clever, but nothing came. "You've made me speechless, I guess."

He laughed and removed the covers that had kept the food warm. A heavenly aroma filled Markie's nostrils. Aurelia had covered baked chicken breasts, with a chocolate-laced mole sauce. Warm corn tortillas with butter and salsa, savory rice and an avocado salad completed the meal.

Justin poured more wine and they sipped and ate slowly, with much conversation, plenty of laughter and some super-charged hand-holding.

When their laughter died at another silly joke, Justin gripped her fingers again. "Do you think you could live out here?"

"I don't know. I was just thinking about that as I drove up the hill this evening."

"That's good." He regarded her seriously. "That you're thinking about it." He tipped his face up to the star-studded night sky. "There's just something about the Hill Country, you know?"

Markie's gaze turned up with his. "Yes." Then her attention fell to the night landscape that spread below the hill. Beyond the small meadow and the stock pond, she could see Robbie's place where the yard light threw a circle of light on the little white clapboard Victorian. "I don't know if it's because I'm staying with Robbie or what, but I've admitted to myself, on this trip, that I truly love this part of Texas. It's gets in your blood, you know?"

He nodded. "This is where I want to settle for good."

"That's because you've found your life's work, and that work is here." She looked at him earnestly. His face, in the intimate circle of candlelight, had never looked more beautiful to her. "But, Justin, my work isn't here. And neither is my life."

"Are we going to start talking about the bright lights of Austin again?" In the flickering candlelight she could read his eyes, and she saw that he meant no disparagement of her lifestyle by that.

"It's who I am, Justin."

"Yes. But isn't this who you are, too? And if you really do decide to marry me, wouldn't it be nice if we actually lived together?"

"Don't be like that."

"Like what?"

"Sarcastic."

"Sorry." And again, his eyes told her he truly was. He toyed with her fingers. "I just want us to be together. Now. I want us to have a life together. Markie, I'd like to…to have a family." He gripped her fingers tightly. "To have another child if we can possibly be so blessed."

For one instant Markie felt like she'd been kicked in the gut. Then the next it was as if a hot star had exploded in her mind. *Another child.* For so long she'd been looking back, always tethered to, pining for, the child she'd lost. She hadn't even considered that perhaps they could redeem the past by having another. "I…I hadn't thought of that."

"Well, think of it." He leaned toward her earnestly, with his elbows propped on the little table and his hands folded over hers in front of him. "Think of it all, Markie. Our whole future together. This is real. The real thing. We shouldn't settle for anything less. And that future includes choosing where we want to live."

She slid her fingers away, surprised at herself for being so skittish on this subject. She hadn't had time to even consider that marrying Justin might mean living in Five Points. "It's not that simple for me. If I move back here to be with you, I'll be moving back to the same town where my mother lives. The small town where she rules, I should say."

"So?"

"So she's a witch. You don't know her, Justin." Markie cupped her hands over his folded ones. "You can't imagine how interfering, how controlling, she really is. She stole my diary, back when I first moved to Austin."

"The diary you wrote when you had the baby?"

"Yes."

"That's weird."

"There's more. I had a picture…" Tears from the old self-pity shot to her eyes before she could stop them. She swallowed, trying to regain her composure.

Seeing her distress, Justin frowned and clasped her hand. "You had a picture of what?"

"I had a picture of the b…baby," she blurted out. "And now it's gone. It's not in there. I know it was in that diary. I wouldn't have put it anyplace else. I think she got rid of it."

"Oh, sweetheart. She took your picture? That's horrible." He left his chair, dropped to one knee by hers and hugged her tightly to him.

After a while he said, "But you still have the diary?" He seemed genuinely concerned that she did. "I mean, I was hoping I could read it." That one word *could,* as if he would consider it a privilege, made Markie love him all the more.

She nodded. "I found it in a box of old junk when Robbie and I were cleaning out the attic room for her boys."

"Did you confront your mother?"

"Oh, yes, I most certainly did."

"Good girl." He stroked a stray strand of hair behind her ear. "And what did she say?"

"That she was trying to protect me, whatever that means."

"Wait." Justin said as if he'd just thought of something dreadful. "If your mother read it—"

"Oh, you can be sure of that."

"Then she knows you gave the baby up for adoption?"

"Exactly. And she will find a way to use that against me someday. That's how she operates. The point is, I had to figure out a way to live at peace with her. So I've avoided her all these years, and I've been very happy doing it. I think my sister Frankie has the same philosophy. That's why she's so invested in her husband's success. That was her ticket off that farm, away from mother."

"What about your father?"

"I think he actually loves her. Or at least he's loyal to her. That's his code. And I love him, but even as sweet as Daddy is, he can't make up for the things my mother does. I really don't want to be around her at all, much less in the same town."

"But what about your sister Robbie? She needs you now. She'll need help when the baby comes."

"Oh, now you're not playing fair."

"I'm not out to be fair." He leaned closer, caressing her in ways designed to give him full advantage. "I'm out for one thing only, to be with you."

Markie melted against him. "And I want to be with you, too."

"Then why can't you come and live on the Kilgore and *be* with me?"

"I don't know," she confessed miserably. She just couldn't. Not yet.

"You don't know *why,* or you don't know if that's what you want?"

"I just don't know. About any of it. This is

all happening so fast. I can't make up my mind about anything until after the election." Markie caught a glimmer of something out of the corner of her eye. It was the headlights of Robbie's van, winking through the trees as she pulled into the drive down below. A sudden reminder that it was getting late and it was time for Justin to keep watch over the caves. For one more night, at least, they would have to leave the question of their future hanging.

CHAPTER FIFTEEN

Sometimes I think about what it will be like if I ever have to face my baby someday. CeCe told me that even in closed adoptions, sometimes people look up their birth parents by mutual consent. I know I would never stop my baby from finding me no matter how my life turns out. I don't care if I ended up being the president of the United States, I'd want to see him.

But what would I tell him about the reasons I gave him away? How will I make him see that I loved him too much to keep him? And what if he asked me about his father? (After I put *unknown* on the forms, my palms got all sweaty. But I am done for good with Justin Kilgore.)

Facing the baby someday. I can't even

imagine what a nightmare that would be. I couldn't take it.

FROM HIS HIDING PLACE where he had parked the Explorer back in the trees, Kurt Kilgore watched as a beat-up little Dodge van bounced along the driveway to the Tellchick house. He had hoped the family was gone for the night, perhaps to the mother's place, but no such luck.

He hunkered his girth down into the bucket seat of the inadequate, small SUV to wait for his opportunity in the wee hours. It thoroughly irked him to be hiding out like this, with his gut crunched under the wheel of a second-class rental when back in Washington he had a spanking-new and perfectly comfortable Lincoln Navigator sitting empty, racking up a fortune in garage storage fees. But a man had to do what he had to do.

He had considered sending some lackey from the campaign into those caves, but the fewer who knew about this matter, the better. He had learned that lesson well when he had been investigated back in '86. A bad, bad year that simply would not go away.

Eighteen years ago. He certainly did not need this busybody mother opening the can of worms that went back that far. The campaign-finance investigation that year had been a close call. It was one thing to eliminate a handful of unfortunate illegal aliens, who had no business being in this country in the first place. It was a much more complicated matter to quiet some little campaign geek who might crack under pressure. Since that awful year he had learned to keep things to himself. And ever since that awful year, he had not sold any more of the artifacts he had hidden in these caves. They had waited, buried as they had been for centuries past in the jungles of Mexico. Who was the wiser? Except for the farmer. Stupid man. Stupid, stupid man.

But now the time had come to make use of that handy Mayan mural—if he could get his hands on all the pieces—in such matters one had to strike while the iron was hot. Kurt's contact, a pompous expert in pre-Columbian artifacts at the Chicago Art Institute, had said there was a British dealer, more of a collector, really, since the woman never sold the precious items she bought, who was virtually obsessed with obtaining the pieces. So the time had come and the money would be substantial—that is, if the deal could be cinched soon.

And soon couldn't come fast enough for Kurt Kilgore.

Curry was closing the gap in the polls, thanks to Markie McBride's machinations. He wondered if this was a personal vendetta for the girl? Undoubtedly. Little vixen.

He would need advertising money to counter her efforts. And television spots were so damned expensive these days.

He readjusted his girth with a grunt of satisfaction. That's what made this thing so fortuitous, the collector appearing right when the campaign needed the money. Of course, there was the not-so-minor question of how to launder the money. The collector might be desperate enough to make her payment in the form of a direct contribution to the campaign war chest. But campaign finance reform had made these things tricky. How to explain a British art collector supporting a Texas congressman's bid for reelection? It was in his stars, Kurt decided. He tilted his head to look at the real stars overhead. *In his stars.*

"Doesn't this collector want the other pieces?" Kurt had asked, because he knew that they were out there somewhere, possibly still at the original site in Mexico. He wished again that his men had nailed the Morales brothers. They knew, he was sure, where the other pieces were hidden. Why else would those brothers be poking around in those caves to get the original piece? Same as he had, they had learned that the other entrance to the cave would soon be inaccessible, thanks to the plan his son had to quarry limestone, leaving the only entrance to the caves on Robbie Tellchick's farm.

His son. His son. His *son*.

The ridiculous set of circumstances that tied Kurt's fortunes to the McBride family had started with his son and it had ended with his son. If only Justin hadn't taken up with that worthless girl. If only Justin hadn't decided to take in illegal aliens as if they were a bunch of stray pups.

Headlights at the top of the hill caught Kurt's attention. He sat up and adjusted his glasses to peer into the dark.

Before long he could make out a newish-looking Jeep Liberty as it rolled into the yard, puffs of dust preceding the high beams, and when the vehicle made a turnabout under the yard light, he could barely make out the ghost of a face in the windshield. Markie McBride. What had she been doing up on that hill? She got out and walked slowly into the house.

Within minutes she appeared under the yard light again, trotting toward the Jeep. She jumped in and then he watched the Jeep jolt back up the narrow rutted road that wound up the hill.

"I CAME BACK," MARKIE breathed as she climbed out of the Jeep and slammed the door. She ran into Justin's waiting arms.

"I'm glad you did." He kissed her temple and rubbed his hands in a sensuous circle on her back. "But why? Did you forget something?"

"Yeah. I forgot how much I want to be with you. How much I'll always want to be with you."

Justin tensed and reared back, obviously unsure of her meaning, obviously hopeful.

His dark eyes peered down into hers, full of questions.

"I went into the house and when I started to tell Robbie about my quandary, I realized it was only a quandary if I made it into one. I think it was the way she was looking at me, as if I was crazy. Sisters can do that."

"Remind me to send Robbie some flowers."

"She'd prefer chocolate."

"Okay. Chocolate. Lots of it."

"It all seems so clear all of a sudden. How could I think my career was more important than a future with you? I mean—" Markie chuckled at herself "—it's silly, right? The reason I threw myself so headlong into my career in the first place was to forget about you. And now, here you are—"

"And here *you* are." He squeezed her tighter.

She smiled up at him. "Yes. Here I am."

He kissed her as if it had been years since he'd done so instead of a little less than half an hour.

"Come on." He led her to the spot where he had spread a couple of serapes. After they'd settled in and snuggled into each other's arms, watching the landscape below, he said, "What about all that stuff about your mother?"

"I think I've been reacting to my mother just about long enough. She'll never change, and I have to accept her the way she is. But not let it dictate what I do with my life. I only wish Daddy could see that and you know, free himself up a little bit. You know what Robbie told me, just now?"

"What?"

"She said Mother came out this afternoon while I was in town, ostensibly to clean her house for her, but she was asking about that diary."

Justin frowned. "That *is* odd."

"You'll get used to it. Then again, maybe not."

"Why would she want that diary?"

"Who knows? Why did she take it in the first place? She claimed she was packing up the boxes and wanted to put it back where it belonged."

"That's so weird. I mean, I know she's your mother, but…your diary, *that* diary. Wow. Robbie didn't give it to her?"

"Of course not. But she said mother got sort of agitated—this is nothing new, either—and they had a little spat, started yelling at each other. Robbie never used to raise her voice at anybody, ever."

"Ooh. Bet that was a goody. A pregnant woman and an old hellcat going at it." He glanced at Markie. "Sorry."

"It's okay. You don't have to pretend you're going to have a nice, normal mother-in-law. Come to think of it, Robbie didn't seem at all upset by the fight. She was in an amazingly good mood when I got home this afternoon. How was she when you took her the movie money?"

But Justin didn't answer. He seemed to be holding his breath. Finally he breathed, "You mean it?"

"Mean what?" Markie had lost the thread.

"What you said about your mother just now, about her being my mother-in-law?"

Markie smiled. "Guess that thrills you, does it?"

"Only if it means you've decided to marry me."

She turned in his arms, serious now.

"You still want to marry me after all that's happened?"

He didn't answer. He kissed her so hard she thought their lips would bruise. When it was over, he breathed, "I'm gonna make you so happy!"

"I know."

"I mean it. We can do this. We can mesh our lives."

"I know," she said again. "You got me to thinking about teaching English at the Light. That sounds so good, so real. I actually think I was getting a little burned out on politics."

"Are you sure you wouldn't miss it, after a while? That stuff gets in your blood."

"It's just a job, like any other job. A frustrating, stressful and at times disgustingly dirty job. Besides, it never got in *your* blood, and you grew up around it all your life."

"Ah. I forget. You don't know my father."

KURT KILGORE'S HEAD jerked up. He stared around the dark interior of the Explorer, thoroughly disoriented. Scrubbing a hand down his face, he realized he must have dozed off. Long campaign hours always took a toll.

Squinting toward the house, he couldn't see the Jeep, but he was satisfied that all was dark. Time to go. In and out, that was the ticket. No witnesses. No assistants. Nobody else involved.

Out of a fat briefcase on the seat, he retrieved an automatic pistol and slapped a magazine into it, then started the engine and quietly rolled down into the ruts of the narrow ranch road that led to the area of the farm where the cave entrance was. After he'd bumped along at a snail's pace for about a hundred yards without headlights, he thought he saw something move in his rearview mirror. He slowed even more and checked it intently. Nothing. Again he scrubbed the hand over his features, deciding he must be seeing things. Now was not the time to get spooked.

BRANDON SMITH FELT A little goofy, shrugging into a denim jacket on a July night in Texas, but he needed the pockets, and people said that deep in the caves it was cold, even in summer. He slipped the camera phone his mom and dad had given him last Christmas into one pocket, a flashlight into the other.

The water bottle in the cup holder caught his attention. Nah. Overdoing it. He wasn't going to mess around that long in there. He was going to get in, take his pics and run.

He hoped he got a good red-handed shot of the old boy with his mouth agape and the goods in his grasp. He could see that photo now, all over *Time* and *Newsweek,* altered in hilarious ways by bloggers on the Net. Yee-haw. Chad and Ben would probably call him Hot Shot Smith. Brandon smiled at his own pun, then folded a stick of gum into his mouth and chewed it into submission. Never hurt to have fresh breath when you were doing a little espionage.

With satisfaction, he watched Kilgore's vehicle roll out of the trees, then off into the darkness. With no headlights. He chewed his gum calmly and waited until a flicker of brake lights up ahead confirmed that the road was bumpy. Was this guy actually a congressman? No headlights, but pressing on the brakes every two feet. Blink. Blink. Follow me. Follow me.

Easily done. He'd been following the congressman around for days. All the way to

Twin Sisters one evening. Somehow he'd known he'd come out to the caves himself. Whatever was hidden in there, all Brandon needed was one good, clear picture. He pulled his pickup out of the shadows and obliged the blinking brake lights. The trick was to inch forward in Drive with little gas, no gunning of the engine. The trick was not to get all antsy, not tail too close. Sheesh. How did he know this stuff? TV?

His quarry disappeared around a bend, and he stopped just below the crest of a small rise with the engine idling to get his bearings. There were small ravines and washouts all over this land—he didn't exactly think it'd be cool to pitch the pickup off into one of them. He inched around the bend, able to make out only shadowy shapes by the light of the moon. But up ahead, the unmistakably rotund silhouette of Kilgore emerged from the Explorer, accompanied by the weak cone of a flashlight.

Brandon braked to a soundless stop behind a waist-high thicket of sow thistle growing along a barbed-wire fence. Easing out, he pressed the door shut just enough to kill the dome light. The cone of light disappeared from view. Moment of truth. Now he *had* to close in. He sure didn't want to lose sight of that light inside the caves.

He made his way in the dark over clumps of weeds, around tangles of brush, and was stalking the guy like a bobcat, when suddenly he thought of the bats. Last summer he'd gone down to Austin with a carload of friends, right about this time of year, actually, to watch the bats that roosted under the Congress Avenue Bridge exit at sundown. He could still remember the swirling columns, rising like agitated smoke to disappear high up in the darkening sky. Were there bats in these caves? *Steady, boy,* he told himself, *this is not the time to get all creeped out.* But the chill bumps that crawled up his arms, anyway, told him that he just might be in over his head this time.

MARKIE WAS FAINTLY AWARE that she was dozing, at first drifting into the pleasant maze of a disjointed dream about the river, but when everything grew darker, as if she were in a tomb, or a cave, she couldn't seem to struggle out of her trance.

She felt paralyzed as she saw a faint glimmer of light, deep in the blackness. Two round dots of silver emerged and took shape like twin chrome disks. And even before the face came into relief in the dim glow of a candle she suddenly found herself holding, she knew who it was.

"Congressman. You scared me. What are you doing here?"

"I could ask you the same thing, Miss McBride." He didn't step any closer and his voice was not apologetic, not kind. "This is rather far off the campaign trail, don't you think? What are *you* doing here?"

"I asked you first." Even in her dream state, she thought how it was the most trite of things to say, but she stood her ground, heart drumming, candle shaking. She tried to see into the blackness beyond Kilgore's shoulder. Then a strange foreboding told her that Brandon was back there. Panic gripped her. Was he okay? Should she call out to him?

"Markie, sweetheart. Wake up." Justin's voice jolted her to consciousness. "I think you were having a bad dream."

Markie sat up straight. "I was. It was

weird. I was holding a candle, of all things, and—look!"

Justin grabbed his binoculars, focusing on the open rocky area in the meadow below. "Somebody's down there. I can make out a flashlight moving along, but not who's carrying it. Ugh. Lost it."

"That or whoever it is disappeared into the caves," she reasoned.

They looked at each other meaningfully. "Oh, my gosh. Today. Brandon. He said something about your dad's appearance schedule, and then…what did he say that set off my alarm bells now?" Markie said.

"I'll go down there and check it out."

"And if it's those guys Brandon overheard in the bar?"

"That's what this is for." He produced his revolver from under the edge of the serape and Markie jolted backward.

"Yikes!" she yelped. "You really are a Texan, after all. Where on earth did you get that thing?"

"It was my granddad's." And it was a fine, functional old piece, too. Inlaid mother-of-pearl grip. Embossed side plate and barrel.

He stood and fished the bullets out the pocket of his Levi's, then quickly dropped the cartridges into the chamber. With this gun, he could blow the head off a rattler at thirty paces, so he felt confident in almost any encounter. But because Markie was looking just a tad grim he winked at her and said, "I'll be *beck*," in his best hokey Arnold Schwartzeneger voice.

"Now, wait just a minute." Markie scrambled to her feet, staring at the gun. "You can't be serious." Then up into his eyes. "Don't go down there, Justin."

"Then what was the point of all this watching and waiting? Look, if it's the Moraleses, I'll try to reason with them, try to get them to tell what they know to the sheriff. If it's the coyote-types, I'll get the drop on them before they see me coming. And if it's Brandon Smith, I'll send his little rear packing back to town. I'll know what I'm dealing with when I get a better look at that vehicle."

"Let me go with you," she pleaded as she grabbed for his arm. Not the one that held the gun, he made certain.

He studied her earnest features in the

moonlight and sighed. "I suppose arguing with you will only waste our time, won't it?"

"I'm going." She was already hopping around on one foot as she tugged on her sandals.

AT FIRST, IT WAS A MATTER of striking a balance between keeping the dim light ahead in sight and hanging back enough to avoid detection. Brandon found it surprisingly easy to keep quiet as he palmed his way along the damp walls of the cave. If the coyotes, who had bragged that they'd already looked here, hadn't found anything, then the artifacts were probably really deep in the caves. Assuming they had a ways to go, he bided his time.

He had the camera phone flipped open so that it provided a greenish glow along the cave walls, more of a night-light than a flashlight. About the time his eyes adjusted to the darkness, the brighter light ahead vanished.

He crept along, not sure if this was a trick of vision or if he'd lost the guy. Not good.

A click, a sound no louder than the tick of a clock, caused Brandon to freeze even before a smooth, deep voice behind him commanded him to do so. A flashlight flared on.

The man who emerged out of a black hollow in the wall, holding a gun, was huge. Brandon, a big boy, felt dwarfed as Congressman Kurt Kilgore, incongruously dressed in smart golf clothes, stepped around from behind a rock. "What in the hell are you doing in here, boy?"

"Congressman, sir—" Brandon started, then belatedly thought to throw his hands up. "I…I saw a light from the road." *Weak.* Do better. "I was putting up signs. They've had trouble with illegals out in these caves. And I… I came to check it out."

"With that thing?" The congressman waved the gun at the camera phone. "And no flashlight? Give it to me." He held out his palm.

Brandon handed over the camera.

With one hand expertly working the camera's buttons and the other holding the gun trained on Brandon, the congressman scrolled through the images stored on the phone.

"You were planning on taking my picture?"

"No, sir." His dad was right. Brandon was a very poor liar.

Kilgore's eyes narrowed. He dropped the camera phone in the dust and, without looking down, ground it against the rock beneath his boot heel until it shattered and broke into pieces.

"Where have I seen you before, boy?" The eyes behind the glasses were coldly assessing. "Never mind. You are trespassing out here. And it looks like I just might have to shoot you."

"No!" a female voice screamed. The flare of another flashlight sliced the darkness as Markie barreled around the opening of the small chamber, followed immediately by Justin Kilgore.

"No!" she screamed again, and threw herself between Brandon and the pistol. "For God's sake, don't shoot him! This boy is your own grandson!"

As monumental silence followed, as all the air seemed suddenly sucked out of the underground chamber.

Markie stared wild-eyed at the pistol in Kilgore's hands. "Please. Put it down. You don't want to hurt this boy."

The congressman's arm fell by degrees

until the gun was finally resting limply beside his thigh. He fixed his gaze past Markie. At Brandon. "My grandson?" he mumbled.

Markie turned slowly, steeling herself to face what she had done. Brandon and Justin both stared—from each other's faces to hers and back. The shock and horror in their nearly identically shaped eyes grew, and the hallmark crease between their brows deepened as they digested the truth.

"Markie?" Justin whispered.

She found the strength to address Brandon first. "Brandon, please. Don't hate me."

Brandon's mouth worked, but nothing came out. Finally he turned to Justin, of all people, with some kind of instinctual plea for help in his eyes.

Justin, who had had his revolver up all this time, still held it steady in the congressman's direction, but his eyes were fixed on his son, not his father.

"You're…?" Brandon said, all his confusion and disbelief summed up in that one word.

Justin only shook his head in equal disbelief. "I had no idea. Honest."

Markie stepped closer to Brandon, her hands

up now, pleading. "It was all my fault." She crossed her palms over her chest. "He didn't even know about you. I… I was young and very stubborn. I gave birth to you in secret—"

Brandon threw a hand up to stop the rush of her self-recriminating words. "I *know* that I'm adopted," he said roughly. "But I had no idea who—you two are…you're…?" His hurt gaze turned to the congressman. "And he's…"

Finishing the questions seemed unnecessary. Even in the dark of a cave, even by the dim glow of flashlights, his resemblance to the people facing him was plain to see.

The congressman's gaze swiveled from Brandon's face to his own son's. His nostrils flared before he spoke. "Put that thing down. I am not the one in the wrong here." He jerked his chin toward the ceiling of the cave. "That is *my* land over our heads and this kid was sneaking around on it like a cat burglar."

"That land—" Markie started forward, but Justin grabbed her arm.

"We heard you threaten the boy." Justin did not lower his gun. "And this farm is not legally yours. What are you doing in here?"

"I don't have to explain myself to you or

anybody else. And this land will be mine again by morning. I'm all prepared to call in the note. No one can fault me for stopping a trespasser on my own property. In the meantime, you can claim whatever you want. I'm leaving." Ignoring the gun, he made to move past the three of them.

Markie's blood was suddenly boiling. She felt like a tigress ready to pounce. Kurt Kilgore had just been told that this beautiful young man was his own flesh and blood and apparently all he cared about was covering up his misdeeds. "I'm taking this to a grand jury," she said, but the threat was hollow. No one had a shred of evidence that the congressman was hiding anything in these caves.

"Do what you want. I'll be maintaining that I thought he was a trespasser on my land." Kilgore shoved past Brandon, who now looked the picture of shock as his shoulder was jostled by the larger man's.

"Let him go," Justin said as Kilgore disappeared into the dark vault beyond. "We'll deal with him later. Are you okay?" he said to Brandon.

"You guys are my birth parents?" the shell-shocked boy said.

"I guess so." Justin stepped over to him and put a steadying hand on his boy's shoulder. "What are you doing out here in the middle of the night like this?"

"I've been following him around. I was gonna try to get a picture of him and whatever he came in here for." He pointed out the remains of the camera phone on the cave floor.

"And did you see anything?" Justin prompted.

"No, it was too dark. He got the jump on me."

"He had a *gun,* Brandon." Markie wilted against the rough rock wall. "He could have shot you."

"Yes, ma'am. I was just trying to score a hit for the campaign."

"No political race is worth risking your life. Think of your parents. They would have never gotten over that."

"Yes, ma'am. You're right." Brandon studied her face as if he were seeing his past, present and future all rolled into one. But he spoke to her as if she were nothing more than a friendly acquaintance. "Markie?"

She looked up at him.

"Why would I ever hate you? I mean, my mother couldn't give birth to me. So somebody had to."

At the thought of how wonderfully he must have been raised, Markie wilted all the more. Someday she hoped to have the opportunity to thank Brandon's parents for the fine job they'd done with their son.

She looked to Justin to see if he was equally moved. But he wouldn't make eye contact with her. A strange chill that had nothing to do with the temperature in the cave passed through her as she realized that Brandon might forgive her for her deception—he already had—but Justin… Justin wouldn't even look at her.

He jammed his gun into the back of his belt, then clamped a hand on Brandon's shoulder again. "That's a great attitude… son." The word had seemed to come awkwardly to him. "Come on. Let's get out of here."

As Markie followed Justin's flashlight out, feeling her way unsteadily along the cold walls of the caves, she feared everything had shifted. They had come so close, so close to genuine happiness. If only she had told him the whole story earlier.

CHAPTER SIXTEEN

THEY TOOK BRANDON BACK to Robbie's house. When she heard them coming in the back door, Robbie, who had been enjoying as sound a sleep as any mama bear, stumbled out into the kitchen in her old robe, barely coherent. She nearly sank to her knees when they told her who the young man with them was.

Justin took her elbow and guided her to a kitchen chair, where she sank down, breathless. "He looks it," she finally said, gaping at Brandon. "He does. He could for sure be my Mark's cousin."

"Mark?" Brandon said. He was standing in a manly pose beside Justin, legs spread wide, arms folded over his chest.

"You've got three cousins," Markie explained. "Frank, Rob and Mark. Twelve, ten and five. They're racked out back there." She aimed a thumb toward the bedroom behind the kitchen.

"And one more on the way." Robbie placed a hand on her great girth.

Brandon shook his head as his gaze panned around the humble farm kitchen, looking as if he'd woken up on the moon or something.

"It's a lot to absorb, I know," Markie reassured him.

"Poor boy," Robbie said soothingly. "Come and sit down and let me take a good look at you."

The rest of the story took an hour to tell. When they got to the part about Kilgore saying he would lay claim to Robbie's ranch by morning, Robbie sat up straight and frowned.

"Something's weird here," she said.

"What do you mean?" Markie sat forward, at her sister's tone.

"Mother. After we argued about your diary, she came out from dusting that bedroom back there—" she inclined her head toward the room where Markie had been staying "—and insisted on taking down the sheers. She wanted to take them home to wash them. Said she didn't want to tax my septic tank with all that wash water. She'd already done four loads. I told her not to bother, but next thing I know she comes out with them in a stack and makes a beeline to her car."

"I heard the car start and she took off. I figured she was still upset about our little spat. You know, about the diary."

"The diary!" Markie dashed back to her room and the others followed.

They watched while Markie pawed frantically in the dresser, and then her shoulders sank. "It's gone. And now I think I know why mother wanted it so badly." She locked eyes with Justin. "I wrote an entry in it about the night we saw your father taking those boxes into the caves."

THEY WASTED NO TIME. Markie hated to wake her father in the middle of the night, but sooner or later all of this had to come to light. She had lived with the lies for far too long.

Giving Markie a cryptic look, Justin reasoned that he and Brandon should stay and watch over the sleeping children. There was collusion, but no warmth in his eyes.

"I agree." Markie said. No telling what

horrid things her mother might say in front of Brandon.

After Robbie hastily pulled on some stretched-out sweats, she and Markie jumped into Markie's Jeep and made it to the McBride farm in record time. They had nothing to say as they climbed the steps to the porch. Markie banged on the screen door, causing it to clatter noisily in the still night air.

Marynell opened the inside door and didn't seem all that surprised to see her daughters. But P.J., coming up behind her, said, "My stars. What are you girls doing here? Is everything all right? Are the children all right?"

"They're fine, Daddy," Robbie said.

"P.J., I want you to go back to bed." Marynell's tone was short.

"But I'm wide awake."

"Then go on down to your barn shop!" Marynell snapped. She narrowed her eyes at Markie. "Go sharpen a saw or something."

P.J. frowned at the kitchen wall clock. "At two in the morning?"

"Just go," Marynell said testily.

He went off mumbling, but not terribly

distressed. His barn shop was his refuge from his shrewish wife. Full of pleasant pastimes and homey comforts.

"What are you doing here?" Marynell said flatly when he was gone. She had not said *sit down* or even *come in,* though the girls had wedged their way inside the door.

"I think you know," Markie said. "Where is it?"

"Where is what? I do not know what you are talking about." Marynell fastened the top snap on the same pale green house duster she'd worn for the past twenty years.

"Mother," Robbie interceded, "are you aware that Kurt Kilgore plans to foreclose on my land?"

"No." Marynell shook her head. "You're wrong. He doesn't want that land anymore."

"Yes, he does. He threatened to take it back out in the caves this very night."

Marynell dropped her defensiveness long enough to look shocked. "In the caves—what on earth is this about?"

"It's a long story, Mother, but Kurt Kilgore just told Markie that he intends to foreclose on me in the morning."

"By God, he will not!" Marynell lashed out. "I will put a stop to that!"

"And just how do you plan to do that, Mother?" Robbie said mildly.

Markie admired a cunning she'd never seen in her sister before.

"Very well, then," Marynell said when she saw that the girls had cornered her. "I was planning to use that damned diary, if you must know. I can force Kilgore to sign over this farm if I can prove to him that I will expose his family's dirty laundry. And he doesn't seem too keen on the idea that I have a record of him being out at those caves." Marynell turned smug. "I believe that is where I really had him."

"What about Brandon?" Markie blurted, horrified at her mother's attitude.

"Who is Brandon?" Marynell's query was all innocence.

"Your grandson, Mother," Robbie supplied. "He's a very nice young man, and he's here in Five Points. Another long story. What about *him?* You'll be exposing him, as well. Would you think nothing of dragging an innocent child's name out in the limelight?"

Robbie's eyes grew suddenly moist. Young people were her weakness.

"That won't ever become necessary. I will give the diary to Kilgore and he will sign over the land, just like we planned. End of story."

"Mother." Markie would try to reason with Marynell. "I'm telling you, there are reasons why Kilgore has changed his mind about this…this *plan* of yours. He wants that land. What if he calls your bluff? Are you actually prepared to go to the media with this diary? Have you thought about the actual damage that would do?"

"Damage to *you,* you mean. To save your own reputation, Miss Hot Shot Political Consultant, you would see your own sister and her family thrown out in the cold."

"No!" Markie raised her voice. "It has nothing to do with *me.*"

"It has *everything* to do with you. None of this would be happening if you had kept your end of the agreement."

"What agreement?" Robbie said, but Marynell's lips clamped shut.

Robbie stepped up to her mother. "Are you

telling us that Kilgore gave me and Danny the land in the first place because you held Markie's pregnancy over his head?"

"It wasn't like that," Marynell defended. "He merely wanted our…discretion, and I merely wanted to see you and Danny settled with a good home. It was mutually beneficial."

"You wanted us next door to you," Robbie said as full comprehension dawned. "That's why you wanted Markie to get rid of the baby? Because Kilgore agreed to hand over the farm if she did?"

"Everything would have been fine," Marynell said, remaining adamant in her self-defense, "if Markie here hadn't been so bull-headed. I was trying to do what was best for both of you."

"Mother, give Markie her diary!" Robbie demanded.

"No. It's the only way to make sure Kilgore signs over that farm."

"Stop saying that!" Robbie yelled. "I don't want that farm! I *hate* that damned farm!" She pushed open the screen door and went running clumsily down the porch steps.

"Now look what you have done," Marynell turned a look of pure wrath on Markie. "I wouldn't be surprised if she delivered early. All because of you!"

MARKIE CAUGHT UP WITH Robbie at the door of their father's barn shop. P.J. had lit the bare bulb that dangled on a cord above his work bench. He was sitting up on the cracked vinyl seat of an old bar stool, reading a Larry McMurtry novel.

Robbie barged in. "Daddy, I want you to take me to town first thing in the morning, as soon as the bank opens."

"Robbie, you can't." Markie rushed in behind her and grabbed her arm. "Where will you live?"

"I'd be happy to take you, sugar." P.J. slid off the bar stool, wary at his daughter's vehemence. "But may I ask why?"

"I'm signing over my farm. To Kurt Kilgore."

"What?" P.J. closed his book and removed his reading glasses.

"Are you crazy?" Markie gaped at her. "You've got a baby coming!"

"Yes, I do," Robbie said calmly. "And

that's what I want to think about now. It's time to face facts. I can't keep that farm going. If I'm going to start a new life, I want to do it before I have the baby. The boys and I are moving to town."

"But how will you live?" Markie couldn't imagine what Robbie was thinking. She only had a high school education.

"In peace, I expect. I'll get a little house, a little job. Danny's family will help us."

"Your mother and I will help you," P.J. volunteered. But his deeply etched frown clearly conveyed that he didn't understand any of this.

"No Daddy, I doubt that will happen. I don't think that Mother is going to like this idea one bit, but she'll have to adjust, won't she?"

"Robbie, I won't let you do this for me," Markie said.

"I'm not doing it for you only," Robbie said. "I'm doing it for that fine young man back there—" she angled her head in the direction of her farm "—and for Justin, who doesn't deserve a father like that, and for me and my boys."

"Then I'm going to town with you." Markie got tears in her eyes as the sisters hugged tight, while P.J. stood near, scratching his pate and looking worried.

JUSTIN AND MARKIE DIDN'T have another moment alone. Justin took Brandon back to town that night, and after too little sleep, Markie and Robbie were up early the next morning. They fed the boys breakfast and made a big deal out of their going to school in Grandpa's car on the way to the bank. P.J. rolled up in his latest Ford sedan at seven-thirty on the dot.

"Your mother gave me this." He stepped into the mud porch and held out a plastic Wal-Mart bag. Inside was the diary.

At Markie's questioning look, P.J. said, "She's shut herself up in her attic room this morning. Didn't even cook me any breakfast. Are you girls gonna tell me what's going on in this family?"

Robbie looked at Markie, deferring to her wishes in this delicate matter. But Markie shook her head. She desperately needed to talk to Justin first. Too much damage had been done to their relationship already. She wasn't going to make one more mistake.

The day in town was a little bit crazy, a whole lot surreal.

Markie had followed P.J.'s car in her Jeep so that she could go to the campaign headquarters and do some work after the deal was done at the bank.

The banker seemed amazed that Robbie appeared while his key was still opening the glass door out front. But he did have the foreclosure papers ready. Kurt Kilgore had struck already, true to his word.

Looking at her sister's back, rounded and shapeless in the denim maternity jumper, her simple French braid curling over one shoulder and one arm barely moving as she signed her delicate scrolled signature several times, made Markie sad and fearful for her sister. She vowed she would never forget Robbie's sacrifice and she would help Robbie get through this, somehow. If it was the last thing she ever did, she would get to the bottom of Danny's death and she would find a way to unmask Kurt Kilgore.

After the business at the bank was done, P.J. took Robbie to the doctor for her prenatal checkup and Markie did some hurried business, then she took a break at midmorning to drive Robbie around to look at rental houses.

Her sister said, "What have I done?" and got weepy about the farm once, but only once.

Then they had lunch with Brandon, and Markie felt like pinching herself the whole time as the three of them got better acquainted. But Justin didn't show up at the Hungry Aggie and the apprehension that had started in Markie's heart the night before grew stronger.

By evening she was back out at Robbie's to help with the packing, which had to begin immediately, since Robbie only had ten days to clear out. She claimed she wanted it that way.

Justin showed up with the Mexicans, ready to help in any way they could. Robbie said to go ahead and move the remaining livestock over to the Light at Five Points. They all knew Kilgore wouldn't care about the animals.

Everybody worked like Trojans and Markie only saw Justin from a distance until the sun went down, when they all crammed themselves around Robbie's kitchen table to eat a stew she's made in the Crock-Pot. Four

Mexicans. Three nephews. One sister. No privacy.

After the Mexicans retired to the rock house, Markie went out on Robbie's back porch, wondering where Justin had gone to, hoping at last to have some time alone with him. The full moon, sliding between two thin ribbons of cloud, made her heart ache. She stared at the silhouette of the windmill and listened to a coyote's wail in the distance, and imagined the animal atop a ridgeline, his neck stretched. A lone silhouette.

After a while Justin came walking down the hill. His footsteps were slow, but sure, as he sauntered up to her.

"Interesting day." His voice floated out of the darkness as he stopped short of the porch.

The moon had peeked out fully, and in that soft light his handsome face, the deep shadows of his eyes, the line of his dark head, affected Markie so strongly, she wanted to hurl herself down the steps and collapse against him. She loved him more than words could tell.

"What do you think your dad will do next?" she said without going to him yet. "Do you care?"

"No. Only if he hurts Brandon."

"He's such a fine young man."

"The best."

"You didn't come and have lunch with us in town." She hoped she didn't sound accusing, because it was actually fear that gnawed at her.

"I needed time to think."

"Justin…" She had to say it, had to risk it. Nothing else mattered. "If you can't forgive me for keeping the truth from you, I'll understand. But I want you to know that I love you. I'll always love you. That will never change for as long as I live."

He stepped forward then, with his arms out, and she flew down the steps and poured into them, like water gushing from a swollen stream. Emotion flooded her as their chests pressed heart to heart, and his hand went up to cradle her head tightly to his shoulder.

"I love you, too." He pressed his lips against her hair.

"I wanted to tell you," she croaked out, "but I was afraid. I was afraid for Brandon."

"You should have known I wouldn't do anything to hurt him ever."

"Yes. I should have trusted you. And you had the right to know, especially after you met him."

"There's someone else who has the right to know, don't you think? What about your father?"

Markie burrowed her head against him, loving him even more for saying that. "I need your help, Justin. I can't do this by myself."

He held her tightly to him. "You are not ever going to have to face this by yourself again, I promise you that."

"I think," he said after he'd hugged her a moment longer, "that P.J. would want to know about Brandon as soon as possible. Especially since Robbie and Frankie already know."

Markie trembled, despite Justin's warm embrace. Her dad, the only person who had ever truly, fully believed in her besides Justin, would be so shocked when he heard about this, just as Justin had been, just as Brandon had been. It would shatter all his previous notions about Markie.

But when they told P.J., he took it amazingly well.

They went back over to his place and stood

out in the yard, under the skittish moon, as if
the story could not be shared inside the same
house where so many wrongs had been done
to Markie.

They told him together, both adding details, both defending the other. P.J. repeated
Brandon's name many times, had to have
some details clarified, but when they were
done, he seemed to understand. And accept.

He looked toward the dormer where
Marynell was still shutting herself up in the
attic room. "Marynell has never been what I
would call a happy woman," he admitted. It
was the first time Markie ever remembered
hearing him voice even the slightest disloyalty to his carping spouse. "I admit I
shouldn't let her talk ugly to me the way she
does sometimes, but nobody understands
how fragile she is except me. At first I tried
to please her. But then, seemed like the harder
she tried to control everybody and everything,
the unhappier she got. I never dreamed she'd
go so far. Markie, sweetheart," he said as he
clasped his daughter's shoulder, "I am so
sorry for the way you have suffered."

Markie was not sure if he meant the way

she'd suffered abuse as a child, or the way she'd suffered in her ordeal of bearing and giving up Brandon. It didn't matter. What mattered was that this sweet man did not end up blaming himself for everything that had happened.

"I'm happy now, Daddy. And Brandon is, too. He's a great kid. I've made my peace with mother. And most of all, I have Justin."

"We've decided to get married," Justin announced as he hugged her to his side. "I hope as soon as possible."

Hearing Justin say the words out loud, Markie felt as if her heart would burst.

"Well, I'll be," P.J. breathed. "That is fine. That's just fine." He smiled as his eyes misted up. "And I expect my grandson will like hearing that, as well."

"We're going to tell him right away," Justin said. And Markie loved *him* all the more for saying that.

KILGORE WON THE PRIMARY, and nobody was surprised, not even the hapless Doug Curry. A week later when the offer to go to Washington for the Cattlemen's Association came through, Markie was elated but torn. She didn't want to be leaving Justin when she'd only recently found him again, and she wanted to be in Five Points to stand by her sister.

"You have to accept it," Justin said. "You've worked too hard for this opportunity."

"But what about you? What about the Light at Five Points? And what about Robbie and the boys?"

"We'll all be waiting right here for you to come home. If you and I haven't forgotten each other after eighteen years apart, a few little plane rides back and forth from D.C. aren't going to change anything. We're all going to look after Robbie. She's not alone."

"But what about our wedding?" Markie continued to worry. "I thought we'd have all this time to plan. I guess we could put it off until the general election is over."

"Oh, no. We've waited eighteen years too long as it is. Besides, if we wait, Brandon won't be able to attend it."

Markie's eyes got huge. "Oh, Justin. Do you think he would do that?"

"We can ask. He's a pretty levelheaded

guy. He's been helping us out at the Light while you've been busy with Robbie these last few days. We'll make it clear there's no pressure. No disloyalty to his parents. Nothing like that."

"Do you think they might consent to meet us? Someday?"

"Again, all we can do is ask. So what do you say? The sooner the better? I want to have a simple wedding, right here in Five Points, before you leave."

"You mean like go to the courthouse?"

"What? No drab old courthouse for us, girl! We're in *love*. I want a real wedding."

"But how are we going to get a wedding done before I have to go to D.C.? That's only a month from now!"

Justin grabbed her hands to quiet her anxieties once and for all. "Now that we've made our decision—" he looked into her eyes "—I don't want to wait. Everything else is just details."

And he was right.

When Markie asked Nattie Rose if there was anybody in Five Points who might whip up a wedding cake on short notice, she said, "Why, I can, honey!"

When Justin asked the Mexicans staying at the Light if they could help with a hurried wedding out there, Rigo and Carlos grinned and winked at Justin, and Aurelia clutched Markie's arm with bright eyes shining. "I cook it," she said in the little bit of English she'd already learned.

When Justin called upon his old friend Father Augustus to do the ceremony, the aging priest had jumped at the chance to see some of his old parishioners. He even agreed to stay on at the Light, shepherding the people there until Justin returned from his honeymoon.

Markie was proud of Robbie when she pried her mother's fingers off of herself once and for all on the day she moved to town. She had found a vacant house to rent and got back her old job waitressing at the Hungry Aggie alongside Nattie Rose. It was sure to be hard work late in a pregnancy, and Markie worried about the strain, but Robbie seemed to be coming back to her old self in that bustling environment. The owner let her take plenty of breaks, and Robbie mostly sat on a bar stool and ran the register.

"The house is one of those old wrecks

down in the historic district, but the owner agreed to let me keep the dogs in the back-yard." Robbie told Markie this while they packed the few remaining things Robbie wanted to take with her. "It has big trees. Bad plumbing. Lots of charm. And I love it!"

Markie hadn't seen her sister this excited in a long time.

Everything was perfect, except that school was starting up soon and Brandon Smith was heading back to his real life.

But at least their son had consented to attend the wedding. The quick road trip up to Dallas to meet Brandon's parents had been stressful for Markie, but Justin's strength fortified her. And Brandon's. Markie was amazed at this young man she had given birth to. He had spent hours on his cell phone, smoothing the way for his parents, and for her and Justin.

The Smiths wanted to meet in the Reverend's office at the church. Justin and Markie could understand that. The four of them were strangers after all, and yet somehow, not.

Mrs. Smith was gracious and soft-spoken and Markie loved her immediately. Her name was Hope, and she told Markie she'd been through this type of meeting before with her older son's birth mother.

While the men were looking at the football pictures of Brandon and his brother that lined the walls of Brandon's father's study, Hope led Markie to sit with her on a small leather love seat. On the wall above it, the Reverend displayed a sampler that read, "He restores my soul."

"I have a little gift for you." Hope reached to an end table for a small package, wrapped in baby blue.

Markie was overwhelmed and flustered. "Oh, I… I'm sorry, I didn't bring a gift for you."

"You've already given me the greatest gift any mother could wish for." Hope Smith's eyes grew teary as she looked at her son across the room.

Markie's own eyes got misty as her heart swelled with all kinds of emotions. Gratitude. Shared pride. Loss and longing. Maybe a touch of envy for the years the woman had had with Brandon.

"Open it." Hope smiled. She was an attractive woman. A good fifteen years older than Markie. Composed and confident.

Markie's trembling fingers undid the wrappings. As she peeled away the last tissue layer, her eyes did fill fully with tears. They came up to meet Hope's warm, understanding ones, and Hope patted her hand. "Your husband-to-be told me you had lost your copy."

Markie swallowed and tried to speak but found she could say nothing. She lifted the tiny ceramic photo frame and pressed her lips to the glass that covered a picture of Brandon, the newborn picture her own mother had destroyed. *All things,* she thought. For her, not just her soul, but *all things* had surely been restored.

CHAPTER SEVENTEEN

Yesterday I was too exhausted to write anything.

Yesterday, all I could do was cry.

Because yesterday, the baby came.

And in forty-eight hours he'll be gone. Right into the arms of his new mother.

He was having a little trouble with his breathing (he's okay, the doctor said) so they took him right out of the birthing room to check him over in the newborn nursery. They practically had to tie me to the table when they carried him off. I guess I panicked. I guess I thought they were taking him away for good, right then. They calmed me down and said the nursery nurses have to observe him for at least twenty-four hours. I've been allowed to hold him pretty often. The nurses have been so sweet. Everybody has been so sweet. Even that a-hole Kyle showed up with Frankie when she brought me a teddy bear. He had some flowers with him, fancy that. I could tell they were from a grocery store, but still, he gets an A for effort. I am sending the bear along with the baby.

He has black hair. Lots. Like Justin.

(Well, okay. My hair's dark, too. Deep brunette, Robbie-the-redhead always calls it.)

He's such an incredibly pretty baby. Perfect! Smooth skin. Great big eyes.

I looked into his eyes right after he was born and it took my breath away. He looks like Justin. I keep wondering what he'll look like when he's older.

When I talk to him, it seems like he recognizes my voice. The first time was when he turned his little head in the delivery room. That's when I had that panic attack after they carried him off. That's when I started all this crying.

One of the nurses gave me a little newborn nursery picture of him to keep. I didn't know I was going to get to have that, and so I started crying then, too, and the nurse said, It's okay, honey. They all keep saying that. It's okay, honey. But it's not okay. I am losing my baby and I am not going to marry the man I love. I am probably never going to see either one of them again. I am probably going to spend the rest of my life trying to recover from all of this. They don't want to admit it, all these people who keep saying, It's okay, honey, but my life is never going to be okay.

Because when I finally saw my baby, it felt like I was falling down a big black hole. And it feels like I haven't stopped falling since.

I am only seventeen years old and my life is already over.

THE BIG HOUSE ON Kilgore Ranch seemed magically transformed. True, the coats of pale blue paint the Mexicans had applied to the stucco walls of the great room looked as if they had been slapped on with a lick and a promise. And the fall flowers and foliage that festooned the steps and the fireplace mantel had been picked in the fields that very afternoon. But the metamorphosis Markie's eyes were seeing wasn't about appearances. It was about life. And love.

She gathered up her long, flowing skirt and stepped one foot onto the landing to peek downstairs.

The afternoon sun canted low in the west and cast a golden glow through the floor-to-ceiling windows that looked out over the Hill Country.

Though everybody down there was talking excitedly, there was a great peace and contentment about the room. The flagstone floor had been swept and mopped. All of the aged, carved wood, even the heavy beams in the high ceiling, had been waxed by the guys. From those beams fluttered dozens of paper cutouts of doves and swans with Markie and Justin's names inscribed on them. Markie smiled. It must have taken Aurelia and Rigo's wife days to make those good-luck symbols. Markie decided she wanted those to be the only decorations except for the mantel dressing and the simple tallow-colored candles that flickered in plain glass hurricane lamps along the walls. Four rows of folding chairs, brought out to the ranch by Nattie Rose from the storeroom of the Hungry Aggie, sat in a semicircle facing the massive fireplace where a gentle fire glowed and sent up an incense of burning cedarwood.

The aroma of chicken enchiladas drifted up from the kitchen. Nattie Rose was probably back there with Aurelia, making sure the snowy-white Mexican wedding cookies were stacked into perfect little pyramids.

Outside on a small table on the patio, protected from a cool evening breeze by a careful tent of Saran Wrap was Nattie Rose's concoction of a cake. Solid white. Four giant tiers that would likely never be eaten. Hearts. Roses. Doves. Nattie Rose had plastered everything remotely related to weddings onto that cake, including the clichéd plastic bride and groom at the top.

Robbie's boys and Nattie Rose's husband, Earl, had seated themselves along the front row like stiff cowpokes waiting out a barn dance. Behind them, Frankie and Kyle were properly seated, as well. Hoping to set an example of wedding decorum for the others, Markie imagined. Her sister and brother-in-law looked a little out of place, dressed to the nines, with their legs primly crossed and their dress shoes shiny, when practically everybody else had on denim and cowboy boots. But P.J. and Justin's stepmother, Vivian, the Mexicans and the staff from the Light at Five Points, along with Markie's co-workers and friends from Dallas and Austin, persisted in milling about like aimless cattle.

The congressman had made it easy for them, pleading a sudden emergency in Washington and sending a ridiculously expensive gift. After the incident at the caves, no one really expected him to hang around and answer questions in Texas once the primary was sewn up.

Marynell, of course, was not in the room, either. Markie thought she might show up for appearance's sake, after all. It made her sad, to be rejected this way by her mother, but she reminded herself that the evening—the vows now and the meal and party later—would be so much more relaxed without the presence of Marynell's pinched, disapproving face.

Robbie came up behind her to peek over her shoulder. "Where's that man of yours?"

"Quaking in his boots, perhaps?" Markie grinned at her sister.

But even as she made the joke, Justin appeared under the arched doorway of the dining room and Markie's jaw dropped at the sight of her future husband. He looked astonishingly handsome, dressed completely in black. He was wearing a black linen *guayabera,* the Mexican wedding shirt, buttoned high at his neck with a black leather bolero vest over it, fitted black pants and hand-tooled black boots. His dark hair was gelled back, matador-style.

Robbie jaw dropped, as well. "Did you plan this—to complement each other this way?" Her face lit with a surprised smile as she looked her sister up and down.

For Markie was wearing a floor-length pale gray satin dress that flowed over her slim curves like liquid silver. It was topped with an ivory bolero jacket, embroidered with silver thread and carefully placed silver bugle beads. She had completed the effect with an antique lace mantilla veil that draped modestly over her dark hair and an antique silver-and-beige fan in lieu of flowers.

"No! I had seen this veil in a shop in an old hotel in San Antonio and I thought it would be a wonderful way to honor Justin's heritage. So I called them and had it shipped here. I wanted to surprise him."

"Well, all I can say is, *wow!* Good job. You will look amazing in the pictures."

Lorn stepped into the room behind Justin, decked out in dressy cowboy black, as well. And then Brandon appeared.

He was the image of a conservative young man—dark suit, white shirt, club tie. Except his hair was gelled up in short spikes and he hadn't removed his shades yet. The three men stopped and joshed with the guests as they made their way up to the fireplace area.

Watching them together, Markie got teary-eyed.

"Oh, for gosh sakes," Robbie said. "You'd think you were the pregnant one instead of me. Come on. You're going to ruin your makeup."

They stepped back around the corner into the former master suite, where the Ramos family was living these days. A large antique cheval mirror still stood in the corner, left over from the old Kilgore homestead days.

Markie stood before it for one last check. Robbie came up behind her and gave her heavy lace mantilla veil a gentle fluff. "Okay. So are we ready?"

Markie put a hand on her heart and drew a deep breath against the press of it. "I guess so. I can't believe this is happening."

"I can't think of two people who are more right for each other," Robbie murmured in her soothing voice. Then she frowned, turning sideways to the mirror and adjusting the voluminous folds of what Markie could only think of as Robbie's "costume." To dignify the garment by calling it a bridesmaid's dress would be a stretch. It looked like Robbie had fashioned a multilayered muumuu out of yesterday's drapes. She had informed Markie that the fabric—a milky floral crepe in autumnal colors—had only cost her a buck a yard at the Hancock's in San Marcos. Unwilling to dampen her sister's recently unleashed creative spirit, Markie had merely breathed, "Imagine that."

"You sure I look okay?" Robbie eyed her

reflection skeptically as if she'd now come to her senses.

"There is nothing sweeter than a maid of honor who is expecting," Markie dissembled.

It didn't matter. Neither did all the other odd little details that had merged to form this unconventional wedding. What mattered was Justin, and the fact that they were starting their lives together, even after an eighteen-year delay.

"Thank you again, for letting us use your house for…later tonight," Markie said.

Robbie waved a palm at her. "No problem. It'll save you precious driving time. I didn't realize it, but being out there on that farm was kind of keeping me down. The boys are griping about the move, but I think I'm going to be ten times better off in my little house in town. I just hope that old house doesn't fall down around your ears. You realize the floor furnace is broke. Who'da thought we were going to have a cold snap this early?"

"We'll be fine. If we need a little heat, we can always turn on the kitchen stove or the wall heater in the bathroom. It's only one night." Only one night, and then she'd be gone. But Justin would not let her sacrifice the opportunity in Washington. They were going to be fine, the two of them, making a life together that was full to overflowing.

"What time does your plane leave?"

"Ten."

"And then when do you get back from Washington?"

"In two weeks."

"And then you're all set for three weeks on the white sandy beaches of Cancún! You will be spoiled rotten when you get back."

"Just don't have that baby until I do."

"Did you hear your auntie?" Robbie said to her huge tummy. "You stay put until the second week in October."

"Let's all sit down," Markie heard Father Augustus's reedy voice call out, though she had not seen him before. "And we'll begin." She was grateful that the old priest had made it. She wondered if he was tired, if the long journey from Jalisco had exhausted him.

There was a rustle of activity as people took their seats. Robbie and Markie went out on the landing.

The simple strains of Rigo softly playing

a Spanish guitar accompanied the sisters' slow descent down the stairs. Markie's steps only faltered once, when her eyes connected with Justin's, who was standing beside Father Gus with his hands stacked at his front in the classic groom's pose.

He stepped forward and took her hand as she came down the little pathway between the chairs, and they went forward to kneel on cushions placed for that purpose on the broad stone hearth. Robbie and Lorn stepped up behind them.

Father Gus held his hands over their heads and said some quiet words in blessing before he took up a lasso beaded like a rosary, another Mexican tradition. He wound it in a figure eight around their wrists and then made the sign of the cross over their heads.

"Nothing gives me greater joy," Father Augustus began as he smiled at the assembly, "than to celebrate something in the worldly realm that has already taken place in the spiritual. Today, Justin and Markie have decided to pledge their lives to each other before God and this assembly, but in fact, their spirits were pledged one to another long ago. I have just blessed their union. Now Markie and Justin will say their own vows to each other. The covenant that seals a man to a woman, that makes them one flesh, is made by the two of them, not by a priest. We are all merely the witnesses."

Robbie was already fishing up her sleeve for a Kleenex.

"Justin," Father Gus invited with his palm out.

Justin cleared his throat. As he looked at Markie, his eyes misted and he swallowed and closed them very briefly, then opened them and started. "Markie, you have always been the only one for me. Nothing could ever take you out of my heart, and now nothing will ever take you out of my life. I will do my best to honor you, to help you, to protect you, and it will be my joy to stay true to you as long as we live." He stopped abruptly and bent his head and kissed her hand, causing a tug on the lasso, and her heart.

"Markie." Father Gus indicated that she was next.

Markie, who could write a press release in a minute, who could pen memorable speeches for politicians, who could spin words in her sleep, had found herself in a state of torment over writing these few simple vows. What could she say to Justin? she had agonized night after night as she tossed on her pillow. What could she say that would demonstrate the depth of her love? The sacredness of her commitment?

She looked down at their loosely tied hands as Justin gave her fingers a little squeeze.

Strengthened by his touch, she looked up at the man who was to be her husband, the man that she would spend her days, and her nights, with until her life, or his life, was done. Her heart's desire stood there, looking into her eyes.

"Justin. I have waited so long for you." Her normally strong voice seemed to be tapering off to a whisper. "When I look into your eyes, I see my one true love." He gave her hand another small squeeze, and Markie swallowed. "I promise to love you, no matter what comes, for the rest of my life. I will cherish our love every day, and I'll do everything in my power to be a good wife to you.

I promise to always be truthful *with* you, and true *to* you, to always speak my heart in love, to always bring honor to you and your household." This last part of her vows was so important, so meaningful, to Markie, because she was determined that the lies that had kept them apart were forever behind them.

Wordlessly, they exchanged their rings with a little help from the priest because of the lasso.

When the rings, simple bands of purest gold, were in place, Father Gus smiled, raised his arms and announced in Spanish, *"They're married!"*

The couple turned to the small assembly and Justin raised their lasso-bound wrists high above their heads before he gave Markie a showy, movie-finale kiss while everyone applauded and dabbed at their eyes.

Then the party started.

First, they went out on the flagstone patio and enjoyed the delicious dinner by the warming glow of clay *chimineas* and hundreds of small twinkling white lights that the men had strung in the low-limbed live oaks.

After the cake was served, everyone took turns toasting the newlyweds.

Robbie's boys and Nattie Rose's girls danced silly and kidlike to *ranchera* music provided by Rigo on his strumming guitar, souped up by the bleating of an annoying accordion that Carlos had scared up from who knows where.

Lorn and P.J. were a little too conscientious about making sure that Father Gus's glass of sangria stayed topped off so that in the end Rigo and Mrs. Ramos had to help the aging priest upstairs.

Justin started getting antsy to leave soon after the cake-cutting and the toasts, but Markie wanted to enjoy the party just a bit longer. She had never felt so loved, so at peace, so at home. These were going to be their people all their lives, she was sure. Hers and Justin's.

Markie had just finished hugging some of her friends from Austin, when Justin bent and whispered in her ear, "Let's dance."

The song Justin had requested was Brooks & Dunn's "Unloved." Rigo and Carlos did a credible rendition, even if the rhythm was slightly more *ranchera* than country and western. It was the words that mattered to Markie in any case.

As Justin whirled Markie around within the circle of friends and family, she realized that all the years of being unloved had been partially self-inflicted, for both of them. And that being unloved was now over, for both of them. How intentional Justin had been, choosing a song with words about giving all you've got and watching all you've got walk away. From across the patio, Brandon was smiling at them.

And Markie knew that the song's promise was true. As long as she was in Justin's arms, she'd never go unloved.

Justin's arms were firm around her, unfailing as his heart. "We've got one more stop to make—" he looked in her eyes "—before we head to the honeymoon cottage."

Markie smiled. That's what he'd taken to calling Robbie's unoccupied farmhouse, the place where they'd spend their first night, a night which would have to last them until they could take a delayed honeymoon.

He took her to the Rocks.

In the narrow trough of the river below, the midnight moon reflected off a swirling blanket of autumn mist. As they made their way carefully along the bank, memories came back to Markie like visions rising out of that mist. Memories that could still torture her if she let them.

Justin gathered up the hem of her long silver dress and helped her climb up onto the crown of the rock. They stood for a moment in silence, holding hands. Then Justin dug something out of the pocket of his dressy vest.

"Wedding gift," he said as he unfurled a gold chain that sparked in the moonlight.

Markie gasped. It was his mother's locket.

She took it and coiled the chain around her hand, kissed the heart shape of it. "If only…" he started, but then he simply opened his arms.

She sank against him. His hands caressed her back as if he already knew what she was thinking. "It's all right," he said. "At least he came to our wedding."

"He *is* beautiful," she whispered, "isn't he?" She felt her own tears pushing up behind her eyelids.

Justin trapped her where she was, pressing his lips to her temple. "Markie, don't," he said.

"Don't—" she swallowed, gulping and trying to stem the flow "—what?" But the tears leaked out from under her eyelids, anyway. She swiped at her cheeks, and when she opened her eyes, she saw that there were tears in his eyes, too.

"Don't look back—" His voice choked off and he pressed his lips to her temple again. She could feel the hot moisture of his tears, his breath, against her skin. This night was supposed to be a happy time, something they wanted, had planned for, a gift to each other.

"That has been always my rule. Don't look back. But now I want to, I have to. Rereading my old diary wasn't as painful this time. It made me see how much I've grown, and how very much we did love each other, even if we were young. I won't spoil what we have now with regrets."

From deep in his throat there came an involuntary sob, and he choked the next words out. "I wanted this moment to be romantic. But I can't...you can't expect me not to feel something when I've lost all those years and I'll never get them—I'll never get *him*—back."

"Look at me." She framed his face with her palms. "The only way you'll survive the sense of loss, the separation, is to keep reminding yourself that he's not yours, he's not mine. He is the Smiths' son now."

He nodded and looked at her. As they caught the moonlight his dark eyes were beautiful in their intensity. His massive shoulders heaved and he pinched the bridge of his nose between thumb and fingers, trying to gain control.

"Maybe we needed something more than a romantic moment out here," she said comfortingly. "Maybe we needed… I don't know. Something deeper. Come here."

She rubbed his back now, the roles reversed as she became his comforter. "We were young and stupid, Justin. Careless. This is simply the price we have to pay."

"No one should have to pay a price this high. To be robbed of our own flesh and blood? We should have been given a choice."

"You mean *you* should have been given a choice," she reminded him. "Unfortunately,

I did make a choice." She pressed her face against his vest and breathed in his scent. "I made a choice for both of us. For all three of us. For you and me and Brandon. I made that choice. The guilt is mine."

"No." He arched forward, pulling her to his chest by her upper arms. "Don't do that to yourself. You were only seventeen," he said as his thumb gently caressed away a tear on her cheek. "You were strong for all of us. It was *I* who failed you. God forgive me."

His whole face—eyes, nose, mouth—seemed to crumple as if crushed with the press of sorrow. "I'll want—" he swallowed "—I'll want to know everything, everything you can tell me, about that time."

"Yes," she whispered, then swallowed and bit her lip. For a moment her voice left her completely. She clasped his shoulders for strength. "I will," she promised more strongly. "You can read the diary. Every word."

They nodded their heads together in concert. Then, as if their mouths were living entities with separate volition, they sought and found each other.

Their salty tears, their contrition, mingled

into a forgiveness that was unspoken but total, as all their years of frustration, all the loss and longing, all the loneliness, melted in the fire of that one kiss.

"Let's go, Mrs. Kilgore," Justin said when it was over. "I need to make love to you now."

JUSTIN PUT THE CANDLE on the bedside stand, then sat quietly on the edge of the mattress, waiting for Markie.

She was in the little bathroom down the hall, changing into something that would make his blood run wild, no doubt, but he wanted to always remember the image of her in that simple dress and lace mantilla. She had looked so beautiful tonight. He was fiercely glad that also tucked away in his heart he carried a million poses of Markie when she was young. Markie looking down at him from the saddle of a horse. Markie riding in a Jeep with the top down, her dark hair blowing wild. Markie, her curves lined in moonlight on the banks of the Blue River.

He heard her come out of the bathroom, then the padding of her barefoot steps as she stole down the hall. She hadn't wanted to spend this night in Robbie and Danny's bedroom and he didn't blame her. This little room with its antique double bed was good enough for them. Anywhere with Markie was good enough for him.

Markie slipped into the bedroom and closed the door slowly, jimmying the glass knob until the latch clicked, pausing to press a palm to the panel, as if there were someone in the house she did not want to disturb.

She was wearing a white gown, thin as the moonlight. He had seen the plunge of it before she turned away. She stood for a moment, facing the door, as if noting the worn paint, the smudges of fingerprints around the doorknob. The room smelled closed up, as the whole house had been, since Robbie had moved to town. "It's stuffy in here." She crossed to open the single narrow window.

The near-full moon showed through lace sheers, reflecting shadows onto a small area rug, an old rocker, the simple counterpane on the double bed. As she stood in the moonlight, her posture was self-conscious, as if she could feel Justin watching her.

"I'm sorry there's no electricity," she apologized senselessly, now looking around at the shadowy pattern of the antique wallpaper that her sister had no doubt hung herself. Why couldn't she bring herself to look at him? They had been lovers once. They were about to be again. But it was as if she felt shy. No. That wasn't it. What was she feeling? The same thing he was? As if something momentous was about to take place, something from which there would be no turning back.

"Are you okay?" Justin made sure his voice came softly as he moved up behind her, the words as physical as any caress.

"Of course." She turned to face him. She looked so very beautiful. He could see the chain and the locket between her breasts, trailing down the open neckline of the gown. She tried to smile, but the effort failed. She seemed too nervous. No sooner had he finished the thought than she said, "I'm just a little nervous, all of a sudden."

She managed a small laugh that sounded more apprehensive than lighthearted. "It's weird. I felt so strong and sure a couple of hours ago, when we said our vows."

"You aren't sure now? I mean, this is what you want, isn't it?"

Justin wondered if it had been a mistake to take her to the river like that, to dredge up the past. The locket shone softly in the moonlight.

Markie McBride Kilgore looked into her husband's face. He was the same sweet Justin, in so many ways. And that simple realization gave her courage.

"Yes. Of course it's what I want. And I don't want to ruin the little time we have just because I've got the jitters. This may be the only chance we'll have to be together for a while. I don't want to go to Washington without this…this…" She couldn't put a word on it. *Consummation* certainly wasn't right. *Validation?* Too cerebral for something that felt so emotional. But this act felt suddenly weighty. Nothing like with the other men who had come and gone in her life. Not that she was ever casual about getting involved with a man. But they had all been mistakes. Chiefly because Justin had been there, alive in her heart all along. She remembered a few years back when she had given up, sick of the cycle of a false connection followed by an uneasy severance. "It's just that I haven't done anything like this in a very long time," she admitted.

He smiled. "Isn't this ironic? When you were a teenager, you acted like a wanton woman. And now that you're a full-fledged, thoroughly married woman, you're acting as shy as a school girl."

She smiled, too. "I know. It's just that I feel like I'm starting all over again here, getting a second chance, and I don't want to do anything to ruin it."

"We're both starting all over together. And we're not going to do anything to ruin it." His gaze was steady on hers. "Come here."

She crossed the room to him. When she sat down beside him, he reached over and took her hand in his lap, wrapping his palms around it protectively.

"Maybe it would help if we talked for a little while first." He raised a hand to guide her head into the hollow of his shoulder.

When she settled into him somewhat stiffly, he said, "You really are nervous."

"Talk to me."

"Okay." He pushed her hair back behind one shoulder, smiled with his eyes, then looked around the room for something to say. "So. This is the room where the princess stayed during her exile."

She looked around the modest, cramped room. "Yep. Quaint, ain't it?"

"Yeah, but comfortable-looking."

"Yeah. Comfortable." Robbie was amazingly good at crafting a comfy environment with very little money.

Seconds stretched while Markie could feel Justin looking around, searching again for something else to say. "O-kay, then." He threw his other arm around her and clasped her to him in a chummy way. "We've talked. So now can we do it?"

That got a giggle.

"That's better." He tilted her chin up.

He rubbed the flesh of her lips absently with his thumb while he looked into her eyes for a long moment. "I can't believe this," he whispered.

She glanced up and saw that he had tears in his eyes.

"What don't you believe?"

"All of it. Any of it. That you're here, that I'm actually holding you. That we're married." He raised her hand to his mouth and crushed his lips against the back of it. "That we have a son," he whispered against her skin.

Markie studied his profile, so handsome, so beautiful. When his eyes slid closed with an expression that was a mixture of torment and bliss, she pressed her own eyes shut.

"But, Markie," she heard him say. He eased her backwards to the bed, rolling her to her side as he folded her in his arms, gathering her close, clasping her to him. He ended up with her face cradled in one palm as if he could hold her thoughts. "We'll always have each other."

As always with the two of them, one kiss became many. One moment became many. All night, while the verdant Hill Country landscape stretched out on all sides of the little farmhouse, quiet and timeless, they made love.

When the first rays of sun peeked over the rim of the land, Markie was still awake, feeling high, feeling reborn, feeling full of life. Then it occurred to her. Was she? Was she, at this very moment, pregnant for the second time? She turned on her side and looked at her husband. His sleeping face was the picture of a satiated man, one at peace with his life.

Redemption. That was the word she had been seeking earlier on this amazing night, when she'd said her vows, when she'd stood facing Justin down on the Blue River, when she'd felt suddenly overwhelmed coming to his bed. That was the thing they had needed tonight, the thing that would now make all their tomorrows right. That's what they had finally done. What they had done was nothing short of a redemption.

****

Watch for Darlene Graham's next book in
THE BABY DIARIES *series,*
Lone Star Rising, *coming in August 2007.*

0707/23b

On sale 20th July 2007

CELEBRITY BACHELOR
by Victoria Pade

When millionaire tycoon Joshua Cantrell visited Northbridge College, Cassie Walker was assigned to be his 'minder'. Gorgeous, wealthy men like Josh always made small-town girl Cassie feel inferior, but behind his public image was a down-to-earth man who knew Cassie was *truly* special.

ACQUIRING MR RIGHT
by Laurie Paige

When businessman Lance Carrington bought the company Krista Aquilon worked for, she feared the worst. But was Lance an utterly ruthless corporate raider or a kindred spirit trying to save the firm? One thing was certain – his takeover of Krista was complete.

RIGHTFULLY HIS
by Sharon De Vita

Max McCallister had been the sperm donor for the woman he'd always loved and his brother. But now his brother was dead and Sophie was raising two fatherless little girls alone... It was time to claim what was rightfully his – Sophie and his twin daughters...

Available at WHSmith, Tesco, ASDA, and all good bookshops
www.millsandboon.co.uk

4 FREE

BOOKS AND A SURPRISE GIFT!

We would like to take this opportunity to thank you for reading this Mills & Boon® book by offering you the chance to take FOUR more specially selected titles from the Special Edition series absolutely FREE! We're also making this offer to introduce you to the benefits of the Mills & Boon® Reader Service™—

- ★ **FREE home delivery**
- ★ **FREE gifts and competitions**
- ★ **FREE monthly Newsletter**
- ★ **Exclusive Reader Service offers**
- ★ **Books available before they're in the shops**

Accepting these FREE books and gift places you under no obligation to buy, you may cancel at any time, even after receiving your free shipment. Simply complete your details below and return the entire page to the address below. You don't even need a stamp!

YES! Please send me 4 free Special Edition books and a surprise gift. I understand that unless you hear from me, I will receive 6 superb new titles every month for just £3.10 each, postage and packing free. I am under no obligation to purchase any books and may cancel my subscription at any time. The free books and gift will be mine to keep in any case.

E7ZED

Ms/Mrs/Miss/Mr ....Initials ....

BLOCK CAPITALS PLEASE

Surname ....

Address ....

....

....Postcode...

Send this whole page to:
UK: FREEPOST CN81, Croydon, CR9 3WZ